The Golden Coins
Of
Lombardy
by
Tony Berry

The Stuart Kings of England

1603 to 1685

James I 1603 to 1625

Charles I 1625 to 1647

The   COMMONWEALTH

Charles II 1660 to 1685

The Earls of Northampton

1540 to 1681

1st Earl Henry Howard

(1540 to 1614)

Lord Treasurer

2nd Earl Spencer Compton

(1601 to 1643

Royalist commander Killed at Hopton

Heath

3rd Earl James Compton

(1622 to 1681)

Royalist commander survives

The Commonwealth

Chapter One (1621 Lombardy)

Father Trabbini liked rabbit, and to his shame he remembered that the thought of hot sizzling rabbit, had filled his mind, whilst holding early morning mass. He had not yet devised his penance but had decided that Monsignor Vatelli would know nothing of this, his minor sin. The Archbishop of Torino's emissary was too disciplined to understand, or easily forgive such signs of humanity in the clergy he supervised. The Monsignor had arrived on his donkey, the day before and would stay for two nights. He was someone Trabbini had rarely met before. Perhaps a share of the rabbit would soften his inspection and his report, At the moment the Monsignor was in his village meeting his flock. Maosta was a prosperous village in a part of Lombardy that was rich in fertile earth, and enjoyed plenty of water. Sunshine and human effort had done the rest. With the resulting prosperity, Trabbini felt certain that there would be enough evidence of a village faithful to both its church and its Arch bishop. As he contemplated his village from the road that would eventually lead to the great city, he was confident that he could easily satisfy his need for soft meat. A short walk over the hill to the widow's farm, some conversation and gossip and he would have his reward. The farm bred rabbits and the widow was a faithful member of church and community. An hour's walk, and his midday meal for both himself and his guest would be found. Although short, part of the journey would require care. Plenty of large rocks, trees, and dense undergrowth covered the hill, but there was a path difficult at times, but familiar to the entire village. He turned to start his journey he rearranged his robe, grasped his staff and set off. He followed the main track that led to Torino, and then he turned to the hill that led to the widow's farm. A June sun, a windless day and an uphill gradient, slowed his progress to a regular steady pace. He was pleased that he had remembered his familiar straw hat. At his age almost sixty, it was a necessary precaution.

As the open grassland gave way to the forest that covered the hillside, he followed the turns and twists of the path, as best he could. Quite soon he was enjoying the cool shade from the forest canopy, but increasingly he found thick undergrowth fringing and narrowing his way. It was a wayward branch that caught his hat. The branch flexed and then the hat was catapulted into a stand of bushes, some ten to twelve feet from the track. Father Trabbini restrained the oath that sprang to mind. His hat was clearly visible and easy to retrieve. He had only to find his way through some undergrowth to recover it. He approached the stand of bushes from behind. He strode confidently to recover his property. Suddenly he felt the ground give way beneath him. He was falling into a hidden hole. In desperation he clutched at the bushes, but only grasped spindly branches that slipped through his fingers. They failed to hold him. His own weight continued his downward fall. For a moment fear gripped his stomach as he faced an unknown descent into darkness. The drop was short, but he still landed heavily bruised but basically undamaged. He was lying on a stone floor strewn with dirt, leaves, branches and small animal bones. The air was thick with dust. For some minutes he lay still. In his mind he examined his hurts. Generally relieved at what he found he slowly climbed to his feet. From the dim light above, he could see he was in a chamber that had served as a store room. About several arms' length away he could detect the outline of a table, and nearby there was a chair lying on its side. Around the chamber there were a number of broken barrels, some clay jars and what appeared to be an old olive press. He could smell an overpowering feral reek, and then heard a scuffling and clawing. Two pairs of eyes in the dim light confronted him. For a second two foxes stood their ground offering a challenge. He turned towards them and they in turn fled to an opening that led first into darkness, but then to a dim light showing in the distance.

The foxes had frightened Father Trabbini, but when he had calmed himself, he blessed their presence, for where foxes could enter a man may secure an exit. He determined that the foxes had made their way out into the forest, and that the dim light in the distance was his own way back to the outside world. His staff had followed his fall. He picked it up thankful for the extra security he felt from it. He decided to examine more closely the objects around him. He remembered that there were those who had enjoyed unexpected fortune on finding the ruined properties of the ancient Italians. He had sufficient education to know of the Roman Empire and its wonders of roads, aqueducts, temples, and villas. He had clearly fallen into such an ancient ruin. He pulled himself to his feet. The room did not look at all promising. His mind was very firm the first task was to find a way to safety. A quick upward glance confirmed that his point of entry offered little hope of a way out. He had to examine the route taken by the foxes through the dim light at the end of darkness. He tentatively climbed over a mound of rubble. His sandaled feet suffered a few cuts and grazes but he was soon standing on a flat stone floor. With his staff held in front of him he entered the deeper darkness, tapping his way forward towards the light seeking salvation. After a few moments he was at an opening where rubble was covered by bushes and undergrowth. but the light of outside was filtering through onto the ground. He guessed that beyond was a well-hidden exit and a way used at the moment only by small animals. However, he was confident that even a sixty-year-old man could make his way out.

Father Trabbini gave a sigh of relief. Having found a safe way out he became calm, and reflected that it was perhaps worthwhile retracing his steps to ensure that there were after all no small items of value to be found. He made his way back to the chamber. He began by carefully examining the oil press. The dim light made touch as important as his sight. His hands moved lightly but his search yielded nothing. He moved towards the table. He found a rusty knife and a broken clay cup. He turned his attention to the clay jars and stooped to pick up the first of the four. He straightened up with nothing in his hands. The jar was incredibly heavy. He tried to remove the top but it was sealed. This was neither oil nor wine. A thought at the back of his mind began to churn his stomach. More determined he placed his feet either side of the jar and with knees locked he wrapped his arms around the jar and lifted. It was too heavy he lost his grip. The jar fell to the stone floor. It gave first a heavy thud and then a loud crack. Father Trabbani stood in wonder as a cascade of golden coins streamed over his sandaled feet.

Monsignor Vatelli listened carefully as father Trabbini explained his discovery. It was past mid-day and the serving woman had been sent home, and there was just the two men facing each other across the kitchen table. In the Monsignor's hand were the three coins the priest had brought to verify his story.

"They are very old he stated. There are some small inscriptions some names and insignia, two have words of Latin and one is recognisable as Greek. On two we have the word Imperator. They are made of gold!".

He paused for one last examination.

"Four jars you say? This father Trabbini is a Roman hoard of gold!".

The two men looked surprisingly alike. Elderly clerical gentlemen dressed in their sober cassocks, with grey hair, thin faces, and both just under six feet in height. Of the two, father Trabbini looked the most nourished. Monsignor Vatelli was especially thin of body and gaunt of face. He placed the three coins in the centre of the table between them.

"Well, father Trabbini what are we to do"?

The parish priest and the Monsignor were not friends but they had always maintained a professional relationship, sometimes cordial, sometimes a little colder. But they both knew that they were now locked together in something that made them both a captive of the other. They were conjoined in their futures.

"This is so dangerous," exclaimed father Trabbini.

"I wish I had never found it. Gold corrupts, men lose all their reason over it. Any knowledge of this will bring every man whether honest or a brigand to my door. We are both in mortal danger. In this we trust no one".

"I agree "replied Vatelli and he wiped his brow with the cuff of his sleeve.

"Such wealth as this brings great power over men and women. Armies spring from it. I think even with the protection of holy church I fear for my life".

He looked fiercely at father Trabbini.

"We must keep it secret and pass it on to great men, who are powerful enough to hold it and protect it. Such men may reward those who deliver it to them!".

"The Church "cried father Trabbini. "This must all go to the Pope, our blessed Pope Gregory. He will use it and he will protect us."

Monsignor Vatelli peered closely at the priest.

"Not Rome, "he said.

"I hear that Pope Gregory is a good man but perhaps a little worldly to use such a blessing in the most beneficial way for the Church. Besides how can we hope to take this in secret to Rome? It would take days weeks. We would be discovered, robbed and killed."

Father Trabbani's moment of hope was lost. He had ignored the reference to a worldly Pope but indeed Rome was a very great distance from Maosta. Monsignor Vatelli rose to his feet and began to pace around the kitchen.

"I know what we must do but I am not yet clear as how to do it. It must go to our Archbishop in Torino. It will join Christ's Holy Shroud and the body of Saint Maurice. It will be but a two or three-day journey. Our Archbishop is also a good man and his ambitions lie within the Church" He returned to his seat.

"Father Trabbini we must devise a plan to recover and move these coins of yours to the Arch bishop In Torino. We will be free of our burden, and have the best chance of a reasonable reward."

Having decided on some action they made their own supper and both took to their bed the weight of the problems facing them. Father Trabbini's sleep was broken by fear and worry. Monsignor Vatelli in place of sleep exchanged searching for answers to their difficulties.

It was two women of the village that provided for father Trabbini's domestic needs. One was employed from daybreak to mid-afternoon and the other the rest of the day until after dinner. The chores of cooking, cleaning and shopping were shared equally. It was an arrangement that had some advantages not least the mild competition to secure father Trabbini's approval. It was Madam Lucetta who had been up early and there were eggs and bread sizzling in the breakfast pan when the two clerics emerged from their respective rooms. Father Trabbini was pale and subdued even remorseful as he sat at the table... Monsignor Vatelli, however, was more alive with a subdued energy. During the night he had thoughts that he wished to share. He sat fidgeting after breakfast as Madam Lucetta was instructed in her share of the day's duties. Father Trabbini had the sense to make shopping in the market her first duty.

"For heaven's sake Trabbani. I thought that woman would never leave... "Exclaimed Vatelli. "Sit and listen I have had thoughts on how we can solve our problems".

The parish priest sat at the table and with inquiring mind listened to his superior.

"You tell me that there is a quantity of coins that would fill some six saddlebags. Well we do not have six saddlebags. We have my two saddlebags but if we tried to buy or borrow the remainder our purpose would be impossible to explain".

Father Trabbini just nodded assent this problem he had seen for himself. The Monsignor continued.

"Double sacks would serve us just as well and be strong enough to carry coin. We must quietly obtain at most ten to twelve single sacks, the sort that has been used for carrying vegetables, fruit, corn, whatever and then double them.

" I have some", cried Trabbini. "I have four used sacks in my cellar that the women use for carrying wood. I am sure I can take these without raising suspicion. It should not be difficult to find the rest".

The Monsignor sat back on his hard kitchen chair.

"Excellent, in this way we can carry our coin."

Father Trabbini leant forward to speak but the Monsignor forestalled him.

"We have two further problems. How do we transfer the gold to the sacks and how are they to be taken to the Archbishop?"

Father Trabbini's urge to speak disappeared. He realised his superior had more to say. The Monsignor was about to reveal the results of his sleepless night.

"Let me describe how we will deal with these matters and yet retain absolute secrecy. You will tell your congregation, your prosperous congregation, that the church in Torino is mounting an assault on poverty in its slums. It is calling for donations not of money but of unwanted but still serviceable goods. This village is to make its contribution in pots and pans, basins old furniture, cups, plates. Things of little value here in Maosta but will be welcomed by the desperately poor of Torino. You Trabbani shall organise this collection and it will be so successful that we shall require to borrow a horse and cart to transport it to Torino. There will be no need of saddlebags or strings of mules. We shall ensure that our sacks of coins are buried deep in the cart's load"

Monsignor Vatelli sat back pleased with himself and his ideas, eager for the response from his fellow conspirator. Father Trabbini was fulsome in his reception of the Monsignor's plan, but he felt his contribution to the debate was to underline the remaining obstacles. "Monsignor" he pleaded. Hoping that his superior had answers to his questions.

"How will we bag the coins and load them on to the cart and the village will want to help us and escort us on our way.

"This I have thought of" replied Vatelli "When all has been collected from the village, we shall set off with you driving the cart".

For a moment Vatelli stumbled.

"You can drive a cart, manage and look after a horse"?

"Er yes my Lord came the reply."

Vatelli ignored his sudden raise in status.

"With you driving the cart" he repeated.

Monsignor Vatelli was becoming a little concerned that Father Trabbini may not be the man he needed to successfully complete their task.

"Now Trabbini, listen carefully. Where the Torino road is at its closest to where you say the coins are to be found, there will be a small accident and you will fall off the cart to the ground. You will be badly winded not seriously hurt but will require to rest. As we will have set off late afternoon, we shall make camp for the night. How far will we have travelled before this becomes necessary"?

"A mile and a half" replied Trabbini.

"Good". Monsignor was pleased that his night time thoughts were possible.

"We shall insist on being alone. No doubt there will be many offers of hospitality to return to the Village. But we shall insist all you need is rest. There will be brave men willing to stay with us but we shall point out that we are not so very far from the village and insist that the good lord's protection is all we need".

Father Trabbini began to breathe heavily. He could see the next part of the Monsignor's plan. He waited and listened.

"During the night we shall go to the place of concealment and fill the sacks and transport them to the cart and hide them. It can be done Trabbini."

His voice became insistent.

"You must take me to the cache. We will both carry a single sack that will be the most we can manage at a time. This will be the moment of maximum danger. After that we shall in turn guard the cart and secure additional sacks."

The two men fell silent thinking over their plan... They both had feelings of hope for success.

"Even if our escort returns in the morning they will soon grow tired and return home. You on the cart and I on my mule will steadily make our way to Torino."

"Our church has clever men in it "spoke an admiring Trabbini. The Monsignor smiled.

"Come", he said. "Let us inform the people of the village of the generous donations they are about to make".

Chapter Two

The plan agreed by the two clerics worked perfectly in its early stages. They had agreed that their aim was to get an acceptable response from the village, nothing that would over fill the cart or leave it looking bare. The pressure of the Monsignor, with the less than enthusiastic support from father Trabbini, produced a horse and cart and sufficient donations from the faithful of Maosta, that just met the requirements for the task ahead. A load that contained everything that was old, damaged and well used, reflected parishioners who followed their instructions to the letter. It was a three quarters full cart accompanied by a few villagers, that left the village in late afternoon for Torino. Father Trabbini was driving the cart, and by its side rode the Monsignor on his mule. Father Trabbini's fall, and his need for rest produced the halt for the night, in exactly the right place. The few villagers that accompanied them were easily persuaded that they were not needed, and should return to their homes. Thus, the two clerics were left alone for the night and after a simple meal they gathered themselves for their night time exertions. They were to find that the dark night the thick undergrowth together with the weight of the sacks were to hamper their attempts, to transfer the hoard to the cart. They had a lantern but they had to keep its use to a minimum. Father Trabbani blundered around vainly searching for the hidden entrance. What had seemed dangerously obvious in daylight, at night seemed impossible to find. He received at first gentle understanding from Monsignor but when this failed to bring the required result, the Monsignor temper exploded. A series of harsh words finally drove father Trabbini to the right place, such that he could lead them to the dark hidden room. By now a good part of the night was lost. They found that each of them could only manage no more than one filled sack at a time. Their progress to the cart was painfully slow. They were drenched in perspiration after their first effort and having deposited their sacks by the cart. a large pull from their wine flasks was required to get them back onto their feet again.

"We must take the chance of leaving the cart alone Trabbini but we must place this first sack back into the tree line, so that anyone around who approaches the cart, will not find them. When they are all retrieved, we will load the cart together."

This effort of speech wearied further the tired Monsignor, but giving father Trabbini a gentle pat on the shoulder, they moved their first load back up to the tree line and then moved on to secure those that remained.

The sun was well up when with a final effort they loaded unobserved their sacks on to the cart. They then lay down to sleep in the cart too exhausted to enjoy the success of their efforts, and caring little about the chance of interference. After an hour Monsignor Vatelli still tired and with aching limbs, forced himself to rise. He drank copiously from his water skin and roused father Trabbani. Reluctantly, they tended the morning needs of their horse and mule, but as they continued their preparations to resume their journey, a growing feeling of triumph invaded both men. Their plan was working. They had already achieved so much. It was not so far to Torino. The Monsignor managed a light laugh.

"Come Trabbini" let us be about our own and God's work. Two days, perhaps three will see us before the Archbishop. Our only danger will be from others on the road. We must be pleasant but not over friendly. God must protect us from the evil of others."

"Amen" was father Trabbini's short reply.

As the sun moved into late afternoon and shadows lengthened, the cart and the clerics stopped at a wayside cabin, where fruit and fresh water could be purchased. The air was cooler now and sitting on a bench they were comfortable enough for an overall consideration of their situation.

"So far Trabbini we have done well. Those we have met on the road have respected the cloth and sought our blessing, rather than offer us harm. We have been lucky."

The words of the Monsignor rang true, but father Trabbini could sense a possible change coming in their journey.

"As we near Torino, the numbers we meet will increase and we may face more offers of protection or indeed worse, those who force their well-meaning company upon us".

"I see the danger, "replied the parish priest, "but we can hardly demand that people leave us alone".

Both men stood up and for greater privacy continued their conversation whilst ensuring that the horse and the mule were comfortable and not unhappy. The Monsignor came to the point of his concerns.

"There are two routes we may follow. There is the main well-travelled road to Torino but we could from here take a less busy but more difficult path, towards the village of Fruselli. From there we could take not the road down to Genoa, but rather that quieter road up to Torino. There are some difficult parts for a cart but we shall almost certainly be free of other travellers. Have you some thoughts on this"?

Father Torino readily agreed to the Monsignor's change of plan. It made sense and he was once again beginning to feel weary and ready to accept anything that made their day simpler. The road to Fruselli was good in parts. Certainly, the Monsignor was correct that there were few other travellers to meet. A general tiredness began to fall upon horse, mule and the company. They seemed to collectively adopt a common plodding pace set by the horse. All was well until the track began to wind around a modest hill, but one with a steep ravine to its side. The chosen way began to narrow as they increasingly found themselves hemmed in by great walls of bare rock. On their other side the ravine grew deeper and the ground fell away steeply. The main dangers for travellers were the ugly rocks and deep vegetation at the very bottom of the ravine. To fall here, meant likely death and disappearance. The cart's horse seemed calm and happy to maintain its steady gait. However, the Monsignors' mule became skittish rolling its eyes, ears erect, it began to try to turn around seeking to rid itself of its rider. Monsignor Vatelli dismounted and sought to calm the animal. Sensing danger father Trabbini leapt down from the cart to provide assistance. The two men frightened the mule even more. With a heavy blow from its rear it knocked the Monsignor to the very edge of the ravine. Father Trabbini left the mule and rushed and grabbed his friend. The momentum of his efforts drove them both towards the edge each clinging to the other. The mule gave a final great shake, and the two clerics clutched in each other's arms fell without a sound, to break against the great rocks, and then disappear silently deep into the vegetation. A silence fell upon the scene. Rid of its tormentors the mule ceased its violence. The sound of birds suddenly seemed very clear. The horse resumed its steady momentum, and the mule quietly followed. The horse could at first sense and then see that ahead in the distance, the track widened to become a plateau, with thick grass a stand of trees and a small bubbling stream. Slowly horse, cart and its golden coins plodded forward followed by the once wayward mule, to enjoy the lush grass and sweet water.

There were five men in the party that left the main road to Torino, and directed their mounts and mules, to the downward track that skirted the high cliffs that loomed over them. Their leader was Spencer Compton the 2nd Earl of Northampton. He was a friend of King James I of England and now a confidant of his son Charles, The Prince of Wales. Some men are so blest, that they grow to become tall, handsome and easy on the eye. They have a self-confidence, and authority not just to lead others, but to inspire their loyalty. All who meet them, feel better for the experience, and wish to be like them. These men are remarkable, but to find one with all such advantages in his early twenties is rare. This was Spencer Compton. Twenty-two years old and he was the sixth richest man in England. A life of exercise and some excitement had kept him fit and in good health. He was dressed in a leather jerkin over a white shirt, black britches, hose and stout boots. This day on his horse he had remained relaxed despite it being the tenth day of their journey. His mission was accomplished and they were going home. Now with evening drawing in he was searching for a place to halt and establish a camp for the night. His Secretary Giles Middleton a law student, rode at his side fresh from university. Although young and new to his employment, Giles through his enthusiasm and hard work, enjoyed a special position with the Earl, and being of a common age he was a friend as well as a secretary. Thus, he enjoyed a familiarity with the Earl not given to others, a situation that he always used to his advantage. "How far to Genoa Giles"? asked the Earl.

"Some three days yet my Lord but I have some doubts as to our exact whereabouts. The guide is a fool he understands neither French nor Latin. Lord Compton snorted.

"Do we press on as we are"?

Giles thought for a moment and looked at the guide.

"The sulky fellow seems to say yes".

For a moment the party stood in silence looking at the narrow track before them. It curved gently around a high rock but there was room for two to ride side by side. The deepening ravine to the left was the main feature that required constant attention. Thankfully ten days on the same mounts had given them a level of skill such that they could face the challenge with confidence. The company was ready to move on but the Earl was taking a moment to muse on the outcome of his mission. He had been the personal emissary of King James. His task had been to provide diplomatic support to the "Grey lords" a name given to the leaders of the Protestant families that lived in the alpine villages of the Valtellina. They were a mountain people who controlled an important route across the Alps, but were surrounded and threatened by Cardinal Richelieu of France, the Hapsburg Emperor and the Pope. All three powers coveted the Valtellina especially the Hapsburgs, for it was the main land route between Spain and their Austrian territories. Compton had brought messages of the King's support but that had been only diplomatic words, together with some small packets of gold and jewels. Their hosts had smiled and welcomed the support but realised that England could do little more. A month of talks had not resolved the matter. Compton had enjoyed the banquets, the balls and the ladies, especially one in particular. But with no peaceful outcome in sight, he and his entourage had made their adieus and were now on route for Genoa and England. The day had been hot but with its ending, a soft wind was producing a cooling on the Earl's neck. At this prompt he led his party on to the path. There was room enough for them but the path was rough and with the steep cliff looming over them, the failing light demanded extra care. Giles Middleton followed his master. The guide was behind him with the mules. The two retainers brought up the rear. There was no conversation as the men and their mounts fixed their concentration to navigating a safe passage. Their progress was slow but as they rounded a slight turn, they could see that the track led to a grassy plateau, with a stand of trees and a pool of water.

"My Lord" exclaimed Giles, "there appears to be a horse and cart amidst the trees but I can see no one in company with it".

The Earl grunted and said nothing but focussed on making certain that they moved safely off the track and on to the plateau.

"We will rest here" he commanded. "Hugh and Michael have a look around. There must be someone here."

They all dismounted and Giles sent the guide to look to the needs of the mules. Lord Compton strode over to the cart. The horse stirred and moved a few paces forward, and then resumed eating the grass. He appeared comfortable with the English Lord. Leaning over the sides of the cart Compton began examining its contents. At this point a mule emerged from the trees and moved over to be with those of the Earl's party

" This is all very strange" cried out Giles, "but he instructed Hugh and Michael to hobble the new mule with their own. For a moment the Earl looked at the new arrival, he then resumed his inspection of the cart and its contents.

"Worthless rubbish" he declared, "clothes, largely broken furniture, rusty spades, nothing here".

He moved to the centre of the plateau and began calling out in English trying to arouse those who owned the cart and the mule, whilst at the same time announcing their own presence. He walked across to the trees. There was little undergrowth no one hidden, dead or comatose. Whilst the Earl was so engage, Giles had turned to inspecting the contents of the cart.

"My Lord" he called in a short gasp. "Something here to see"

The Earl recognised a level of excitement in his Secretary's voice. He returned to the cart.

"Well" he said.

Giles spoke softly but urgently.

"I touched a sack pushed forward under some old clothes. It felt solid, very solid. Using two hands I grasped it more firmly. I swear I felt coins"

"Show me" commanded the Earl, "but slowly".

Between them the Earl and his Secretary revealed the four sacks that the two priests had laboured so hard to deliver to mother Church. The Earl with a knife had confirmed the promise of the sacks.

"Gold Giles, more than you can think of, treasure to fill a mad man's dreams. We must keep calm. Let the others rest where they are. We can re-join our party and reflect later on this amazing fortune."

After a hurried supper, Lord Compton ordered the guide and his retainers to their blankets. Giles, he ordered to follow him over to the track well away from the cart.

"Giles I am one of the wealthiest men in England, with what we have here in these sacks I could match anyone in the land. This has obviously been lost by someone but it was hidden, one suspects no legal ownership".

Giles looked at the Earl, he knew his next words.

"I will lay claim to this Giles and you shall prosper from my ownership. The devil is how are we to get this back to England. No one must find out about this. Gold drives men mad. I trust you Giles but Hugh, Michael and our guide must know nothing."

The two men stood a while quiet with their own thoughts. Then they began an intense discussion on getting the new-found wealth to Genoa and then on to the Northamptonshire estate at Castle Ashby. They would keep the cart remove the rubbish and replace it with their baggage, the presents and artefacts that had been the load of their mules. This, they would supervise very carefully. They both realised the dangers ahead, the long road, the ocean voyage and the cities they would pass through. One mistake and in an instant their treasure would be known, their ownership challenged, and perhaps their lives lost.

Chapter Three (1651 England)

.

Newly arrived in London from France, Captain John Ketch, strode up Whitehall carefully avoiding the rubbish, waste and excrement, that still covered the streets and alleyways of England's capital. He was followed by a porter carrying two large leather bags. His new rank and its pay allowed him to take advantage of such services, for in the past he had carried his own bags. Ketch was now twenty-eight years old. He still retained the short brown hair and steady blue eyes of his early manhood, but his physical frame had been distinctly strengthened by time. His shoulders were more firmly set. His chest was larger and his waist not so painfully thin. His torso, arms and legs displayed a new solidity and even his pale face had darkened. As a military man he was at his physical peak. His good sense and intelligence had not been lost, however, and he kept a wary eye on the porter, ready to intervene if he tried to slip away. In the early part of his army career at the onset of the war against the King, he had the rank of trooper. But four years ago, he had been recruited into Cromwell's Secret Service. He now worked under instructions from the Secretary of the Committee for Extra Papers, John Thurloe. He was a secret agent of the Commonwealth working from within the army. In that capacity he had served his masters well. In three particular instances he had managed a crisis, that avoided serious damage to England's new rulers. In general, he enjoyed the work. There was no such thing as routine. But from time to time he remembered, that a Captain of cavalry would usually lead a troop of up to 200 men. Also, a life he would have found satisfying.

London was a place of energy and opportunity, fear and dirt. Thick black smoke covered the city, the product of thousands of coal fires. The gloom was thickened by low winter cloud and an absence of wind. A damp murk embraced all, from which his cavalry officer's uniform was limited protection. His progress along Whitehall was delayed by the throng of men and women all going about their own business. However, his passage was easier than most as few would jostle a Roundhead cavalry officer in his full uniform. Thus, with back and front breast plates over a buff leather top, strong dark woollen trousers, boots and a sword at his side he had a martial air that would brook no interference. Not that such an event was likely. It was October and in London the army was popular. A month earlier the Royalist army of Charles Stuart had been decisively beaten at Worcester, and despite the loss of summer England felt real hope that a long period of peace was to be enjoyed.

He was but 15 minutes from his destination the White Hart tavern down by the river where the great palace of the Duke of Lancaster once stood. His reception on arriving was welcoming. Mrs Dunn was at her customary station behind a heavy, long wooden table, on which stood bottles and jugs, together with spigots, tankards, spoons and other requirements for providing ales and spirits for customers. The table itself was at one end of a large public room. Facing the table but at the far end of the room, were the large doors of the entrance. Between these two points was a cluster of tables, chairs, and benches. It was late afternoon and usual clients, those seeking refreshment after a day of toil, had not yet got to their favourite place to relax. The room was not empty, however, there were a few idlers and old men nursing their tankards and conversing with their neighbour. Mrs Dunn always found a room for Ketch even if it meant moving one of her large sons into his brother's room. She liked Ketch. He was in the prime of life, attractive, generally clean and she had never seen him drunk. He was not one of these extreme Puritans and he always paid his bill in coin.

"I have a room for you Cornet," she said unaware of his promotion.

"This lump George will help you to it with your baggage".

George was the larger of her two large sons. Unlike his brother Henry, he had a happy disposition and shared his mother's appreciation of Ketch's worth. Unknown to his mother he had a dream to join the army. He had mentioned it to Ketch but had received no encouragement, Ketch had no wish to come between George and his mother. As they moved towards the stairs Mrs Dunn called out after him

"There will be food in an hour, we have a leg of sweet lamb in the pot, Oh and a Major Blake says he will collect you early tomorrow."

Major Blake had been responsible for recruiting Ketch into his secret life. The message could only mean that his superior Thurloe wanted to see him. Soldiers were a common sight at the White Hart, but for the regular customers an obvious officer and one with special treatment from Mrs Dunn may have news.

"Have they got him yet, "called out one of a group of old men who largely spent their time playing cards.

Ketch turned. It was just a month after Worcester and as far as he knew Charles Stuart, the hopeful King, was still a fugitive somewhere in England hunted by the army and the public alike.

"Not as far as I know," he called out as he made his way up to his room followed by George.

The room was up one flight of stairs to the floor above, not large but it had a window on to the street below, a bed, a chair, table and a wash stand. Ketch relieved George of his baggage and slipped him a copper coin. Finally, alone, he took off his sword and lay on the bed to both rest and collect his thoughts. After a few minutes he rose to take off his belt and boots and with a taper set a light to the prepared kindling, for a fire in the small fireplace. He proposed to sit by the fire and recover from his visit to France. As the warmth of the fire grew and his body began enjoying its warmth he slipped into a pleasant reverie. His mind moved between the major parts of his current life. Above all he thought of his wife Anne, at home in Northampton in their small house on the market square. Married for three years, Anne was used to the burden that his work placed on her. As an agent for Cromwell 's security chief he was often away and occasionally in danger, but this time he had been away for over four weeks and in a foreign country. He knew they had friends who would support her in his absence, but never the less he felt he needed to be home soon. This need to see his wife moved his thoughts on to his next meeting with his master, John Thurloe. Ketch admired Thurloe, his knowledge, his intelligence, his commitment and in a strange way his honesty. He knew that spies especially Chief of Spies dissembled and lied, but as yet to Ketch's knowledge, Thurloe had never lied to him. Thurloe was a man of enormous power and yet he did not frighten Ketch. He frightened other people especially his colleagues Holditch and Tull. Ketch knew, however, that Thurloe cared for his operatives, expected remarkable things from them, but protected them jealously. Ketch's mind turned to their last meeting high up in the Palace of Westminster. It was there that he was given his instructions for France. He fell into a dep reverie that took him back to his last meeting with Thurloe.

It had been an unusual meeting. Thurloe, sat as normal. behind his desk. He was dressed in the traditional puritan uniform of black Jerkin, britches and a dazzling white collar. There was, however, another person seated in the room. He was dressed the same as Thurloe except around his neck was a large white ruff. He sat at a chair alongside the desk, and to his left hand was a small table, and there sat a clerk with papers, pen and ink. The table had its own papers and a large magnifying glass. Thurloe opened the meeting. He gestured Ketch to a chair facing him across the desk.

"You are going to France Ketch, not for me, not for the Committee for Extra -papers, but for this gentleman on my left. Let me introduce you to him."

Ketch turned to face the newcomer. He saw a man of advanced years but one who looked comfortable and relaxed in Thurloe's company. This was a man of substance and significance. He was of a medium height with black hair that was turning grey, cut short in the Parliamentary fashion. He had a slim oval face with a prominent nose. His mouth was small with a large lower lip. He took a cursory look at Ketch and then continued to hold the papers he was reading, up close in front of his face.

"This is Mr Milton" said Thurloe. "He is the Secretary for Foreign Tongues and you are going to France for him. You will know him as a great writer and early pamphleteer in our recent struggles against the former King."

The man called Milton handed his papers to his clerk and turned towards Ketch. "I cannot see you too well young man" he said

"But you have Thurloe's recommendation and that is sufficient for me. What you have to do requires some background, so listen with care".

Ketch shuffled in his chair. Milton's voice was low and mellow but there was an unexpected authority in his words.

"Besides translating the correspondence received by the Commonwealth from foreign governments I also advise our leaders on our foreign policy."

Ketch gave Milton his full attention. He was involved in serious matters of state.

"You will know that that at this moment Charles Stuart is in Scotland waiting to invade this country. As such it is vital that we fully understand the policy of France in this matter."

Ketch nodded, like everyone else he knew that the son of the beheaded King had been in Scotland for over a year trying to reconcile its varying factions to support him in common cause.

"It is all about family Ketch."

These last comments of Milton totally bemused Ketch.

"What *on earth has family got to do with this?*".

He kept his thoughts unspoken thinking it best to say nothing until Milton spoke again. Milton continued with his explanation.

"The pretender in Scotland has useful connections .He has a sister. His father, Charles I, who we beheaded, had a daughter who married William of Orange, essentially the leader of the Dutch Republic. This William has been a source of men, munitions, materials and   money."

Ketch cast a look at Thurloe, his return glance said

"listen this is important"

Milton continued.

"However, it is our good fortune that this William of Orange died in March" and he turned towards the Secretary Thurloe.

"My colleague here on my right, and John Scott MP respectively Secretary and Chairman of the Committee for Extra Papers, headed a mission to Holland and achieved a total change of policy. No more help for Charles Stuart there.".

This Milton said with considerable relish and allowed a smile to cross his face.

"So far so good".

He paused for a moment and allowed himself to take a drink from a goblet placed in front of him. He continued.

"But that was not the only family support enjoyed by Charles Stuart. His own mother was Henrietta Maria the sister of the late King of France, Louis XIII, which makes his son the present King of France, Louis XIV, his full cousin. And as far as we know his support for Charles remains constant. So, Ketch we have uncoupled the Dutch from Charles Stuart, but not the French."

Ketch began to feel uncomfortable wondering what exactly was his role to be and he threw a concerned glance to Thurloe. Milton carried on with his tale.

"France, Ketch, is different from Holland. It is a country wracked with division. Louis XIV is a twelve-year-old boy. The country is ruled by his mother Anne of Austria and her assumed lover Cardinal Mazarin. They are both extremely unpopular with both the people and the nobility. There have been physical attacks on them which they seem powerless to prevent. The Paris mob invaded the King's bedchamber and he had to pretend sleep in order to save himself. The Queen and Mazarin had to flee Paris for months. Nobles employ their own private armies. A large part of the country is Protestant like ourselves. They call themselves Huguenots, but the majority of the country is Catholic. Spain the most powerful country in Europe spends a fortune meddling in French affairs to pursue their own interests."

By now Milton had become flushed but he had not yet finished with Ketch.

"Beside this, half the country the Bretons, those in Provence and Alsace do not speak French at all."

Milton sat back in his chair and gradually composed himself. He spoke in more measured tones.

"All this division of course is to our advantage but we have no idea as to what France will do about almost anything, let alone give support to Charles Stuart. However, Ketch, think what a struggle we would have on our hands, if we faced even a token Royalist invasion in the South of England backed with French support, coming at the same time as an invasion from Scotland. That could prove to be a very stern test for our new republic."

Thurloe turned to Ketch.

"That is the best we can do in giving you the background for what Milton requires of you. We have a representative in Paris a Monseigneur Rene Petit. The French court will not recognise him as our ambassador they continue to recognise those of Charles Stuart, but he has some sort of accreditation, after all they must speak to us through some one. As you would expect he has established some good contacts and we expect that he will be able to provide you with a report on the true strength of the support for Charles Stuart."

At this point Milton re asserted his ownership of the discussion.

"Your task, Ketch, is to go to Paris meet Rene Petit and return with his report, emphasise that it must cover troop movements, specific regiments, names of commanders, whose advice carries most weight at court. In addition, ketch you must spend some time yourself discovering what you can and assessing the reality of what is a very confusing situation."

Milton turned to his clerk and received a sheet of paper which he held up close to his eyes, and then turned again to Ketch.

"I see you have limited French and some Latin but Thurloe says you have brains and an engaging manner and you can cope with danger. You can trust Petit, Ketch, but remember others may see you as a spy".

Ketch received his information from the two Secretaries with a certain relief. He was to be a messenger, collect a report talk to some people, and then come home. Yes, there may be an element of unknown danger but he was used to that. He had thought he was destined for some more dark and ugly task, but what was asked of him he could do. Thurloe, Milton and Ketch continued to discuss the details of his task and some names, dates, transport arrangements and money were decided. He was finally dismissed by Thurloe but as he started to rise from his chair. Thurloe smiled and said,

"Oh! by the way, to strengthen your diplomatic status you have been promoted to captain. The clerk outside has your new commission. I doubt any Frenchman of substance would talk to a Cornet".

Ketch's thoughts were dwelling happily on his promotion when he was brought up sharply out of his reverie by a heavy banging on his bedroom door. It was George.

"Food is ready Mr ketch, mother says come down whilst it is hot".

Chapter Four

Ketch was enjoying a late breakfast in the large public room of the White Hart. There were a few other customers but Ketch was largely ignored and left alone. Although his meal was most satisfactory his state of mind was not. His work in France had been a total waste of time. Petit's reports and his observations, forwarded to Thurloe and Milton, had been worthless. All their efforts had no influence on the course of events at all. The Battle of Worcester had changed everything. Charles Stuart's army of Scots had been defeated and Charles himself was a fugitive, being hunted all over England. A month away from home could in no way be justified to his wife. What was worse was that he had needlessly been away when great military events were taking place. He was a soldier he should have been at Worcester.

It was with such thoughts uppermost in his mind that his meal was interrupted by the arrival of his close colleague and mentor Major Blake. The Major was effectively Thurloe's deputy, he especially was responsible for informing army leaders on the mood and state of the army. It was he that had introduced Ketch to the world of secrets, not by choice but desperate for support in an urgent task to find an unwise letter written by King Charles. It had been Ketch's contribution in securing the success of the Major's quest that had led to his eventual induction into Cromwell's intelligence service. This was the service run by Thurloe on behalf of his master. The two men had also worked successfully together in the ending of the army mutiny in 1649. Although Ketch had managed to get the Major to his wedding theirs was an unusual friendship in that they met only infrequently, when following the tasks allocated to them by Thurloe. Ketch, however, was always conscious that after the affair of the King's letter, his knowledge of a certain state secret, had made Thurloe, plan his elimination. It had been Richard Blake who had persuaded Thurloe that Ketch's loyalty could be relied upon. The Major was 36 years old, slight of build and dressed as a civilian with black shoes, socks, britches, and jerkin. The overwhelming Puritan black was reduced, however, by his white collar and cuffs and a dark red sash that gave a military hint to his appearance. The Major possessed a restless energy and there was a constant humour in his dark blue eyes. He enjoyed the company and confidences of men and women, a perfect personality for his profession.

"Well Ketch, a Captain! and a visit to France, fortune favours you."

These his opening remarks were spoken softly so that only Ketch could hear. but he was clearly delighted to meet up once more with the man he had always looked upon as his protégé. "Yes" replied Ketch. "I am very happy with the promotion though Thurloe has had little value from it so far. The visit to France brought scant returns. Worcester has changed everything as far as France is concerned. But! What of Worcester were you there, did Thurloe allow you to get involved? What can you tell me?"

"Yes, I was there", replied the Major. "As was Thurloe. We helped a bit but it was basically a straightforward hard fight. The Scots fought well and it was not an easy victory, but a victory it was and one with over ten thousand prisoners."

Ketch looked quizzically at his friend. The answer had not been very forthcoming. "But," he continued,

"You have not got Charles Stuart himself, and unless you have news he is still at large somewhere in England".

He looked expectantly at the Major.

"No doubt you are involved in his capture and I also expect to join in the hunt."

The Major just smiled to himself he knew that Thurloe had another task for Ketch.

"I must return to that search Ketch but first I must take you to Thurloe, you will find much has changed since you have been away. He of course demands all speed and I am charged to tell you that he has received the satchel with all your reports. But we must be away!"

The Major waited whilst Ketch quickly informed Mrs Dunn of his departure and collected from his room, what he thought he needed for an interview with Thurloe. Then the two men smartly left the inn. Ketch was not sure where they were going, but the Major had understood his concern and began to explain how their lives had changed.

"Thurloe is no longer based in the Palace of Westminster, all our clerks, papers, and materials have been moved into the Palace of Whitehall. In some ways this is a good move. There is more room and we are not surrounded by the members of the Commons. There is no doubt Worcester is bringing peace and is forcing changes Ketch. The Commons and the army are testing each other for some sort of mastery. The Committee for Extra Papers has been abolished. Cromwell moved Thurloe into Whitehall and placed him under his own personal direction. They meet regularly but I am sure there will be other changes. At the moment all other matters depend upon the outcome with Charles Stuart."

Ketch pulled a face. He doubted this was good news.

As Ketch and Major Blake made their way to Whitehall the Major looked carefully at Ketch and then said,

"I have some unhappy news for you Ketch, James Hedlow, the former clerk to Northampton Council and your friend is dead. He died peacefully in his sleep three weeks ago."

Ketch came to a halt. His body seemed to freeze with sorrow and grief. He stood silent for a moment.

"He was a very good man Richard in so many ways, to so many people. He was wise, clever, brave and generous. Both Anne and I greatly valued his friendship. He became as a father to us."

His words came tumbling out.

"But there were so many others who knew and loved him. It is a massive blow for the town. Even retired he was the first man of Northampton".

"I also knew him", replied the Major. "We both met him for the first time when we ourselves first met"

Ketch seemed to come out of his immobile state.

"Anne will be desolate. He saved her life gave her courage to face the world. She will need me now Richard. I fear for her, I must go at once"

Ketch turned to retrace his steps but the Major caught his arm.

"Hold Ketch you must see Thurloe. He has already acted to support Ann. He has sent your trusted friend Sergeant Tull to provide her with someone to rely on. There is more in this that you must know."

Richard Blake drew Ketch to one side.

"Clerk Hedlow left a will. He was in fact a rich man and his wealth is divided between you and his nephew Stephen. We have been told that Stephen is to inherit his three farms and you are to receive his house and garden and a number of properties in Northampton. This has been a very large bequest. You are in fact a very wealthy man but your absence has been a problem. The hunt for Charles Stuart has prevented sending Anne any more help than Tull, but you have friends in Northampton and the new Mayor Councillor Lugg has received letters from Thurloe and has given his promise to protect Ann and your inheritance from any challenge. I tell you this in haste Ketch as Thurloe has plans despite all this, to send you to Northampton. He also decided that it was best for you, to hear these tidings quickly, and told by a friend"

Ketch remained still and silent for some moments, as he tried to come to understand all that he had been told. Then in a massive effort of will he seemed to shake off the words of the Major.

"Let us see Thurloe at once."

They entered Whitehall Palace through the main gated archway opposite the great Abby church. It was guarded but seemed a common thoroughfare, used by all those who declared they had business. The guards waved through all who approached them. The palace was one of the largest in Europe. It was a jumbled collection of interlocking building with rooms of all shapes and sizes, for all manner of purposes. There were residential areas, offices, ballrooms, great halls, private meeting rooms, stables, store rooms, kitchens, music rooms and armouries. To its inhabitants the control of accommodation was a mystery largely based on tradition, as determined by the army's senior generals. Through a series of corridors, the Major led Ketch to a passage with a large skylight. At the end was a dark green door with the notice "Enter". Doing as was requested, Ketch found himself in a large high room with a floor to ceiling window, casting its light on a scene of both order and change. In one part of the room various persons were arranging furniture, stacking papers and setting up desks. In another there was clearly decision and management with clerks engaged in their various duties. A door to their left opposite to the great window opened and Thurloe emerged.

"Welcome to our new home "he cried. "We have barely been here three days and we have much to do. Come on in Ketch come in to my sanctum. At the moment I have a carpet, a desk some chairs and a cabinet. I have a window that looks out on to a courtyard, that I do not Know. I have no curtains but there is a table with glasses and some Flemish wine. Come and get comfortable." He turned to Major Blake. "Is everything well".

The Major answered his question with a nod.

"Good! It is important that you return to finding Charles Stuart. He has been eluding us for too long. The trail has gone cold. I fear we will lose him. Quick go!"

Ketch was disappointed to see his friend dispatched to other work when they had barely met and they had so much to say. Nevertheless, he turned and entered Thurloe's new office.
Thurloe, as promised, poured Ketch a glass of wine and it gave Ketch a little time to take a fresh look at the man who guided his life. He found that his new rank, his time in France, even these new surroundings, gave him a new confidence to more closely appraise the man in front of him. Thurloe looked essentially the same except for the loss of his beard. If anything, he looked more relaxed. It was possibly because he was enjoying his move to new premises but Ketch thought it was more than that. It seemed as if the cares of state weighed less heavily upon his shoulders. Thurloe seemed to be actually enjoying life.

"Of course, he thought, "Worcester! Worcester changes everything".

He waited whilst Thurloe returned to his place. When they had settled with Thurloe sitting on one side of his desk and Ketch on the other. Thurloe gave Ketch a look of genuine sympathy.

"I am sorry for the loss of your friend the clerk Hedlow, He was not only your friend but also a strong supporter for the Commonwealth. We here in London shall also miss him."

He looked down at some papers on his desk.

"As we had sent you to France, I felt that we had to take some action on your behalf. I was written to by the new Mayor of Northampton, a councilman Lugg. He claims to know you well and he tells me that you have received a considerable inheritance from James Hedlow's will. He and his friends will have done their best to protect your wife Anne and the inheritance whilst you were absent. You clearly have made a mark in Northampton Ketch. In such circumstances I felt it appropriate that I send Sergeant Tull to Northampton to provide your wife with any assistance she may need."

Ketch had heard of Thurloe's kindness already from Richard Blake, but he was pleased to have it explained and confirmed by Thurloe himself. Ketch was warm in his thanks for this unlooked-for help. Thurloe gracefully waved his thanks aside and turned to their central task

"Well Ketch, you re-join us at an exciting time. You have missed Worcester and you will find out all about it soon enough, but all our efforts are now turned to finding Charles Stuart before he can get back to France. He is still in England but as yet we do not have him. You and I are among the few of the army not actively searching for him."

Ketch was about to make a comment when Thurloe raised both his hands, a sign he did not want to be interrupted.

"We must move on Ketch. I have two matters that I wish to discuss with you. First France. Both Milton and I will read Petit's reports and your own account, but in reality, your visit was overtaken by events. The matter of French support for Charles Stuart is now unimportant.

Worcester has changed everything. Ketch decided it was worth a few words to clear away the matter of his visit to France.

"I agree. Before Worcester few people in Paris would talk to me or Monseigneur Petit. They may be divided amongst themselves but no one had any interest, let alone care for the English. But after Worcester when we heard the news, whilst we were not feted, or even liked, there was a new respect in the air and everyone wanted to know more about General Cromwell. Thurloe re-entered the conversation.

"Charles Stuart is finished especially if we catch him and If Cromwell lasts for ten years, we shall find our Commonwealth fully established…. No more Kings!"

Thurloe adopted a conspiratorial air.

"Between ourselves Ketch I sometimes consider that it might be better if Charles Stuart got away to Holland or France. If we caught him what would we do with him? Chop his head off. I think not. Lock him up. He would always be dangerous and a centre for discontent. Of course, as it is, he has a younger brother and plenty of other relatives who would lay claim to the title."

He broke away from his musings.

"However, all that does not matter, the monarchist cause has no support and no resources and that Ketch brings me to my second point".

Ketch felt he had to speak. He thought Thurloe was seriously wrong in his analysis on one clear matter.

"Forgive me Mr Secretary" he said reverting to Thurloe's old title. "Although my investigation in France has little value, there is one central point that I really must bring to your attention. The English at home and the people of France may or may not have sympathies for Charles Stuart, but the English royalists left in France most certainly do. They in many cases have given up everything for both Charles and his dead father. They have given their wealth, lost their lands, sacrificed sons, brothers and fathers. They will never abandon the monarchy. They have only one purpose in life and that is to bring about a restoration. We heard many times the old comment of Lord Manchester, you may beat the King ninety-nine times and he will still be the King, but to succeed the King has only to win once. We must not ignore the future danger they may present."

Thurloe smiled and laughed out loud.

"Oh Ketch" he exclaimed you are wiser than you know and have the infallible ability of being in the right place for all events "

He paused and in a most determined voice.

"And this brings me to my second point".

Ketch made to speak but once more the hands went up.

"I have a new task for you Ketch but before you say anything let me say at once that this new matter involves your own home town of Northampton. So that it involves an immediate return to your wife. I hope you are happy with that".

Ketch thought it best to say nothing and to let Thurloe continue with his instructions. The Secretary looked hard at ketch and then continued.

" Strangely enough Ketch it concerns the very matter you have just been so keen to draw to my attention, namely the fanatical, continuing, royalist support to be found in some quarters. Those who will never, ever be reconciled to the new order and who desperately need monies to maintain their cause after this their recent calamitous defeat"

Ketch was relieved to be going home. He missed his wife and he knew that she missed him. They desperately needed time together. For a moment Ketch realised that he did not know if Thurloe himself was married. There was no indication of any kind. Presumably he thought, the fewer the people who had any information about Thurloe the better. Certainly, he was a mystery to his own agents, However, he pushed his mind away from such matters and awaited more details of Thurloe's assignment.

"Your assignment Ketch involves the late Earl of Northampton Spencer Compton. When war with the King broke out, he joined the Royalist cause and he became a dashing cavalry commander. He was a hero to his men and a sharp thorn in our side. He was both brave and gallant in my mind to the point of stupidity. But for a few years he prospered very much a talisman for the royalist cause. In 1643 he was the Royalist commander at the Battle of Hopton Heath. There true to his nature he led a daring cavalry charge that captured our artillery. Again, true to his reputation he led another charge where he got too far ahead of his men and was surrounded. He was offered quarter Ketch, but he refused it, fought on and was pole axed. A rash man, brave but very rash."

Thurloe paused for a moment as if reflecting on the folly of bravery. Ketch waited he knew there was more to come.

"We offered his comrades his body in return for our artillery but they refused. We initially honoured him by having him embalmed but they refused to pay for it. So, he was eventually burnt at Derby. A sad end to a brave enemy",

At this point Ketch had no idea how this tale was of importance to him. Thurloe continued.

"At the time there was some interest that on his person he was found to have a leather pouch containing eight rather large gold coins. These coins were not made recently but were of Greek and Roman origin. Now this was sufficient for a search to take place at his home, a rather grand house known as Castle Ashby just outside Northampton. The house and the estate had been sequestered and was administered by our County Committee in Northamptonshire. The house was unfortunately looted by servants and locals at the very beginning of the Civil War and a portion of it had been damaged by fire. Zouche Tate the MP for Northampton was asked to search the premises and grounds to see if any more of these gold coins were to be found. Zouche was quite energetic in his search and upset quite a lot of local people and damaged a certain amount of property but nothing was found, so the matter was laid to rest. No such coins had come to light. At the time I was just a minute clerk for the House of Commons and these events were largely forgotten but here is the important new problem. After Worcester and this is eight years later, a fair number of the prisoners especially the officers were found to have such gold coins on them. Now we know that there was a distribution of monies to royalist forces in Lancashire on the way to Worcester and gold is difficult for small purchases and would have been changed for silver. So, in fact quite a lot may have been distributed that we do not know about. I doubt that we have found it all, also much will have been hidden away when the outcome of the battle was becoming clearer."

Ketch sat back in his chair he noticed he had not taken any of the wine poured for him. He remained silent for a moment and then having taken a drink he joined in the conversation,

"If Charles Stuart should return to France and should there be more of the Earl of Northampton's gold, he may yet remain a problem for the Commonwealth. He still has that support that I observed in France."

"Exactly Ketch," replied Thurloe. "Whilst it does not do to exaggerate matters undoubtedly it does cloud our current happy outlook"

Ketch had two questions for Thurloe.

"Is there an heir to this treasure and can you explain its sudden re-emergence?"

"I can answer the first but not the last", was his answer.

"His son is James Compton and is the third Earl. He was almost as celebrated as his father. He commanded a cavalry wing at Newbury and a division at Naseby. We have lost track of him. We did not pick him up at Worcester. He is probably in France. It does not matter. He has no claim on those coins, they are part of the sequestered estate."

Ketch nodded.

"So, my task is to get to Northampton and find out if any of that ancient gold remains and if so secure it for the Commonwealth and expose any royalist paymasters."

"Yes, Ketch finding any paymasters is just as important as finding the gold."

Thurloe leaned forward he still had things to tell Ketch. I have not been slow in this matter. I have sent our colleague, Sergeant Holditch to Chester. He is to squeeze Chester's gold merchants as to who was dealing in Roman and Greek coins and what do they know of the distribution to the army. He is to join you in Northampton when he has something to report. Further I have written to Lord Wilmington. He manages the sequested estates in Northamptonshire and sends the resulting rents and revenues to the House of Commons. He is a very strong supporter of the Commons Ketch unfortunately he is a House of Commons man who has little liking for the army. But he must be told you are coming and that you expect assistance from him. I expect he will not be happy or an easy colleague. Zouche Tate when he first investigated these matters dealt with a Giles Middleton. He is a former secretary to the second Earl Spencer Compton. I think after Lord Wilmington your focus must be on this man. His is a strange situation. Because of his knowledge of the Earl's affairs, Lord Wilmington kept him on to run the details of the sequested estate. He is still there and he has always denied knowing anything of hidden gold, loudly protesting that the coins found on Spencer Compton could have come from anyone. Zouche Tate died some years ago but his steward was a man called Varley Brent, he also remains in Northampton. He was very hard with Middleton almost to the point of torture. His treatment of Middleton was so unpleasant that it led to calls for the whole matter to be dropped. He sounds very unpleasant but you may get something from him. I fear there will be a need for speed in this matter Ketch. There are those who remember the previous search of Castle Ashby for gold coins and word will also be known of what has been found at Worcester. There may be those who will challenge you in this".

Thurloe turned to a drawer in his desk and produced a piece of parchment with a seal on it.

"You have had one of these before Ketch it is a warrant and a requirement for all citizens to answer your questions and seek to provide what assistance you might need. There are some difficult residents in Northampton who may protest their rights. You may be moving among gentlemen, do not be outfaced by them. The warrant will also help but things are changing. In war time Cromwell's warrants received instant obedience but civil authority is now re-emerging. There may now be lawyers who will detest such things and question their validity."

Thurloe rose from his chair.

"Come ketch we have details to arrange and papers to sign, and monies to be distributed, join me in the outer room and with my chief clerk we will arrange such matters.

Chapter Five

Sergeant Holditch sat in the corner of the large public room of the Bear tavern in the city of Chester. It was gloomy and cold, but he was under orders to draw no attention to himself. Self -discipline required him to refrain from his usual habit of wrestling a warm place by the large fire. He had arrived in Chester the day before and when asked, a cooper's apprentice had pointed to the Bear as a safe place to sleep. On his arrival there the main room was full with men drinking and talking, it had a comfortable air and candles and the bright fire sought to give a feeling of comfort and security. But conversations were low and there was a feeling of concern amongst the company.

"Not surprising ", thought Holditch. *"Everyone knows that Chester had been a royalist city from the beginning of the recent war against Charles I. Only months ago, it had also waved his son on South, wishing him success with his Scottish army. There was now a roundhead regiment in the city searching for the fugitive Charles, but also seeking out those that in anyway, exhibited royalist sympathies. Any excuse was likely to be taken up by hard fighting men to secure a little revenge for lost comrades."* Holditch nursed his pewter pot and reflected on the task set him by Secretary Thurloe. He had to find out how those gold coins got into the hands of the rebel army and who had put them there. This was no easy task but it could be vital information for his friend, now Captain Ketch back in Northampton, in his search for the source of the coins.

Holditch and his closest friend Tull had teamed up with Ketch when they were all troopers in Lord Manchester's regiment at the very beginning of the recent war. They had kept together as they were moved about the regiments, finding that three could survive the soldiers' life, better than one. The three together had experienced different encounters with both friends and enemies but their firm friendship and avoiding being noticed had always seen them safe. For a time Holditch and Tull had lost touch with Ketch during events in Northampton when a Colonel had been murdered. That was when Ketch was again involved with Secretary Thurloe and the army's spies. Sometime later they had met up again with Ketch when the two of them had been of use in Salisbury at the time of the army mutiny. As a result, both Holditch and Tull had been drawn in to working for Thurloe and given the rank of Sergeant. Tull was now in Northampton and it was as a sole agent for the first time, that Holditch had to undertake his task. It was a new experience. The importance that Thurloe attached to his mission was seen in the paper tucked inside his jerkin. Signed by the General it required all to assist Holditch in any task he required. He knew of such papers but until now had never seen one and to date his journey had not required him to use it. He knew his first task was to interview the two remaining goldsmiths still present in Chester. He had overheard a conversation that one had been recently burnt down in the search for royalists' sympathisers. In his own mind at the moment he had rejected his initial thoughts, of immediately seeking the support of the local garrison. "Try not to let others know you are there", had been Thurloe's final words. He was determined to make his initial visits to the goldsmiths alone.

He rose early the next morning and dressed with care. He sought to present himself as a lower order clerk who was clean, reliable and holder of a modest position. This was in fact quite difficult for Holditch. He was by nature outward going, enthusiastic, mercurial. He enjoyed talking and was a natural in the market place. His wit and banter served him well in usually securing the best prices. He determined to rein in the more expansive elements of his nature and fully focus on the task ahead.

Chester's town clock had struck nine sombre notes as he entered the premises of Joseph Torrender, Goldsmith. The shop had a small frontage down a side street off Chester's London Road. The front door with the name above was the only indication that inside commerce was undertaken. The door opened easily enough to the pressure of Holditch's hand and arm. Inside he was in a small bare room. There was no furniture and no indication of what trade was carried on there. There was a grill in the wall opposite, with a small shelf below it and Holditch could see a door set seamlessly to the side. He stepped up to the door and gave a loud and confident knock. Initially there was no response but several repetitions eventually resulted in the grill being lifted and a bearded face appearing behind it. The bearded man's opening remarks were not welcoming.

"Who are you and what do you want? We are closed. Go away."

Holditch made no reply but slapped a large gold coin onto the small shelf, the only one entrusted to him by Thurloe. The grill was raised and fingers were extended towards the coin but before they touched, Holditch's hand was back on it.

"It may well be in your interests to grant me a little conversation", said Holditch. "Nothing dangerous I have no weapons only a tale to tell." His voice was calm but firm and carried an engaging warmth. The face behind the grill studied him. Holditch stepped back still holding the coin, so that all that he was could be seen. He gave a smile of innocence.

Apparently, he was regarded as harmless, the shutter went back down and the door was opened and he was beckoned inside to a small workshop that also served as a living room. On one side was a bench with instruments, lenses and a small collection of tools, on the other side an unlit hearth with chairs and two small tables. The bearded man was tall over six foot, broad shouldered and muscular. He was dressed in a brown woollen shirt, and black trousers, much of which was covered by a dark leather apron. His boots were covered in scorch marks. The face behind the beard was strong with large black eyes and a prominent nose, that had been broken in the past. Sallow cheeks and a clear brow rose to a large bald head. It was not a pretty face rather one that would not flinch from a challenge.

"You are Joseph Torrender" inquired Holditch. "You deal in coinage and all matters to do with metals of value?

The goldsmith gave Holditch a long hard stare before answering, but eventually he admitted that this was his name. He hitched up his trousers and offered Holditch a chair by the empty hearth.

"And what is your name?" he inquired.

"Not yet", said Holditch. "But if you sit with me, I shall tell you about this gold coin and its many friends and you would be wise to hear my tale".

Holditch kept his tone of voice light and engaging. There may be a time for menaces later. He hoped not, the goldsmith was a large man. Joseph Torrender waited and having made up his mind decided to take the chair opposite. Holditch began.

"These are difficult times, especially for those who live and work here in Chester. There is a regiment of ironsides combing this area for the pretender king, Charles Stuart. To date there has been only a little looting and misconduct, but they really want Charles Stuart and if they cannot find him, they will gladly move on to a search for rebels. In particular those who aided him with food and clothing and money changing for his officers and men".

Holditch's voice began to contain a hint of menace.

"There are no rebels in this house", exclaimed Torrender and he stood up and leant over Holditch who remained sitting calmly.

"No, I am sure that is the case for this house", he agreed and with a few more soothing words he had Torrender back sitting in his own chair.

"You know all this" continued Holditch.

"But, let me give you some extra bits of information. First, I am here in Chester on behalf of a very important man in London. A man who serves directly under Oliver Cromwell. This friend and his master know that Charles Stuart made a distribution of monies to his Scottish troops North of Chester. A remarkable number of gold coins just like the one you have just seen, were found on Scottish prisoners taken at Worcester. They were large, heavy and made of Roman or Greek gold."

Holditch stirred easily in his chair, his posture became confidential and supportive. It was one of a friend wanting to be helpful.

"You will know Joseph that such coins please everyone, but are difficult to use in our daily buying and selling. So, we change them for silver in places such as this."

Joseph began to stir uneasily as Holditch continued.
"Now as far as my friend in London is concerned, a helpful goldsmith one wishing to cooperate with London, would be regarded in such dealings as merely following an honest trade. But, to others it may appear as treason".

Here, Holditch stood up and from inside his jerkin he produced his special piece of paper.

"I decide in this matter Joseph who has, and who has not, committed treason. Here is my commission. Holditch thrust the paper towards the goldsmith with his finger pointing at the signature of Cromwell.

"And what if I hit you on the head and throw you in the river", snarled a return.

"You could try", replied Holditch. "But, within a week you would receive another visit involving a lot more heads than one, and you would hang. The choice is yours tell me what you know or be charged with treason".

The goldsmith back in his chair, sat silent and with a heavy vigour rubbed his head with his hands. He spoke.

"If you are what you say you are, then I have no choice. I am in your power. That paper would convince the regimental commanders here in Chester."

Holditch relaxed, he had cooperation.

"Just answer my questions, be helpful and I can leave you in peace with a commendation to the commander."

Joseph Torrender began to speak and having decided to cooperate this large and still at times aggressive man, began to explain to Holditch the number of coins he had exchanged for silver and the problems of trading with the men from the North. He told of such exchanges taking place all over Chester, as merchants were offered gold coins as payment. From his tales Holditch was able to understand that the trading was mainly done by the common soldier with but one or two officers involved. Holditch began to pressure the goldsmith for names. "Impossible", was the reply.

"No one gives names in such matters".

"Surely you asked the source of this wealth", pressed Holditch.

"We all knew it was from the King" came a sharp reply.

"So, you still call him your King".

These words from Holditch were softly spoken but they speedily reminded the goldsmith of the difficulty of his position. He continued.

"Someone was responsible for distribution".

"No persisted the goldsmith, no one was named".

The goldsmith was silent for a moment and gave Holditch a sly almost cunning look.

"There was one man, not a soldier who after the army moved South came to me with a small pouch of these assorted gold coins. His own personal stock he said. I would not trade at first, frankly I was short of silver. That simple honest refusal made him really angry. In a fit of rage, he shook me and said he would not be denied. He had taken too great a risk to be treated thus by merchants he had made rich".

"And his name" asked Holditch.

He stood up very quietly over the goldsmith. This was why he was there. For a moment Torrender hesitated as if to bargain a price for his information, but a warning voice within him stressed the danger such behaviour would involve.

"Dundas Stannard said he would not be denied and that Mr interrogator is all I know".

Holditch rose from his chair.

"So, this Dundas Stannard was likely close to the source of the coins or may have been the actual source of the coins." Torrender just grunted in reply. He was clearly losing his cooperative nature. He had told what he knew. Holditch risked two more questions.

"Did you see him again, here or about Chester.

"No, came another curt rejoinder.

Finally, and belatedly the goldsmith gave a description that could have been anyone. Holditch made to leave.

"Before I depart Chester, I shall mention your help to the garrison commander, it may do you some good." Holditch kept his word although he did add that the goldsmith would be an excellent informant.

He spent the next two days seeking out more information on Dundas Stannard. He eventually found an old woman who said she had provided such a man with lodgings, but he had been gone some time. She did, however, provide a useful description quite different to that of the goldsmith. Dundas Stannard was a small but strongly built man with broad shoulders, thick chest and powerful arms and legs. The old woman described him as dangerous looking with old smallpox scars on his forehead and a lopsided lip. After this Holditch decided he was quite sick of Chester and it was time to move on to Northampton with what he hoped would be well received news.

High up in the Derbyshire hills where no trees are to be found and the land is but rock, moss, and stunted grass, there was a lone cottage. In the pale, watery light of a half-moon it appeared to be abandoned and derelict. It had once been the home of Dundas Stannard. Up to the age of fourteen he had lived there with his sheep farming parents. It had been a cold, hard life, for both parents and their only son. Thin, scrawny sheep produced little in the way of a living. Neighbours were few and far away. Of family and friends there were none. On his fourteenth birthday, he rose from his bed and walked the long miles to the nearest town and never returned in ten years. On this, his only visit he found his parents were long since dead. His former home, however, in its isolation, was a place safe as a refuge for a royalist when roundhead troopers were scouring England for Charles Stuart and any of his former companions. Sitting on a chest by a fire within four sturdy walls Dundas was not uncomfortable. He had secured ample provisions, a warm cloak and a sound horse. He felt secure and far from prying eyes. The nearest human life was at least four miles away. He supped wine from a wooden cup and began to consider his options. They seemed limited. He was a known royalist, not a grandee but there were plenty who knew which master he served. His particular master, Sir Thomas Skeffington, had been a great friend of both their king and the dashing cavalry officer, the long dead Spencer Compton. Sir Thomas in the earliest days of the Civil War had ridden with the Earl of Northampton but unlike the Earl he had survived his military encounters. When all was lost, and the King was imprisoned and Cromwell's star was in the ascendant, he had fled to France and pledged his support to the King's eldest son. It was in France that Dundas had met Sir Thomas. The two men immediately liked each other and he Dundas had become his aide, servant and confidant. They had always been close to the Prince and in June 1650 when he accepted the crown of Scotland they had been in the congregation. It was through Sir Thomas that he knew about Giles Middleton and his guardianship of the Italian gold. Together he and Skeffington had been charged by the Prince to go South and collect such gold as Middleton had pledged to the cause. Dundas had to concentrate to remember the details of those events. They were critical if he was to take the risk of a return to Northampton. He concentrated his thoughts.

Just after Charles Stuart had come to Scotland, a messenger of the Sealed Knot had arrived from Giles Middleton for Skeffington, saying that he had found the hidden place, where the Earl had concealed his gold. It had lain undiscovered for six years. He knew that it would have been the Earl's wish that such gold should be used in support of the Prince's cause. Skeffington and Stannard under orders from Charles had made their way to Northampton and collected a large quantity of gold coins stored in a rather dirty doubled sack. They had stayed but one night with Middleton and they had heard the full story of its discovery and transport to Castle Ashby, the Earl's Northamptonshire home. They also were told of how a similar sack had been given to the Prince's father at the outbreak of the Civil War. Giles had explained how the death of the Earl at Hopton Heath had proved a great calamity as only he knew the final resting place for the coins. Neither his son James nor Middleton himself had been told. Dundas gave a little laugh. Middleton had been about to tell them the full story of its re-discovery, but Skeffington had pleaded tiredness and a long day ahead and they had been spared that tale. Nevertheless, both Dundas and Skeffington were convinced that the Prince had not been sent all that had been found. Middleton was too pleased with his guardianship to have given everything up.

Dundas rose from his seat and began to pace about. He did not know if the arrival of the gold had emboldened Charles Stuart, but it was shortly after, that he had taken the decision to march South into England. Of all his counsellors only, Skeffington had argued against it. Dundas shook his head. These thoughts upset him. Charles Stuart should have stayed in Scotland. Cromwell had tried but failed to defeat him there. Overtime he would have had to return to England, leaving Charles in possession of Scotland, with plenty of time to await events and the long game. But at Stirling, Cromwell had opened the door to England, and the Prince could not resist the opportunity that was to eventually lead to failure and the death of his friend and master. Skeffington had fallen at Worcester and Dundas still mourned his loss.   Dundas poured himself another cup of wine. He was close to a decision. Both England and Scotland were places of capture and death for him. He would have to get to France. He smiled inwardly. That would not be difficult for the man who could pay his way. The Yorkshire coast was full of fishing villages where the locals swelled their income with a passenger trade. No, he had to decide whether to risk a visit to Northampton. He was concerned that any of those gold coins, if found at Worcester, would attract more than himself. Some would remember the efforts of Zouche Tate and Varley Brent. After a short pause, Dundas had made his decision. He would take the risk. It would ensure a life of ease and comfort in France or better still Italy. His intention was to keep the gold for his final years. For all he cared the Prince could either be a prisoner or a pauper, it was time for Dundas to look after his own interests. If he can convince Middleton that the gold would be used to further the royalist cause, so be it. But if not, he would just take it. He had no fear of Giles Middleton. Dundas returned to sit on the chest. He gave more thought to the man who stood in his way to a fortune. What would be going through his mind at the moment. The royalist cause was lost. He had played the part of a secret royalist paymaster. He nominally worked for the House of Commons in managing the sequestered estates of the former Earl of Northampton, to whom he had been both clerk and friend. To Dundas that seemed a mass of loyalties that could only lead to exposure and disaster. In his own mind, Dundas saw himself with the gold, and on his way to France. He suddenly had a most uncomfortable thought. Perhaps Giles Middleton had already gone. This unhappy idea forced Dundas to rethink the timetable that had been forming in his mind. He could stay here only a few days and then he must go South.

Chapter Six

As a young man Giles Middleton had an early stroke of good fortune and it determined the rest of his life. As a student at Oxford he had rendered the Earl of Northampton a service, which led to the appointment as his Secretary. As such, over the years he had been with the Earl constantly, and had become fully involved in all matters of commerce and finance, concerning his estate. Of a similar age to the Earl, the two men had become friends, and thus Giles became his confidant in family and personal matters. The Earl was amongst the richest men in England with estates across the country. His favourite residence and his home was Castle Ashby, a great house some six miles to the South and East of Northampton. Such was the Earl's wealth that his home was embellished and made beautiful by England's greatest craftsmen. He filled his home with furniture, tapestries, gilded mirrors, carpets of the finest quality. High ceiling rooms were given the most intricate of plaster work and large paned windows. The most unique adornment was to be found all around the roof line of the house itself. A balustrade of stone lettering spelt out in Latin the verse from the bible. "Except the lord build the city they labour in vain that built it, except the Lord keep the city the night watch labour in vain." For this home, that matched the finest palace, he kept a staff of eighty retainers which included three chaplains. The responsibilities placed upon Giles were great as was his commensurate authority, but like his master he became selfish and arrogant. The Earl offset his failings with charm and generosity. He entertained his neighbours and gave freely to charity. As a courtier he was close to James I, King of England,

and when the King died equally with his son Charles. Both Kings had employed him in the most important of diplomatic and personal missions. In all matters the Earl was outward going and when battle came, daring and brave. He was an inspiring leader in the royalist cause and his death at Hopton Heath in1643 a grievous blow.

Through most of these matters Giles had been a loyal servant, but the behaviour of the Earl had been no role model for his Secretary. His management of power and authority were quite different. He was respectful to his master and those of noble birth, but to others even men senior in their professions, he was abrupt demanding and given to deceit. For his master he was seen as both clever and hardworking, but for many others their experience was one of dissembling and cunning. Whilst women fell at the Earl's feet, Giles used his position to bully favours and force himself upon maids, serving girls and even low-ranking guests, and many a neighbour's daughter received bruises and pain, as he took his pleasures.

Whilst the Earl lived, Giles was able to maintain his position as a loyal, honest servant not the least because of the part he played in Italy in 1623, but the upheaval of the Civil War changed his life completely. The Earl abandoned his house, and he and his son James Compton went to war for the King. Parliament sequestered his estates and the life Giles enjoyed was gone. Whilst the change in Giles fortunes was absolute, it was not disastrous. Parliament had decreed that each county it controlled should manage its own sequestered estates and send all monies to London, to finance the army. In Northamptonshire, this responsibility was given to a Lord Wilmington. Whilst appreciating the great trust placed in him, his lordship was appalled at the responsibility. The estates of the Earl of

Northampton, were but a part of the charge placed upon him. In desperation he sought some respite in his labours in Giles Middleton. His wide knowledge of the estate was clear but he was also a known acolyte of a major royalist. Wilmington knew there would be criticism of the idea that was forming in his mind, but regardless he summoned Giles for interview. He thought that there just may be a risk worth taking that would solve this part of his problems. For Wilmington the interview went far better than he could have hoped. Giles Middleton was quite prepared to renounce his former royalist associates and freely take on management of what was the Earl's estate. To his prospective employer he described it as an adjustment that was being made on all sides, as the fortunes of war moved around the country. Wilmington was determined that this switch of loyalties was to be clear for all to see and accept. He made available to Giles Wilmington House at the very heart of Northampton, overlooking the market to the North and the road to London to the South. This would become the centre for all commercial activity to do with the estate, and the living quarters for Giles his wife and servants. The risk taken by Wilmington appeared to be successful. In truth Giles became an effective manager of the sequestered estate and monies were regularly transferred to Parliament. In practice Giles and the town accommodated his change of loyalties with little more than a few lingering suspicions.

However, within a few years' events would radically alter this established rhythm of life. In 1649 he found the cache of golden coins hidden at Castle Ashby. The royalist loyalties he had so successfully repressed once more took hold of him. He saw this new-found wealth, as a route to preferment to the very highest level, under a new King. By his own judgement he enjoyed another great triumph, he married Elizabeth Caxton, the prettiest girl in the County. She was a wealthy farmer's daughter and even with his solid status in the town, it was a surprise that she agreed to marry a man twenty years her senior and become Elizabeth Middleton. In fact, for a time they were the happiest of married couples, but a simple tumble from a horse was to result in blindness for Elizabeth. Their relationship did not survive this accident. Giles saw this fall in terms of his own loss and it strengthened the unpleasant traits of Giles's character. He became more mean, selfish, parsimonious and cruel. Increasingly his hidden stock of gold became the centre of his life. Elizabeth's affections remained loyal to her husband but these were no longer reflected by Giles.

As Ketch was approaching Northampton on a cold and dank morning, Giles Middleton sat in his study peering at his correspondence. There was not enough light.

"More candles", he shouted out through the open door. "Mathew you idle cur, bring me more candles now!"

Fuelled by his impatience he rose from behind his desk, and strode into the main corridor of Wilmington House.

"Do you hear me Mathew. More candles."

A slimly built man of some twenty years dressed as a servant, came hurrying from the back of the house carrying a handful of what was being demanded. He placed them on the desk and began to cast around for candle holders. He knelt down in front of a large cabinet and opened the lower doors.

"God you are a fool Mathew. That is where I keep my personal strongbox. There are holders on the window ledge. Just get out". With these words he pushed the servant into the corridor.

"And tell Rose I want to see her"

Whilst he set to with the candles a small, plain, but plump young girl entered the room. She was some sixteen years of age and wearing a white cotton dress covered by a blue apron. She was nervous, apprehensive even fearful. Giles returned to his chair.

"Come stand by me girl" he demanded and he grasped her right wrist with a tight grip of his hand. He pulled her body against his.

"You will come to me again later when I call you Rose, whilst your mistress takes her afternoon rest, and we will be kind to each other."

The young girl stiffened and shook herself away but failed to break his hold.

"Must I, "she murmured in a low faltering voice.

"Oh yes Rose", he replied, "and no word to her of our arrangements. She would hate to see you dismissed and you do love her so".

 He let her go. He was confident she would satisfy him, and what matter if she bruised a little. He turned his attention to the strange letter from the foreign merchant newly arrived in town. "Absolute nonsense", he said to himself, "and he shall know it"

He leaned back in his chair and a frown came over his face. He had a more serious problem than foreign merchants. Down in his cellar was something that could get him hung.

 Edgar Middleton was the younger brother of Giles Middleton and like his brother worked for Lord Wilmington but as an outdoor steward, a jack of all trades. He was forty years of age and a man of great physical presence and strength. Although not the goliath of his youth, he remained initially intimidating to most men on first meeting certainly those without wealth or nobility. Of his features his red hair cut short was the most obvious, but his face was open with a wide mouth, a clear skin and full blue eyes. All women thought he was handsome. Over six feet tall he retained his muscular physique. His tasks around the estate, were those that required strength to complete. In summer he could be found stripped to the waist working alongside the blacksmith, or in the fields at harvest carrying corn stooks under each arm. Winter would see him ditching and hedging and caring for livestock and at that time around the estates, he would be seen in a great woollen and leather robe, striding about with his great staff. This cut from a bough of oak he had topped off with a part of a set of deer antlers, five-pointed bone spikes that could be as dangerous as their owner. This was both a useful tool and a formidable weapon. Regardless of this he was by nature friendly and thought by all to be good company.

His cottage was built up to the brick wall of Lord Wilmington's kitchen garden at Wilmington Hall. The Hall was situated four miles outside of Northampton on the road to Kettering, and was the permanent home of the Wilmington family. A great stone building surrounded by many acres of park and farmland, it had all the amenities expected by the leading Lord of the County. On the morning of Ketch's arrival in Northampton, Edgar had risen to find a day of murk and gloom. He was surprised to see that a note had been pushed under his door. The words were not easy to understand. "James says the End of the World today at noon. Franklin". For a moment all was blank. Then his mind began to race and his heart had a faster beat. This was a note from someone he had not seen in a long time. Edgar like his brother and many other estate workers, had been a loyal royalist at the beginning of the war. But both

County and Town had gone over completely to the Parliamentary cause and those that wished to continue working and living in the same way, had to say the right thing at the right time no matter what their inward thoughts. In this way Edgar like many others managed to live with his neighbours. The note was from someone who had his loyalty, its real meaning was clear to him. It was to meet at the given time at the local tavern with the unusual name "The End of the World." This was located in the village of Ecton a further hour's walk towards the town of Wellingborough to the South East. The note was from James Compton, now the Earl of Northampton, royalist commander, owner of Castle Ashby and the true inheritor of his father's golden treasure. Franklin had been the name of the Earl's first horse. He tried to calm himself with a mug of water. It helped, but he needed to sit by his empty hearth to gather his thoughts.

 "What was the Earl doing here, so close to his home, with roundhead patrols and road blocks all over the County. Whatever his purpose, Edgar knew that the Earl his friend and master was in great danger. There would be no mercy for such a well-known royalist commander or any who gave him aid."

He made up his mind quickly. He would keep his appointment and with little time to spare, he collected his cloak and staff, and walked out into a cloudy, cool day. His emotions did not reflect the nature of the day. It took him a full hour to reach the village of Ecton and he took a few moments rest before approaching The World's End. The tavern had been a makeshift collection area for the seriously wounded after the battle of Naseby. It had been a fierce and bloody affair and one that condemned the King, Charles I, to eventual long-term defeat. Most of those that reached this place saw no more of the world. Thus, the unusual name. The tavern was stone built with a slate roof and a double door entrance. Benches were set either side of the entrance and on one of these sat a young man wearing a buff rustic jerkin together with black trousers and boots. In the thick leather belt around his waist was a wooden cudgel and he was leaning forward with his elbows on his knees, with his hands clasped together. He observed Edgar very carefully and slipped his right hand to rest lightly on the cudgel as Edgar stepped up to him. He sat back on his bench and in a low voice inquired

"Edgar Middleton"?

Edgar knew this was not James Compton.

"You have my name stranger I would welcome knowing yours," he replied.

"Your size tells me who you are" came the answer.

The stranger decided to make his position plain.

"I have a friend whose first horse was named Franklin".

This strange reply caused Edgar to look sharply about him but there were no customers or idlers to hear their conversation.

"I am but a messenger and a guide" added the young man. "It would help if you would come with me."

"And, why should I do this" ventured Edgar.

"To meet a noble friend", came the reply.

Edgar hesitated. There was danger in this but his desire to renew his acquaintance with James Compton decided him to follow on behind the messenger.

"I will go with you "stated Edgar.

"But I am well known in these parts and to be seen travelling with a stranger will be a cause for questions. Lead on but I will follow a goodly distance behind."

The young man nodded and began to walk down from the tavern into the main thoroughfare through the village of Ecton.

The street was the village. Its cottages were strung out along It and although it twisted sharply downhill, Edgar was able to keep to the distance he required. Inevitably, he met someone he knew, a housewife who insisted on showing him her growing baby and their talk was long and loud enough to draw out an old man, the baby's grandfather. He further spoke proudly on his number of grandchildren.

"Thirteen in all and no deaths, County folk are strong eh master Edgar."

Edgar gave the required period of time to talk and make statements of wonder and was able, fairly speedily, to carry on down to the end of the village. Here the fields led down to the River Nene. High hedges flanked the road and after a few minutes his guide stepped out some eighty yards ahead of him and re-united they resumed their march, the young man in front with Edgar following. After some half an hour his guide reached Billing bridge but instead of crossing, he stepped into Billing mill an isolated watermill some quarter of a mile from Billing village. *"What now",* thought Edgar and he strengthened his hold on his staff. He followed into the mill. Its entrance was low and dark. The grinding stones and wooden workings filled the great downstairs room. There was no sign of the miller, a man who Edgar knew well. He was surprised at such a quiet man providing a refuge for royalists. Edgar had no doubt that somewhere near, almost certainly in the building was James Compton.

A side door opened and James Compton stood in hesitation, making himself known to Edgar. The two men recognised each other and embraced.

"My Lord", said Edgar.

"This is dangerous. You should not be here so close to home, there will be those who still remember you and would not refrain from raising the alarm".

"I know", replied James, "but I had to speak to either you or to Giles"

The Earl took Edgar by the arm and steered him in to the side room. It was the miller's parlour, comfortably furnished.

"Sit", he said. "I haven't much time."

"Were you at Worcester" questioned Edgar. "Are you now heading for France".

James shook his head. He wanted to give orders for the future not talk about the past. With an impatient grimace he spoke more sharply.

"Edgar, I was not at Worcester. I was bringing reinforcements from Wales and missed everything. Yes, I am going to France, but for the moment I wish to give you and Giles close instructions on my father's gold, whatever is left of it. It must be kept here in Northampton safe for the future. This Commonwealth of theirs will not last for ever and even if it does, one day there will be a peace that will allow the Earls of Northampton to return"

Edgar stayed silent for a moment carefully thinking his reply. "That may be a problem, I believe that Giles is set on continuing to use these funds to support Charles Stuart. The King is still at large like yourself hunted by Cromwell. Such time has passed, however, that there seems now a real chance that he will escape to France."

James's face contorted with anger.

"The Stuarts have had enough. My father took a large portion in 1642 to Charles I and I know Giles sent another large amount to his son in Scotland before this latest failure. What is left must

63

be held for the family to re-build the estate. Make sure this is done Edgar, make sure Giles follows my instructions. I have not come here and risked my life for nothing".

Edgar looked at James and in solemn tones assured the Earl that a substantial quantity of the gold still existed and he would ensure that his orders would be carried out.

"What now my Lord do you need money or any particular assistance?"

"No came the reply. "I have a small boat and companions close by. We shall follow the river to the sea and hope to get to France".

Giles lowered his voice.

"What of this miller my lord. Can he be trusted? I just know him as generally a good man but will he keep silent on your presence here."

James smiled. "You Middletons do not know everything, his father lives with him and he was with me at Newbury. They are both loyal.

The Earl stood up.

"I must go Edgar. All this will be important for both our futures, make that very clear to Giles."

After a firm hand shake Edgar was steered by the Earl back into the large mill room.

"I must go at once" and with a quick glance outside James Compton left the mill and disappeared through the trees towards the river bank.

The miller climbed down a ladder from the upper rafters of his mill. He and Edgar looked at each other neither saying a word. With a nod of recognition Edgar turned and walked out of the mill and into the day that remained cloudy and dull. In this he took no interest, he had to speak to his brother.

Chapter Seven

Ketch rode slowly into Northampton sparing a glance at the memorial to dead Queen Eleanor the wife of Edward I. He was pleased to see it was still undamaged by recent events and still announced that any journey to Northampton was almost complete. For four days he had endured, the rain, wind and cold of an October storm that seemed to promise a harsh winter. He had protected himself from the worst of the weather with a brimmed leather hat tied tightly under his chin, together with a large woollen cloak and stout boots. But still he felt wet through in much the same state as his horse and mule, who had no such protection. He like them had managed the last few miles on sheer endurance but at last the end was in sight. There had been little on his journey to lighten his mood. The hunt for Charles Stuart had meant that all travellers were checked regularly and required to give an explanation, as to who they were and the purpose of their journey. The inns and taverns along the way were also full of troops and other hard-faced men, who eyed carefully anyone who looked or acted suspiciously. Ketch's new rank and his answers served him well and he had been troubled as little as any.

Most of his journey he had been in the company of others, but he still had ample time to reflect on all the matters that his mind placed before him. He was most moved by the death of his friend and mentor James Hedlow. In a sense it was not a surprise. He was not a young man. It had always been his delight to talk of the Armada beacons he had seen in his early youth. But Ketch had left him vigorous and hearty and enjoying his semi-retirement. It was through Hedlow that he had met his wife

Anne and his wise advice had played a major part in solving some of the dangerous events in Northampton in recent times. Richard Blake had spoken of a will and its contents had led Thurloe to dispatch immediately to Northampton, his comrade Tull to support Anne and to protect Ketch's interests. His wife's beauty came into his mind. He continued to miss her. He quietly cursed Thurloe and Milton for dispatching him on a pointless venture to France. He had missed her and he knew that she missed him. She would have fair cause to blame him for their absence from each other. He had decided to work for Thurloe and had accepted the French assignment. There would be much merit in her case. But he remained concerned. He had secured promotion to Captain and for that she would be pleased, but to be away at the death of the old town clerk a man who had saved her life and whom she regarded as a father was a hard hurt to bear alone. New wealth and Tull's well-meaning support would count for little. In the dull cloudy murk of the October morning his musing had led him through the South gate and up the hill to Northampton's market square. He was not surprised to see that there was no light in their little house so he turned his mount towards the Derngate. There, just beyond was Hedlow's fine house and garden. He expected to find Anne and Tull there. He entered the back of the house through a courtyard to the stables. A young boy no more than ten years old appeared. He looked none too pleased to be taken from whatever warm spot he had been enjoying. The boy was unknown to ketch and without a word he handed over charge of his horse and his mule. Too tired to give instructions he crossed to the back door of the main building, which he knew led to a short corridor. He pushed at the door, it yielded and he staggered into the house. At the end of the corridor there was a shadowy shape of a woman. It was Anne. She rushed to meet him with open arms.

"John", she cried, "At last".

But as she went to hug him, she stopped abruptly.

"Oh my God" she exclaimed, "you are freezing cold and dripping wet. You must get out of those clothes".

She took his weary face in her hands.

"Come, remove those wet things straight away and take yourself into the parlour by the fire"

Without a word he did as he was told. He was exhausted but had at least survived and been well received. As he sat by the fire, she dried his head and face, took off his boots and placed on his feet some fur lined slippers. Still fussing, she exclaimed, "You need food. We have some hot stew that is on the stove. You must have some now",

For the first-time ketch smiled, he was pleased to be home. Then Anne gave him a pointed look.

" After food we must talk."

Their talk when it came ranged over many subjects. But first it was how upset Anne was over the death of the old clerk, how he had saved her life, how he had been the means of their coming together and now the source of their newfound wealth. Ketch could only concur with her words and sympathise with her grief.

"I know I have been away for over a month and at a time when you had a desperate need for me and the support of a husband, but it is the nature of my work, and I am truly sorry for your distress. Almost certainly I shall never be required to go on overseas missions again and what I am currently undertaking for Thurloe requires me to be in Northampton. And when that is completed", he paused.

"Well given our new wealth, we may review what our future together is to be",

This conversation continued until they both felt the need for a midday meal. As they rose to make their preparations there was a knock on the parlour door and an apprehensive sergeant Tull entered the room. Anne and Ketch both looked at each other and laughed.

"Oh, I forgot the sergeant was with us." Said Anne.

"Yes, Tull it is quite safe to come in. Your new Captain has recovered his position as master of the house."

" There are no masters here "re-joined Ketch.

With this little exchange any final barrier between husband and wife disappeared.

"Tull!" exclaimed Ketch.

" I am so pleased to see you and you have done much for Ann, but it is a weary man you see before you. I must have a few hours' sleep".

Tull left the room and husband and wife made their way to bed.

Ketch and Anne came down stairs mid-afternoon to find food laid out on the dining room table. Tull had not only made himself useful in this way but he had also provided for the needs of their visitor. Stephen Hedlow, nephew of the late James Hedlow and town constable sat at the table, finishing a morsel of cheese. Immediately he was given a welcome hug by Ketch.

"It is good to see you Stephen at this difficult time. Anne and I have lost a very dear friend but he was both a close friend and a loving uncle to you. We all know that he cared for you very much."

Anne also embraced Stephen.

"You uncle had been a rock for me in the past at a very difficult time. With no husband present, I only managed with losing him and the matter of his will through your support".

She grasped both men by the arm, re-assurance for one and thanks to the other. Stephen smiled,

" it's good to be useful and when Tull arrived the three of us could deal with all matters thrown at us".

Ketch took Stephen by the shoulder,

"I am also very grateful Stephen and when things are a little quieter, we will discuss this debt we have to you."

He then turned and invited everyone to sit round the table.

"We have important matters to discuss but before we start, I must say that I keep looking around for James. We are in his house and always he was in our counsels. It is difficult and sad that he is not with us".

Before anyone could echo those thoughts, he said,

" let us spend a moment in silent thought of the man we have lost and who has left us his example and such a rich inheritance".

The company complied with Ketch's wishes and for a few minutes sat silent thinking of James Hedlow.

Then Ketch turned to other matters. He felt the time had come to make sure that those close to him were fully aware as to why he was in Northampton, but first he needed the basic facts about the nature of James Hedlow's will. He turned to Stephen.

"Can you kindly lay out for me the outcomes from his will and how certain it all is"?

Stephen briefly conformed to Ketch's wishes explaining the substance of what he and Ketch had been granted. For Ketch, and indeed Anne, it was the freehold on three houses on the market square, a brewery on Abington street, together with a large collection of paper bonds and cash amounting to approximately £1,000. In addition, there is the freehold of this house and some surrounding acres. At this moment he stopped. Ketch was overwhelmed, Anne had known some of this, but she felt it was best coming from Stephen. He was the old clerk's closest, indeed only relative. Ketch was still in shock.

"I knew he was a man of means but he has made us wealthy beyond our wildest dreams".

He turned to Stephen.

"What about you I hope you have been equally blest". Stephen laughed.

"Oh yes, he has not forgotten his nephew. I have three farms to call my own. I have become a very substantial landowner."

Ketch was relieved. Stephen's obvious satisfaction both pleased him and removed a possible source of friction. He was someone whose help he would undoubtedly need in the search for the Italian coins.

"One final question Stephen has anyone come forward to dispute the will with unknown deeds, or emerged with hidden charges or unpaid debts."

"No", came the confident reply.

"The will was lodged with the Town Mayor who is our local magistrate. We have nothing to fear in that way. Besides Ketch you are well remembered for the good you have done in the past for this town, you have plenty of friends here".

Now that the key issues of the will had been dealt with Ketch was anxious to explain the task that Secretary Thurloe had given him in Northampton. It was not only right that his wife and companions were so informed but he was quite sure that he was going to need their help. They also needed to know that Sergeant Holditch was also actively involved at the moment elsewhere. Thus, for the next hour he spoke of the death of Spencer Compton, the Earl killed at Hopton Heath and the discovery of the gold coins. He detailed the attempts by the then Northampton MP Zouche Tate and his robust accomplice to seek out whether or not there were more coins in the family home or held by his family or servants. At this point in his account the October daylight began to fail and some time was spent finding and lighting candles. When once again he had everyone's full attention, he resumed his tale.

"Nothing was ever found and in faith, the Earl could have obtained those coins from almost anyone. The whole matter was seven years ago and has largely been forgotten. However, after the recent battle at Worcester, a number of such coins were found amongst the royalist prisoners. So, the House of Commons and the army are very anxious to know if there is still a royalist paymaster about with gold that could fund another uprising on behalf of the Stuarts. This would be a tragedy, just at a time when a period of peace is in everyone's grasp"

He paused for a moment.

"So, I am here in Northampton either to confirm that there is no royalist paymaster or cache of gold but if there is then obtain it and get it to London".

He shot a serious look at Anne and Stephen.

"You both know the people of this town better than I do. I t would help if you outline where I should begin my search and with which people".

Stephen was the first to reply.

" The death of my uncle has in a strange way been helpful for your task. It has given you a reason to be in Northampton. You are here to claim your inheritance, to secure your property and it will not be unusual for you to be out and about meeting and talking to all manner of people. Also, you are favourably remembered for the assistance you gave to the town during the mutiny. There have been no objections to the will from Council men or magistrates, so you begin your task with the town well disposed towards you."

Ketch breathed heavily.

"Thank you, Stephen, that is encouraging but what can you tell me about the dead Earl's family and what is left of his property." Stephen absentmindedly picked up a piece of bread from his plate and began gently playing with it before taking up his account.

"The Earl's estate including the great house, Castle Ashby, was sequestered by Parliament at the outbreak of the war. All its rents and revenues go to Parliament as was the proceeds of the sale of all moveable property, pictures, tapestries, furniture and the like. When news of the confiscation broke the servants looted the house of as much as they could carry before Parliament's agents arrived. The house now is partly derelict as a result of a fire. The whole estate amongst others is now under the control of Lord Wilmington. He took the surprising step of entrusting the management of the estate on his behalf to Giles Middleton who was formerly the Earl's secretary. I can in part understand the reason for this. Giles would know everything about the estate and all the relevant people involved in it and all the financial issues of mortgages loans and debts. But he was a former royalist supporter, however, he swore support to the new regime, and Wilmington's gamble seems to have paid off. For estate matters are running smoothly. Wilmington also employs Giles's brother Edgar as a sort of steward helping with the physical upkeep of the estate. You will probably want to start your inquiries with Giles, if so, you must certainly talk to Wilmington first. He is not the sort of man to accept hearing about interference from the army after the event"

Anne took up the tale of Lord Wilmington.

"His is not such an old title but he is probably the most important man in the county. He was with Parliament from the very beginning of the struggle with the King and both Pym and Hampden were close friends. He and James Hedlow kept the South of the county and the town of Northampton totally in support of Parliament. He was, however, enraged when the House of Commons was purged and the House of Lords abolished. I must warn you husband he is no friend of the army. For the rest he is wealthy and spends liberally. He has never married and has no children. He was a great friend of someone you know well, the former Mayor of Northampton, Councillor Trussell and generally he seems content with the workings and loyalty of Northampton"

Ketch gave his wife careful scrutiny. She had changed considerably since he went away. In their early years together, she had slowly been gaining self-confidence but the death of her friend and mentor seemed to have resulted in a new strength. Perhaps it was born of necessity he mused, the fact that I was away. Her voice was stronger, she had given up constantly adjusting her hair to hide the still vivid scar on her cheek. When first wed she would barely venture out of the house without Ketch. Her treatment on the battlefield after the battle of Naseby had produced a woman whose life was confined to their little house on the market square and the house of James Hedlow. That weak frightened character no longer existed. Here was a mature woman with a new bodily strength to match her

73

self-confidence. He looked up to see her smiling at him as if she knew exactly what he was thinking.

Ketch paused and looked at the assembled company.

"Right", he exclaimed.

"I shall seek out Lord Wilmington and I had better also visit the new Mayor Councillor Lugg. We have known each other for some time. He must be told of an army investigation in his town."

He looked out of the parlour window the October light was fast fading.

"This must wait for tomorrow, now we need some food."

A clamour of voices broke out.

"What can we do to help you in this difficult task" demanded his three companions.

"Fine," he thought.

"I definitely need help with this". He turned to Tull.

"Tomorrow you must remain here. There must be someone present in case Holditch returns from Chester. Let us hope this is soon and that fortune has smiled on him and he has some news for us."

Tull was a few years older than his army companions. He was a taciturn West countryman, who spoke slowly, but with a delightful accent that predisposed people to listen to him and what he said was usually valued. He was a man rarely without tobacco despite the scarcities of war. Somehow probably with the aid of Holditch, he always had on his person the weed that King James had called noxious. It was therefore no surprise that his first movement on being called into action was to take his empty pipe from his pocket.

"That is a simple enough task captain. I shall enjoy sitting in your newly obtained garden awaiting the arrival of Holditch".
"Do not get too comfortable", retorted Ketch.
"We must all keep our wits about us".

He then spoke to Stephen and inquired as to his role as the town constable. He was heartened that for the moment despite his inheritance, he was to continue in post. Ketch was happy to outline a task for him.

"May I suggest that tomorrow morning you patrol the town centre in your normal fashion looking out for strangers and listening to local gossip, especially about the Middletons and Lord Wilmington."

Stephen nodded his assent and sat back clearly satisfied with his role.

"And what about me" demanded Anne.

"I have no intention of being left out of this, I am not staying in feeding Tull with food and drink, when I also could be out in the town gathering information."

Ketch could not but agree.

"In addition," added Anne," tomorrow there will be a market in the town square. The Middletons live in Wilmington House on the very corner of the square and Giles Middleton always takes his wife and her maid to this market, and generally guides them around."

Anne could see that this was news to Her husband so she continued.

"I suspect John you have no idea as to the Middleton household and yet I suspect it may be an important part of your task"

Ketch with a slight nod of his head acknowledged his ignorance. Anne continued.

"You know that Giles Middleton lives and works in Wilmington House and there with him lives his wife, Elizabeth and her personal maid who is called Rose. Besides these, there is a manservant Mathew and a housekeeper Maria. All fairly normal so far but the important difference is that the wife Elizabeth is blind. Giles and Elizabeth were married some two years ago. The marriage was a great surprise. Giles is some twenty years older than Elizabeth he had never been married and she was the beauty of the County. She was the daughter of a wealthy local farmer and she had been with horses all her life. But from a simple fall, she hit her head and the result has been blindness. As such Elizabeth needs a personal maid and Giles had to employ a housekeeper. It is hard to tell what has been the effect on their relationship. Giles has the reputation of being a difficult if not a hard man but as yet they seem to have established an acceptable way of life".

Anne sat back pleased with her explanation and her clarity. Ketch was quick to thank her.

"That is all very useful information. Now I know the likely key persons to be questioned".

Ann was not quite finished.

"While you are seeing Lord Wilmington and Stephen is around the town, if you agree I shall play the part of the housewife and go shopping in the market tomorrow morning. It may be that I shall meet the Middletons and converse with them. That can only be useful."

Ketch thought for a while, no one knew he was in Northampton or would be surprised that he was here and knowledge of his other purpose was confined to this room. He was happy to assent to Anne's task. He moved to stand up and bring their meeting to a close but Stephen spoke up again.

"I am sorry to prolong matters Ketch" he said. But< there is some other information that I feel sure will be useful and I suspect I am the only one here with it, namely some details about the lay-out of Wilmington house. You are after a cache of gold I am sure these details will be of value"

Ketch returned to sitting down and bade Stephen to continue.

"Wilmington House is a large square house at the corner of Mercer's row and the Drapery. It has but a ground floor and a first floor but there are a considerable number of rooms. It has a double front, with steps leading to a large solid front door. From this door a corridor leads straight to the back of the house dividing around a central staircase. On entering the house immediately on your left is the study where Giles both relaxes and conducts his business. Then there is a dining room, a kitchen and then store rooms a room with a pump and an indoor privy."

Tull could not but comment. "All very comfortable."

Stephen smiled and continued.

"To the right on entering there is a large reception room, then the maid's room two empty rooms and then behind the staircase are two rooms that look out onto the market square. These are occupied by Mathew and Maria. Stephen paused looking for comment but as there was none he carried on.

"The upstairs rooms are unused but you may ask where is the master bedroom? In fact, the main reception room has been transformed into a large bedroom for man and wife. It is also where Elizabeth spends much of her time, and there are extra facilities for Rose to spend the night with her mistress should Giles be away or working late. If he is working late, he has a couch in his study. Now all this is largely normal but the distinctive feature of Wilmington house is in the study. Everyone was quite silent as Stephen came to the heart of the matter.

"His study is a front room with a large window out on to Mercers row and one on to the Drapery, and below this last window there is a flight of steps that go down to a cellar. The steps are partially masked by a wall about three feet high which comes out from the front wall about half way into the room. Thus, the steps are largely hidden from visitors. The entrance to the cellar is a solid wooden door that is usually locked but in the cellar itself there is a large metal door, also kept locked, which leads into Northampton's underground network of tunnels. It is this that I think you must know Ketch".

Stephen paused to collect his thoughts.

"To speak of tunnels is a little grand. There are a few medieval tunnels that run from market square properties to the Church of all saints, some from the Peacock inn to Wilmington house and St Andrew's Priory. There are said to be similar tunnels from the castle to the White Friars monastery, and from the Grey Friars to the Rood in the Wall Tavern. Some of these intersect others and have been joined with new wine cellars and storerooms built around the square. Some of these have collapsed and are dangerous. Over many years the great conduit in the market square has been built, closed and then repaired often re-directed. The crypt of central churches has often broken into or been flooded by new sewers. Occasional underground springs have forced channels which have since dried up. All in all, Ketch this is a dangerous part of the town. It is so unstable that nobody goes very far into them. From time to time some foolish youth will test his courage and will require to be rescued by brave men with many lanterns also there have been unlucky boys who have never been found. That is why Giles keeps that heavy iron door locked. No one will get into Wilmington House that way without gunpowder".

A long silence followed the end of Stephen's account. But Ketch eventually spoke up.
 "That has all been absolutely vital information.
He smiled at his wife and friend.

"Anne, Stephen, you have both been so helpful, my heartfelt thanks".

This time he stood up and stretched his arms.

"Right", he said. "We all have our tasks for tomorrow morning. I suggest we take our ease for a few hours. Stephen you are welcome to stay but you may wish to go home."

For the rest of the evening each of the company relaxed in their own way.

Chapter Eight

On leaving his newly inherited house ketch decided to return to his original home on the market square to secure some fresh clothing. He had worn his military clothing on the road from London and he saw advantages in now being dressed as a civilian in his own home town. He was pleased that in commencing the walk to Wilmington Hall that many passers bye smiled in recognition of him often with a cheery wave. Wilmington Hall was a good one-hour uphill walk and ketch was looking forward to the exercise. He thought that riding horses was the most effective form of transport and could be enjoyable but sometimes the body told you to use your legs. The Hall was built on the edge of a hill and was surrounded by large gardens, rather than an extensive park. These gardens seemed to be a serious contribution to the life of the Hall for there were several gardeners at work tending various plants and fruits and ketch could see several large greenhouses one of which seemed to sport a small chimney. The building itself was of dressed stone with fine stone steps leading to an impressive black door embossed with gleaming brass boss. The windows were plenty and in good repair. It was not a large building but it gave out a strong message of being both well cared for and comfortable. At its back there were plenty of out buildings in similar good repair. Ketch knocked confidently on the main door. It was answered by a manservant. Ketch quickly stated who he was and his rank and that he wished to speak with Lord Wilmington. He was shown into a library whilst the manservant discovered whether or not he was to be received. The library was that of a cultivated aristocrat. Besides the shelves of books, in the centre of the room was a leather topped desk with a finely moulded chair. Not all the walls were covered with books, however, for there were also hung a number of fine tapestries. Ketch had time to inspect two glass topped cabinets holding ancient maps and documents and examine some of the other pieces of fine furniture. With something of a flourish, Lord Wilmington entered the room. He was a tall man about sixty years of age and very thin, almost cadaverous. His arms and legs were long and he seemed rather ungainly with both a long stride and a far reach. His head and face were thin and his complexion was more that of a country man than an aristocrat. His blue eyes were watchful and despite his gait he moved towards Ketch with energy and purpose. Thinning brown hair betrayed his age but overall, he appeared both an astute and careful man. The manservant departed and Ketch was directed to a chair by the window facing a large desk. Both men sat down.

"I know you Ketch" were Lord Wilmington's opening remarks. "You have done good service to this town which it would appear has in return made you a wealthy man."

He smiled to himself.

"I was a great friend of James Hedlow. He was a man I respected and in many things our judgements were the same. If he has given you so much of his inheritance, he must have thought a great deal of you".

There was a short silence between them but Wilmington took back up the conversation.

" How can I be of help to an army officer?"

Before Ketch could reply to this question, Wilmington leant forward with a clear intent to make a firm point.
"I should make it plain to you that I do not like the army. They have won their war but it is time to send the soldiers home.

Cromwell and those around him know nothing of government and they have taken all power to themselves. They have purged the House of Commons of those members who do not agree with them. They have removed the Bishops of the Church of England and then the greatest folly of all abolished the House of Lords. They may abolish the House but they will never get rid of lordship. I remain and the noble families of this country will remain, and we always will Ketch. Things must change or we will be back to tyranny and many will then ask what was the war and all its death for?"

Ketch was not expecting such a flow of words. He did not know what to do. He certainly did not want to get into a debate defending the army. Wilmington was not finished yet.

" I was in the House of Commons Ketch until my father died. I now provide money to a crippled House that should be restored and replace those army leaders who have taken all authority unto themselves. We need to restore those institutions that have provided us with stability for centuries."

Ketch shuffled in his seat. This was not a good beginning. During Wilmington's denunciation of Cromwell and the army he was fingering in his pocket the signed warrant from Cromwell that had so often in the past produced help and obedience from all who saw it. Clearly it would be of no use with Lord Wilmington.

"My Lord", commenced Ketch.

"There is a matter of importance that I have been asked to investigate".

He got no further. Wilmington had more to say
. "You have arrived in Northampton and you have your inheritance to secure but you come to see me. Your army

masters must have serious concerns if they want something from me and my county".

Though the words were harsh, Wilmington was quite controlled. He sat relaxed in his chair. There was no threatening note in his voice. He had laid out his position on national affairs to his own satisfaction. He had said what he wanted to say and now was the time when he expected Ketch to speak. Ketch started again.

"It is probably best, my lord, if I do not take up matters with you on the role of the army. However, I will say that Charles Stuart is still at large weeks after Worcester. If he gets to France, he will always pose a threat. At the moment he is without troops, ordinance or money but he will still have friends in this country indeed in this county, but more importantly in France. The French King is his cousin and he will use Charles to France's best interest."

Lord Wilmington made a noise in his throat that could be treated as dissent or agreement. Ketch decided to plough on.

"Alone in France, Charles Stuart will be dependent on his cousin but if he had money if there were royalist paymasters who could supply a large sum in gold, that dependence is lessened. Charles may propose courses of action that the French King could be asked to support, rather than fully finance".

A furrow crossed Lord Wilmington's brow. He looked intently at Ketch.

"Go on", he said. Ketch took up his theme.

"You will remember my lord, Compton Spencer, the Earl of Northampton. He was killed at Hopton Heath some years ago, and a few golden coins were found on his person and this led to inquires in London, as to whether or not Northampton was the source ",

At this point Lord Wilmington meant to interrupt, but Ketch ignored the signs wishing to get to the end of his tale.

"I have to tell you my lord that some quantity of similar coins was found on prisoners after Worcester and I have been sent to pursue similar inquiries. "

Lord Wilmington did not look happy.

"This is unwanted news Ketch," he remarked.

"We have had all this before. Our late member of Parliament, Zouche Tate took up the matter very forcibly. He and his retainers virtually sacked the Earl's home of Castle Ashby even though it was already a shell. It had been looted by his servants on the outbreak of war. But, Zouche broke down panelling, dug up gardens and smashed open walls. Nothing was found but a terrible gold fever led him and his retainers, to question very harshly Giles Middleton and his brother Edgar".

Much of this was already known to ketch but he thought it best to let the lord tell the tale in his own way.

"Zouche had a manservant called Varley Brent basically a ruffian who beat very badly Giles Middleton. Giles is essentially a clerk interested in books and computations. He took it very badly but he swore he knew nothing of gold and that the source was neither the Earl or Castle Ashby and that it must have come from someone else."

Lord Wilmington sighed at this remembrance of past events.

"I do not like this Ketch. It could be a troublesome waste of time."

"What about the brother" asked Ketch.

Wilmington gave a smile. "I have a great affection for Edgar. He is not easily bullied. They were gentler with Edgar for he is the Sampson of the County. Despite their numbers, they relied on words rather than blows. It was just a pity that he was not there when they questioned his brother."

Wilmington clearly enjoyed Edgar Middleton's strength. He leaned back in his chair and from a draw in the desk he produced a badly mad wooden pipe. He looked at it fondly.

"Young Edgar made that for me when a boy and I treasure his present. Almost wistfully he replaced it and resumed his explanation.

"They both work for me ketch in the management of the Earl's sequestered estate. Giles knows all particulars about rents and mortgages, debts incurred and loans given. From many years' experience he knows every farmer, merchant and worker on the estate. Edgar is involved in the more physical maintenance of the property. "

At this point, Wilmington became more confidential.

"Both men have a burden that is shared by others, Ketch. They were supporters and employees of Royalist nobility and now they work to support a Puritan government. Former royalists regard them as traitors and those that support the Commonwealth view them with suspicion. For me that lies in the past, all that interests me is that they are providing a valuable flow of monies to the House of Commons. As far as I am concerned Ketch, they are both loyal and reliable servants."

Ketch understood that at least as far as Wilmington was concerned, he placed little credence in the story of gold and he did not want any disruption which would interfere with the flows of money to London.

Ketch was not totally convinced by Wilmington's argument and it showed in his face. Wilmington was annoyed.

"Giles Middleton is not without courage. He saved Spencer Compton at the cost of earning the hatred of the people of Oxford. I believe It is a tale worth telling."

Ketch felt that good manners required him to hear what it was that Wilmington was so determined to put before him. Wilmington started again.

"Just as matters between Parliament and the Crown were coming to a head, Spencer Compton decided to take a closer look at the royalist city of Oxford that was so close to Northampton which in turn was a town that strongly supported Parliament. He took Giles with him and they quietly examined fortifications and the repair of the city walls. Giles had been an undergraduate at Oxford and that evening his college was commemorating their Founder's Day with an outdoor feast and festival in their Great Courtyard. Not just food and drink but also musicians, jugglers and fire eaters. When the college learnt that a former student was visiting the town with probably the richest man in England. The two men immediately became guests of honour."

"Yes, I understand that such colleges always need benefactors", interjected Ketch. Lord Wilmington nodded his agreement and continued.

" The celebrations had fallen on the day of the town's market and as evening was falling and the festivities had begun, many of the local townsfolk and their families came and stood outside the college to listen to the merriment. Slightly the worse for drink in a moment of magnanimity the Earl instructed Giles to invite some of the townsfolk into the courtyard. When Giles waved his arm to the people outside a mass of people just surged in to take up the offer. Such was the crowd and the tumult that the Master of the college ordered the closing and locking of the great wooden doors. Those townsfolk inside began to help themselves to food and drink and in the spirit of the moment began hugging and kissing the fellows and their wives. They demanded that the musicians, jugglers and the fire eaters should all perform for them. The mood was a happy one but inevitably arguments broke out over behaviour and offence was taken by some and the packed courtyard became a scene for a riot. Tables were turned over with food, bottles, and plate falling to the floor. What was dangerous was the sudden outbreak of fire, almost certainly from the fire eater's equipment. The riot turned into a tragedy with men women and children fighting and screaming to get out. But, the exit of the great doors was closed. Giles knowing the college, dragged the Earl to safety through one of the staircases. However, these escapes were quickly closed by the scholars, concerned for their rooms and property. Giles went back into the courtyard by a window, and with a silver candle stick smashed the locks on the chapel and dining room doors which provided an exit to safer spaces for the crowd. But those left behind were in a sorry state. The fire in fact had not been great and was eventually dealt with. It was the panic that caused the deaths and injuries. In the end three men two women and seven children, had been killed and many others were grievously hurt. All the dead were either family members of merchants from the market or those of tradesmen, butchers, shoemakers, carpenters. The college paid out monies to the families affected and the Earl made a large donation to the college. No one, however, remembered the efforts of Giles to ease the crush. The people of Oxford had an easy scape goat in Giles as the man who invited them in. The deaths were laid at his door. He was got out of Oxford quickly and it was as well that they did for there were many with heavy grievance against him."

Lord Wilmington shifted in his chair, he was conscious that he had over told a tale that had meant to be helpful. He could see that Ketch was not interested in events in Oxford ten years ago even if they did reflect well on Giles Middleton.

"I have taken up too much of you time but I believe I have made my point.

"I can see that you have great confidence in Giles Middleton and you wish him to be troubled as little as possible", replied Ketch. "But I have my orders, my lord. It is inevitable that I must follow the path, without the violence of Zouche Tate and press closely the Middleton brothers as well as searching Castle Ashby".

Lord Wilmington nodded a silent assent. He rang a bell on his desk and a manservant appeared and Ketch thanked the nobleman and moved towards the door.

"One other matter, "said Lord Wilmington.

"Watch out for a Varley Brent. If he hears that the search for gold has returned to Northampton you will have a dangerous competitor."

There was much for Ketch to ponder as he made his way back to Northampton. He was pleased at the civility of Lord Wilmington but there had been no offer of assistance rather it had been made quite clear, that if serious disruption arose, he would be held to account. He began to find his walk irksome. The joy of such exercise he had lost and he was much relieved that a passing carter was prepared to take a passenger for a few copper coins. For a short while the debate with Lord Wilmington was forgotten as the carter enjoined him in conversation on the weather, the harvest and the foibles of the nobility.

Chapter Nine

It was not long after Ketch had departed to see Lord Wilmington that Stephen and Anne left the house together. Anne turned left to enter the town and make the short walk to the market square. Carrying her basket, she was seen as a regular housewife undertaking the morning's shopping, a task performed every morning. But for her today was different, she saw her purpose as gaining information in support of her husbands' mission. Stephen had walked alongside her whilst pinning to his chest the cloth badge of office as town constable. The town crest picked out in coloured thread showed up strongly against his black jerkin. He was a powerful figure of authority. On reaching the town he turned away and entered a series of alleyways and poor wooden housing, that led firstly to St Giles church and then Abington street, the major road to the North and East. Here, where the road forked was the edge of his jurisdiction and a place where idlers and troublemakers gathered, looking for a chance, to fund their drinking and gambling. They were not, however, beyond honest work and from time to time travellers would employ them as porters or guides, for the journey to the nearby towns of Wellingborough or Kettering.

As expected, he found a small group of unshaven, unkempt, poorly dressed men grouped around a brazier where a small portion of charcoal gave out a dull glow and a limited amount of warmth. Stephen walked slowly towards them. He wished them a good morning and had they obtained any work. An elderly man rose to his feet and gave a small nod of respect.

"Not as yet constable but we always hope."

A much younger stony-faced man also rose to his feet and looked hard at Stephen.

"Have they caught the King yet", he called out. The voice carried an obvious amused contempt at the failings of authority. *I might have known, thought Stephen,*

"*Varley Brent* always *pushing always trying the little goad looking for the overreaction*. Stephen replied sharply,

"He is not your King Brent and there are many in Northampton who would want words and more with those who would choose to call him their King".

"Sorry constable" replied Brent. "I mean Charles Stuart the one who would steal our freedom and who should have his head chopped off like his father."

Brent was trying hard to make up for his mistake. Such a slip of the tongue could get him whipped. Chastened he resumed his seat. The men looked at each other and avoided Stephen's gaze. He left them to their talk and slowly made his way down the main street towards the market square.

Anne, when she reached the market began to walk around the square strolling amongst the market stalls, chatting to their owners and others like herself making purchases. She was no longer the fearsome maid she once was. The fatherly support she had received from the old clerk Hedlow and her marriage to Ketch, to say nothing of her new-found wealth, had over a period of time produced a new self-confidence. She was popular with friends and neighbours and both she and ketch were well respected in Northampton. Her sweetness of manner and her own good sense resulted in many conversations as she moved about the market. It was still early morning when Giles Middleton and his wife together with their servants entered the market from Wilmington house. As Lord Wilmington's factor and the occupant of his lordships town house Giles had to be respected, but the majority of Northampton residents were distrustful of him. To the minority of those who retained royalist sympathies he was a turncoat raising money for the hated roundheads, the majority who supported the new regime saw him as someone not to be trusted. As Giles steered his blind wife through the market, he spent his time informing her of all about her and the purchases made by her housekeeper. There was therefore, nothing unusual about Anne in her turn conversing with them. Their talk was largely of topics current in all conversations in the market, the harvest and the fate of Charles Stuart. Anne began to outline the difficulties of obtaining certain articles, as travel was still uncertain and merchants preferred to remain at home. Elizabeth took up this topic and whilst agreeing with Anne she mentioned that they had a visit from a man from Southern Germany. He had asked to see Giles on a matter of business. Giles was quick to hear this remark and thought it necessary to intervene in the conversation. He explained that he had no knowledge of the visitors concerns and had been unable to help him.

"Well", interposed Elizabeth he was with you some time and your voices were raised at times."

"Ah!", Giles smiled."
"That is how foreign people do business my dear, they are noisy, excitable and often rude in their bargaining. He is unlikely to come again."

Elizabeth happily received the reassurance of her husband and turned away. Anne could not see that any of this was of importance for Ketch and moved on.

As Stephen walked out of Abington Street, he could see Anne with a half-filled basket talking to a group of people. The central member of this group was a well-built man in his mid-forties, dressed in the black apparel of those of strong puritan persuasion. Only his white collar and his thick grey hair toned down the blackness of his dress. Stephen knew him as Giles Middleton and he was with his full household. There was his blind wife Elizabeth with her maid, his housekeeper who he knew as Maria and his manservant Mathew. Elizabeth was looking especially beautiful. Although wearing a white lace cap, the abundance of her golden hair was evident from the tresses that would not be contained. Neither was her female figure hidden under her navy-blue shift. Her face was clear and she enjoyed a firm brow, large blue eyes a soft nose and blush red lips. With her arms linked to those of her maid and husband, there was no evidence that this beautiful woman had been dealt a blow, that prevented the full life that such beauty deserved. Stephen was moved every time he saw her. He had once had hopes of her himself. From time to time this passion re-surfaced in him. Anne had completed her conversation and moved away to the Northern side of the market, towards the small house that she and ketch for the moment still rented. Giles and his household had similarly moved but towards the centre of the market. Stephen spent some minutes following their progress. After a while he noticed that they were also being carefully watched by a thick set muscular man of middling years with short cut hair and the mark of smallpox on his forehead. He was unknown to Stephen but he conveyed a sense of both energy and menace. Stephen moved forward to question the man, when he in his turn abandoned his observation and stepped straight into the path of Giles Middleton. He just stood stock still quietly forcing himself to be seen. He said nothing and then turned away. Giles did not step back or in any way physically register that he knew the man, but his surprise and concern was to be seen in an angry grimace that filled his face. Giles quickly regained his composure and turned those with him, to begin moving towards the back door of Wilmington House. He was careful to adopt a calm measured tread and even stopped to look at the offerings of one of the stalls. His progress remained steady towards the goal of his home. He was not to get there, however, without further incident. Virtually at his backdoor as he was marshalling people for entry, he was accosted by an elderly man, obviously a stranger, dressed in a dark green, velvet doublet with brown trousers and brown boots. His clothes were of a foreign cut. His thin face showed displeasure and as he spoke angrily to Giles, he grasped his arm and began to pull him about. Giles in turn pushed him away and shepherded his party into the house. Finally, he turned to confront his attacker but he had moved away only pausing to throw Giles a look of dark intent. Stephen felt it was important that Ketch should hear of these matters at once. He made his way quickly back down towards the Dern Gate.

Later, looking forward to lunch, Ketch together with Anne and Stephen sat in the parlour of the new home, exchanging the information each had obtained. Tull had volunteered to collect something for a noon day meal, whilst listening to what was being said and soon a game pie, cheese, cuts of cold meat, some rather dry bread together with a collection of pears and apples covered the table. Ketch explained how he was received in a friendly fashion but Lord Wilmington had very clearly stated his dislike of the army.

"The important thing", said Ketch.

"Is that he did not forbid an approach to Giles Middleton and a general inquiry into the location of any coins. There is a complication, however, as to who would have legitimate right to any coins that might be found. I would not be surprised if Wilmington would not stretch out his hand."

Anne in her account emphasised the unwillingness of Giles to discuss in front of her any details concerning a recent foreign visitor. Stephen outlined the strange behaviour of Giles when confronted by a thickset dangerous looking man and they both remembered the short struggle between Giles and the stranger, that had led him to hurry into the house. As they were completing their accounts Tull had joined them at the table. He had a contribution to make.

"I have been in Northampton Ketch for a few weeks now helping Anne and she may confirm that most people having contact with Giles Middleton, are very careful and very cautious of him, especially women. I think it is more than any hidden royalist sympathies or his position with Lord Wilmington. They always seem to be on their guard with him."

Anne looked quizzically at Tull.

"He is right Ketch, amongst women there are some unhappy tales about unwanted approaches from Giles Middleton."

Matters descended into silence and eating, when noises of a horse were heard at the back of the house. Ketch rose and moved to the backdoor and into the courtyard.

"Holditch!" he exclaimed.

"Welcome, you look both tired and dirty. Let the boy look after your mount. Come inside. You must clean up and have some food".

Holditch slid down from his saddle and grasped Ketch by the hand.

"It's good to see you Captain. It has been a long, and at times, difficult ride but I have news."

He handed his reins to the stable boy.

"You said there was food", he inquired.

"I never seem to be far from hunger Captain, perhaps your good wife can feed an honest soldier".

"Holditch you never change", cried ketch. Always looking for something anything to eat. Come on! Get washed and you shall have food."

Ketch looked fondly on Holditch. In such a land as England at the end of a civil war, he knew a man could rely on few real friends but he was sure of Holditch's friendship and loyalty. His reputation in the army was that of a scrounger, but his well-fed bulky figure and slightly baby face hid a man who was hard and ruthless when required. Many a trooper failed to understand that his benign appearance concealed a soldier of strength and speed, being surprised at the sudden appearance of a knife at his throat. Cheery by nature Holditch had often given Ketch the benefit of his philosophy of life.

"I will wait in line with the next man Ketch, but if someone tries to push ahead out of turn, he will find his face in the mud with my foot on his neck."

Ketch smiled to himself.

"Holditch was a friend indeed"

Ketch returned to the parlour to give news that Holditch was with them. After a few minutes Holditch emerged from the back scullery and Ketch introduced him to Anne and Stephen. Tull and Holditch just clasped each other's shoulders. This was the maximum of affection they ever showed to each other. They were after all soldiers. The party moved into the dining room to hear Holditch's news. The food and drink quickly appeared before Holditch and he began his tale. He always had a great enthusiasm for life and a great deal of natural wit and humour. This was unlike his constant companion Tull who was by nature a taciturn West countryman. Holditch was determined to present his news as a great adventure and as usual in the telling of his tale he lightened the mood of his listeners.

"Basically, Ketch he said. Thurloe was right there was a distribution of monies to the army of Charles Stuart North of Chester, somewhere in Lancashire,"

As he spoke Holditch liberally filled his plate from those that had been brought from the parlour and placed before him. "Amongst the coinage distributed, were gold coins and efforts were made to see that everyone received at least one. But there were not enough for this and inevitably some did better in the distribution than others."

There was a pause at this point as several mouthfuls were taken together with a strong draught of small beer. Suitably revived he continued.

" When the army reached Chester, it was found that gold is often difficult for the purchases that soldiers generally make such as food, drink and ah! Women."

Holditch threw a look of apology at Anne but carried on.

"For this they need silver and as such the moneychangers of Chester not only did good business, they were overwhelmed."

Ketch leaned forward in his chair and lightly tapped the table to ask a question, but Holditch was in full flow.

"They are very difficult those money changers, Ketch. Information has to be prized out of them. Fortunately, there was a regiment of cavalry at hand and the suggestion of their involvement in our discussions eventually secured cooperation"

For the moment Holditch returned to his cup and plate and this allowed Ketch to get in his question.

"You did not have to use actual force", he inquired.

"No" was the answer.

"Plenty of threats was all that was required".

Ketch wanted to know more than this from Holditch but Tull intervened with a question of his own.

"For goodness sake Holditch we already know this what new information have you?"

Tull and Holditch had been comrade in arms for many years. Holditch was not to be hurried.

"It is all very well for you Tull, lording it in Northampton, plenty of food and drink, a nice soft bed and nothing to do. I have been following dangerous orders and my officer,"

Here he nodded at Ketch, "needs a full account".

"Well get on with it", exclaimed Tull.

With a hard stare at Tull, Holditch came to the heart of his information.

"A man central to the distribution of the monies was a sort of English mercenary, not really a soldier but close to the officers. His name was Dundas Stannard".

Holditch held up his hand as Tull meant to say something. Tull sat back in his chair and remained silent.

"Let me describe him", said Holditch.

"I got a description of sorts from the moneychanger but a better one from the old lady that gave him lodgings. She was an acute if rather grasping landlord. She saw him as about forty years of age, not tall but not short, strong about the shoulders, muscular arms and legs and physically very compact. He has a squarish head with grey hair cut very short. Apparently of a frightening aspect and seen as a very dangerous man. She also mentioned evidence of past smallpox which had scared his forehead right up into his brow."

Stephen who had been listening to Holditch's description intently could contain himself no longer.

"I have seen just such a man today in the market square. he made as to directly confront Giles Middleton, but at the last moment turned away. It was clear to me that Giles Middleton knew him. He tried not to give himself away, but he knew him I am sure of it".

"I have not seen him myself" ventured Holditch.

"But he seems a very distinctive man. "

"He is distinctive all right" cried Stephen."

"And, he does look dangerous "

Ketch looked at Stephen and then turned to Anne.

"Did you see this man ", he asked.

She thought for a moment.

"Not myself but Stephen did mention him as we returned back home."

Ketch thought quietly to himself and seemed to come to a decision.

"If Stephen is correct and he seems very certain, we have a link between the man that Holditch tells us helped distribute gold coins to the rebel army and Giles Middleton, a man previously thought to be the caretaker of such a hoard. I had my doubts about this task of Secretary Thurloe but it has become much clearer and more serious."

Anne at this point sought to contribute to the discussion.

"We may also ask ourselves why this man Dundas Stannard is here now in Northampton. What are his plans with or for Giles Middleton?"

Ketch had concern in his voice.

"We must act soon. It seems to me that matters here in Northampton to do with these wretched gold coins is coming to a head."

"Do you have a plan Captain", asked Tull.

It was still new to Ketch to have his rank spoken. He liked it, but from men who were his friends it made him uncomfortable.

"Ketch or John, Tull. Let's keep life simple".

Tull thought for a moment and then spoke up, he had something to say.

"Will we be in uniforms for this search"?

Ketch had his answer. "I have given this some thought Tull. Whatever we wear it will be guessed, at least by some that we have reopened the search for gold. Uniforms will support our authority but civilian dress will be less frightening. I think there must be a bit of both. I will wear civilian dress but Tull and Holditch must be in uniform, but no swords or helmets. Clearly, we will be seen to have the army's authority and indicate we are in deadly earnest and discourage any interference, but without being too threatening."

Anne looked at her husband, she had sat quietly in her chair as her husband made his purpose plain.

"There are three women in Wilmington House which you intend to enter and search and even the army may regret this action in the face of three screaming women, one of whom is blind. I think your search and even your questioning may be more effective if I come with you. They will feel safer if a woman is present".

Ketch was taken aback, this he had not foreseen. He had to admit that if the picture painted by Anne took place the whole event could become a disaster.

"Agreed a woman with us will be most valuable."

He allowed himself a smile.

"We do not have a uniform for you".

"Good" she reposted. I shall be a reassuring citizen, not one of your bully boys."

She made a face at Tull and Holditch. Ketch turned to Stephen.

"Your position is a delicate one, you are the town constable the servant of the town not the army. I think you must step back a bit from these events. We shall not involve you in any search or arrest but of course you should be present, to see that nothing we do causes offence to the Town Council. Of course, there may be a need for you to prevent anyone seeking to interfere with our task. Ketch rose to his feet. The light in the room began to dim, some of the candles were guttering low.

"It is dark outside" declared Anne. I think you should start early tomorrow."

Ketch looked about him. They had talked longer than he had thought.

"My wife is correct," he admitted.

"We start first thing tomorrow.

Chapter Ten

Whilst Ketch and his party were having lunch and engaged in their planning, Giles Middleton sat in his study and turned over in his mind the two events in the market square. The clumsy approach of that meddling fool Conrad Tauber was of no real consequence. Giles was quite happy to see him off back to Germany. No, he was much more disturbed by the appearance and bold confrontation of Dundas Stannard. This was much more serious. It could put his life in jeopardy. He had no wish to be unmasked as a royalist paymaster. He tried to bend his mind as to what did Stannard want? What was his purpose in coming to Northampton? He also was taking a terrible risk. If Stannard, despite the risk to himself, was to reveal that Giles had provided gold for Charles Stuart, neither could remain in Northampton. Giles knew that with his life so at risk he would have to flee to France. There he would be a well-regarded especially if Charles had really escaped. However, it crossed his mind that perhaps Stannard just wanted to be bought off. At this thought Giles experienced a slight measure of comfort. Given Stannard's character that almost certainly was why he was here. Greatly relieved at his conclusion, Giles realised that paying off Stannard would not be easy, it had to be done in great secrecy, avoiding any suspicion. Just for a moment Giles toyed with the idea of leaving Northampton with Stannard. A devil's partnership he thought, but there were some advantages. Then he began to consider such a decision seriously, a view of his life if he stayed or went. Here in Northampton he enjoyed a position of respect. He was not loved but he was an important member of civic life. He had to admit to himself that his life with Elizabeth had changed. Once she was a glittering beauty and he had been envied by all, but she was no longer an asset, rather a liability of extra expense for which he was now pitied. If he successfully paid off Stannard and remained would the remaining gold be of any use or any benefit to him? His suspicions were that the Earl did not wish for the last of it to support the royalist cause, but he could never use it himself whilst the Commonwealth survived. That meant that Giles would have all the risk of its keeping. There may be other vultures following Stannard that would have to be dealt with. France was an appealing alternative. With the gold he would be rich, he would be amongst like-minded friends who would have valued his contribution to the cause. In France a man of means could enjoy all the comforts of property, food, horses and women. In his heart Giles knew that this was an unsure future. Unfortunately, he understood that he could also face resentment, constant pleas for money and the likely-hood of a lonely death in exile. His uncertainty annoyed him. He stirred in his chair. "One thing is certain", he thought. I must deal with the saddlebag in the cellar. It is but one door away from being found.

He needed his wife. He rose from his chair and at the door of his study he called for Elizabeth.

"Come here my love. I have matters to discuss with you."

After just a few moments, despite her blindness, Elizabeth was in the chair facing Giles across his desk

." I have two matters of concern to raise with you," he said. "One is of small significance, the other of major importance. The first is the German visitor of yesterday and the same man who obstructed us in our own back doorway."

"You were quite sharp with him yesterday" replied Elizabeth. "I could hear raised voices and he was clearly very angry this morning".

Giles continued.

"He says his name is Conrad Tauber and he is a wine merchant importing wines to London."

"Anyone selling such goods at a distance needs wealth, strength and good contacts", contributed Elizabeth,

" Why does he wish to speak with you, you barely drink wine? Giles smiled.

" You are right but it was not about wine that he has come to Northampton. In a sense he has come looking for a dowry".

Elizabeth listened in astonishment. Before she could repeat his final word, Giles had raised his hand and continued with his explanation.

"Many years ago, 1623 to be precise, the second Earl of Northampton, my Earl, Spencer Compton was sent by King James to the high mountains of Europe called the Alps. It was a diplomatic mission. I was a young man newly appointed as his secretary. It was a wonderful visit. Unfortunately, from a diplomatic point of view it was not successful, but Spencer himself was very well treated and feted for many weeks. He was very much the favourite with all manner of woman both young and old. The German wine seller who came to see me yesterday and today claims that Spencer got one of his conquests with child and left his lover with nothing but her disgrace."

Elizabeth's face was careful not to show any emotion. Giles continued.

"The mother and child were shunned by their relatives, had to leave the area and lead a life of poverty and misery. The mother has since died but the child now some twenty-seven years old is the intended wife of Conrad Tauber and the current Earl, James, has a half-sister of which he knows nothing. Conrad Tauber intends to marry her and end her life of poverty. He sees no reason why the Compton estate should not make a substantial contribution."

Elizabeth gasped. Giles sat quietly awaiting her full reaction.

"Do you believe him", she asked. "It all seems a long time ago".

Giles smiled in reminiscence.

"Yes, it was but you have to understand that Spencer Compton was wildly handsome and dashing. It is not an impossible story, in some ways a very common one". Elizabeth wanted to know more.

"This Conrad Tauber must be a wealthy man. I doubt that he needs money."

"I doubt that he does", replied Giles.

"But he is a very determined one. He is a Puritan and a strict Calvinist. He is clearly in love with the daughter and will do anything to remove the stain of sin. He is set upon cleansing her past and central to this is a payment that shows remorse and a desire for atonement by that person really responsible for it. I confess that I am always put out by such intense, almost savage, feeling". Elizabeth wanted more details.

"What is the name of this girl? Did you know her? Is it a name you recognise? Has he given any proofs to show that this is not just some high tale and how much does he want?"

Giles lost his smile under the flow of questions. He spoke as clearly as he could, to answer them.

"No, I do not recognise the name of the mother. Tauber writes that It was Silvrina and the daughter's name is Angelica. He has shown me what he calls proofs but I have little confidence in them. There is a note in what looks like Spencer's hand arranging a meeting and a wax seal bearing his coat of arms stamped on a piece of quality paper."

The two Middletons sat facing each other, neither certain what was to be done.

"Oh! added Giles.

"He requires five hundred pounds in gold or silver".

Elizabeth turned her bright eyes, that could see nothing, towards her husband.

"What do you truly think Giles"?

The question hung in the air for some long seconds. Giles made up his mind and for his own understanding he counted his reasons off on his fingers.

"Spencer Compton has been dead for seven years, I think he would have demanded more certain proofs. Conrad Tauber is not really interested in money, he is making a religious point, and of course the money demanded now belongs to the Commonwealth. I suspect that Lord Wilmington would not want money spent in this way". He was content. He turned to Elizabeth.

" Conrad Tauber is staying at the Peacock inn, I shall send Mathew with a note clearly stating my position."

Elizabeth looked carefully at Giles and said," if this was the matter of small significance what are we to consider now?

Giles smiled to himself the matter now to be considered was indeed of a greater significance.
"We shall have some wine for this problem", he said.

Rising from his chair he opened the study door and called Mathew to him.

"Bring me a bottle of the French red wine, two glasses and I want privacy for an hour".

Within a few minutes the wine was brought and placed on the study table. Giles locked the study door poured the wine resumed his seat and turned towards Elizabeth. Whilst Giles had been making these arrangements, Elizabeth had taken to walking around the study. Although blind for a year she had developed a remarkable ability to memorise the location of furniture, and all other objects that might have been an obstacle for her. Although at a continuing disadvantage outdoors and amongst crowds, within the house she was at ease and could move around freely. When the wine had been brought, she re-joined Giles at the desk. He remained silent for a moment and then began to place before Elizabeth the nature of the danger that both of them faced.

" From the first you have known that I have in my charge a great golden treasure that Spencer Compton the Second Earl of Northampton found in Italy and that I was with him and helped bring it all back to England".

Helen nodded. That Giles had been involved in this had always been at the back of her mind as a source of future trouble. Giles took a first sip of his wine and continued his explanation.

"It is a secret that has been well kept here in Northampton with only myself, you Elizabeth, my brother Edgar and James Compton our Third Earl knowing of it. Only once have I been challenged on this and despite the efforts of Zouche Tate and Varley Brent I denied everything and told them nothing. "

He looked at Elizabeth, but she was listening intently so he continued.

"Over the years the hoard has diminished and was not always in my care. Spencer Compton kept control of its location and use in the early years. It was the foundation for the transformation of

Castle Ashby into one of the grandest homes in England. Furniture, tapestries, carpets, wallpaper, everything of the very finest was to be found in the Earl's home."

Elizabeth already knew most of this but she could sense that Giles spelling out this introduction meant something of real concern was to follow. At this point they both refreshed themselves with wine, Elizabeth smiled encouragingly but Giles looked grim. He continued.

"All this happy peace and prosperity was broken with the outbreak of hostility between King and Parliament. Spencer and a large part of the golden coins went to war for the King. He was killed early on and Castle Ashby was looted by the servants and any other local who cared to push himself into that mad scramble. This was in 1643 and as he had told no one where the cache was hidden; for six years it was lost."

"James knew nothing" interrupted Elizabeth. "Spencer had not even told his son?"

"No," replied Giles.

"In 1649 by a happy coincidence I found it. Some other time I will tell you how, but we must move on, we have difficult things to do. I told no one but Edgar and James."

Giles was breathing deeply now as he got further into his tale.

"Last year I received a summons from King Charles in Scotland for the use of the gold."

Giles knew at this point he was bending the truth somewhat for he had offered the gold, but if he was to secure Elizabeth's full cooperation, he wanted his royalist leanings to be not so obviously strong.

"He sent two men to collect it Sir Thomas Skeffington and a mercenary called Dundas Stannard. They received all but one saddlebag of what was left. The point of all this Elizabeth is that this morning in the market square Dundas Stannard stood in front of me. He is here alive in Northampton and with the royalist cause lost because of the defeat at Worcester, he can be here only for one thing. He will try for the gold. He is a very dangerous man."

Giles knew that he had revealed himself to his wife as a royalist paymaster, a very different story than that of holding gold for the Earl. Elizabeth was silent in face of this news. She began to consider Giles in a very different way. His real ambitions were for the return of the king. His level of deceit was far greater than she had ever imagined. He and the Earl of Northampton in the Scottish invasion, had financed the killing of men women and their families. She was appalled and saw that his actions would raise questions about her own behaviour. She became concerned at her own fate. Should Giles be found out in his dealings, a blind wife with a traitor husband would have a bleak future. Giles could see her emotions in her face but he had to continue Elizabeth was of real immediate importance. He had to secure her cooperation.

"I do not know what the future holds. Charles Stuart may yet be caught, may yet get to France. News of the golden coins may get out and undoubtedly some will remember previous events in Northampton and Dundas Stannard is in Northampton. For all our sakes, Elizabeth we must find a secure and secret place for the gold that remains"

Still uncertain of the consequences of what she had just heard Elizabeth nodded her consent. Giles gently raised Elizabeth from her chair. From his desk he took a ball of twine."

Chapter Eleven

Holding the twine Giles placed his hand on Elizabeth's shoulder.

"I think having a blind wife and one with a special talent will provide us with the safest of places for the gold."

He moved them both to the head of the steps that led down to the cellar. On the three-foot wall that flanked the cellar stairs, pots of herbs had always been in place. Rosemary and Thyme, basil and mint gave both a fragrance to the room and some protection from the foul odours that rose from the cellar.

"Enjoy the herbs" he said.

He took a moment to brush both their hands through the herbal leaves. The husband and wife then descended the steps down through the locked wooden door to the cellar. Leaving Elizabeth at the foot of the stairs, Giles expertly with flint and steel lit a candle lantern. The light threw up a cellar generally full of unwanted household bits and pieces, broken barrels, an ancient wine rack, planks of wood and unwanted furniture. But up against the far wall was a solid wooden chest. Elizabeth already felt the damp and clammy air around her.

"Well! Husband" she said.

"What now?"

Giles unlocked the chest and with a grunt of effort brought out a saddle bag with both pouches bulging with the golden coins inside. Placing the saddlebag on the floor Giles took Elizabeth 's two hands and guided her to sit on the chest. He stood regarding her in silence for a moment. Then he put to her the questions that were vital to his hopes.

"I have known and so have the household, that you have developed a skill sometimes given by nature to compensate the blind for their affliction. You have in your darkness developed a memory that allows you to move quite freely and safely amongst all manner of stationary objects. You can climb stairs, walk about furnished rooms with confidence and certainty as long as all things in it are stationary. My hopes hang on this Elizabeth. Am I right?"

There was the strain of both hope and fear in his voice. Elizabeth guessed what was required. They were to go into the tunnels. In her blindness, she was to remember the route taken.

"Yes, Giles you are correct my blindness has given me a new skill"

In her heart she knew she had no choice. She indicated her assent by standing and stretching out her hands to her husband. With the pounding in his heart diminishing Giles unlocked the metal door that led from the cellar into the tunnels. He tied the ball of twine to the wine rack and gave the end into Elizabeth's hands.

"Whatever happens do not let go of this, if all goes wrong it will give us the way home. "

He picked up the saddlebag and threw it over his right shoulder and with his right hand reached out and held Elizabeth's left hand. Kneeling he retrieved the lantern in his left hand. For a moment they stood stock still together, a strange tableau in the dark. Giles spoke clearly, Elizabeth had to understand.

"Together we will go into these tunnels, Elizabeth and we will slowly make our way to a point where I am lost but you can remember exactly where we are. Hopefully it will not be too far and then using your memory and the twine we shall return to the cellar."

For a moment Elizabeth hesitated.

"You must be clear in your instructions Giles. You must watch carefully where I step and have a care for my head. We must be slow and you must relent in your impatience, which I can feel."

Giles mumbled his assent. He guided them slowly towards the entrance.

Giles suffered from the weight of the saddlebag and felt the blackness like a physical force enveloping him. The lantern worked well but it's light was limited to a bright pool a few feet in front of them. He began to comprehend the real meaning of blindness. They could only inch forward, Elizabeth could hardly control her fear.

"You must talk to me Giles, you have the lantern, do not stop, you must keep telling and repeating everything in our path. I need this to keep my trust in you".

The linked couple after a few yards stopped and both sought to control their fear. Giles was determined to see this through. He began as Elizabeth asked a nonstop description of the floor, the walls, the bits of rubbish in their way. The ceiling above them was barely visible. Only a few times did they see hard packed earth, timber struts, brickwork and occasional piping. The walls, however, made of similar material, were ever present, and at times seemed to press on in to them. These were the times of their greatest fears. After what seemed long minutes and having mercifully avoided any major problems, they became a little more confident. Elizabeth had not stumbled or hit her head. Giles was still holding the lantern high. Their progress began to improve. When they first heard the rats, they both shuddered. It was a nasty surprise, neither had given any thought to the regular inhabitants of the tunnels. They were close and were constantly just a few feet away. Fortunately, humans here were sufficiently strange as to be watched but avoided. Elizabeth as a farmer's daughter was able to calm herself over them and keep a grip on her fear. For Giles their squeaking was a nightmare that he could barely endure. Their presence led him to hold so hard on Elizabeth's hand that she twice had to tell him to relax. The pathway began to twist and turn and after a few yards they had to step down into a dry sewer and this they followed for some minutes. Giles noted some stone steps to the left that took them up into what was a brick lined tunnel of a more formal nature. Here the floor was more even and for a short while they made good progress. The tunnel came to a blank wall and to the right there was a room full of broken crates and bottles and from here they passed through a low doorway into another room. In this case a hole in the wall took them into what was clearly a dry stream bed. Here they turned to the left, footing was uneven and progress slow. All the time Giles kept up his flow of words. Any faltering led Elizabeth to stop. In this fashion they continued with their clumsy journey. It felt as if they had been in the tunnels for hours but in fact the distance travelled was no more than a hundred yards. At a point where they met a wide puddle of water much to Elizabeth's' relief he stopped. Casting his eyes about in the light of the lantern Giles found a pile of large stones, bits of wood and old bricks. Leaving Elizabeth standing still he took the saddlebag and carefully hid it amongst the rubble. From one of the pouches he extracted without unbuckling it one of the golden coins which he placed on the top of the rubble. The relief from the release of his load was enormous. He let out a great sigh.

"This is our journey's end Elizabeth. Your memory must include this."

"Thank God" was Elizabeth's reply.

"Now we return and with the twine and my mind I will get us back to the cellar."

Giles felt uncomfortable at Elizabeth's remark. He was grateful for her help but she seemed to be taking charge and he resented it. As it was Elizabeth busied herself with following the twine, and Giles was relieved to guide her without a constant commentary. The return journey was managed much more quickly, but there was a mild outbreak of bickering as their spirits rose at the thought that their ordeal was nearing its end. Back in the cellar Elizabeth waited to be guided back up to the study. Giles, however, sat her back on the chest and stood facing her. He spoke softly.

"That was very brave my darling, you have probably saved us both from serious consequences had that saddlebag come to light. But it is important that I can feel confident that you can retrieve it. After all you are now the only person who can".

Elizabeth scowled. She waited, she had no idea what Giles was going to say. He took a careful breath.

"You do not know but I have placed one of the gold coins, a large one, on the rubble. It will be easy to feel where it is. It is very important that I knowl that I can trust you to find the coins again. On your own if need, be."

Elizabeth made to speak but Giles carried on.

"You must now go back on your own and return with that gold coin. Then we will all have confidence that it can be done. Elizabeth rose from her seat and gave Giles a push in the chest.

"I cannot and I will not do it on my own. I know that I can find that coin and return with it, but I do not want to do it alone. I may slip or fall and then who would help me in there".

It was Elizabeth's turn to forestall speech by Giles as he ventured to reply.

"You can bring Maria or Mathew and I will happily go with them or you can once more come with me."

Giles was not just unhappy, he was very cross. He had no wish to take that journey again. It was unpleasant and he did not like the idea of being totally dependent on Elizabeth who he roundly damned in his mind. They stood in silence for a moment their wills in conflict. Finally, Giles said.

" All right, Elizabeth I will go with you but make sure we both come back alive".

He held her and they both moved to the entrance back to the tunnels. "You can bring the lantern if you wish, "said Elizabeth

In fact, Elizabeth managed the journey without difficulty, Giles carefully hanging on to both her and the lantern. It had taken less than half an hour. Elizabeth had never been so pleased with herself and she kept the coin tight in her hand. On reaching the safety of the cellar, Giles was slowly reconciled to Elizabeth's success. It was after all his clever idea. They slowly lost the tension of the moment. There was success in this for both of them. The husband and wife climbed the steps, both running their hands to release the aroma of the herbs and returned to the study. They both confessed to being hungry and with a need to wash and eat.

"We need an explanation for the state of our clothing", said Giles. I expect one of the servants will notice, especially Rose". Giles thought for a moment.

"I have been down in the cellar and you giving me a loving embrace had not realised how much dirt I had acquired."

Elizabeth nodded her assent. It was probably the best they could do. Elizabeth then called for Rose and Giles went to see about food.

Chapter Twelve

It was still early morning when Ketch flanked by Holditch and Tull marched past All Saints church and up to Wilmington House. There were plenty of by-standers about who saw them mount the stone steps and hammer on the door. Most of them would also have observed the town constable and a woman following up behind them. A young man answered the door plainly annoyed at the noise.

"Open up in the name of the Commonwealth", demanded Ketch, and he gave the door a push and crossed over the threshold. Tull, Holditch and Anne followed him. Stephen on the other hand remained at the front of the house to ensure no external interference and to sooth the concerns of those who were now taking an interest in what was going on.

"Go immediately to your bedroom and wait to be called" instructed Ketch.

Mathew the manservant, annoyed at being pushed and not really sure as to what was happening began to obstruct Ketch. But seeing two soldiers in uniform he thought it best to keep quiet and when ketch repeated his instruction, he deemed it prudent to do as he was told. However, he lingered long enough to see Giles coming out of his front reception room that doubled as a bedroom for Elizabeth.

"What is this ", demanded Giles. "Who are you people? Mistress Ketch Why are you here?"

Having caught sight of the uniforms a dark ache grasped his stomach. He feared that he knew why the army was here but he was determined to maintain his stance of innocence. Doors were opening along the corridor and two women, Maria and

Rose appeared with Mathew behind them. He sought cover for not retiring to his bedroom and wished to see what was to happen next. In a calm voice Ketch sought to steady the household and explain his purpose.

"I have army authority and permission from Lord Wilmington to search this property. I shall discuss the purpose of the search with the head of the household. First the remainder of you return to your rooms, you will all be questioned and searched."

Ketch turned towards Giles,

"Where is somewhere private where we may talk"?

Giles opened the door to his study. Ketch gave instructions to Tull, Holditch and Anne to wait in the corridor. Tull and Holditch were to ensure the servants stayed in their rooms. Anne was to find Elizabeth and comfort her as she could. Then he followed Giles into the study. Closing the door behind him Ketch saw Giles staring out of his front window trying to get Stephen's attention.

 "The town constable is part of our arrangements," stated Ketch.

"My name is Captain Ketch. I am a commissioned officer in the army, you would do better to sit down and listen to what I have to say."

 Giles, with bad grace, took to his chair. Ketch sat opposite him.

"I fear you have a very serious problem" said ketch.

" We have pointers that confirm what some in the past have thought about you, namely you are a royalist paymaster and even now with the collapse and ending of your cause, you have a cache of gold ready to fund the renewing of hostilities. This is treason a capital crime".

Giles stared back at Ketch. Those words aroused a deep fear in his heart but he was determined to resist. He knew he would need such resolution; His life could depend on it.

"You clearly have no bench warrant. The army may be in power but Englishmen still have rights. If you want to accuse me then take me before the magistrate. This war was about fighting tyranny. It was too bloody for us to bear tyranny of the army."

Ketch felt a little unhappy at these remarks. There was an unpleasant truth in them. He had virtually no evidence and really only the permission of Lord Wilmington for any action he was taking. It seemed to him that his orders from Thurloe in London, had been made without realising that civil law was returning in the new state of peace in the land. But he had to get the job done.

"You have been through this before Giles", he said in a more reasonable tone. "You know what some people think. It is in your own interest to cooperate with this search. If we find what others believe you are hiding then the matter is decided. If you are innocent of hiding gold in this house, then we shall find nothing and to that extent you will be publicly cleared of wrong-doing".

Giles was pleased he had restored the balance of power with this stupid soldier. *There was no gold in this house. He should allow this search, but against his stated opposition. They will find nothing and then he will complain. He will make so much trouble. All Northampton would know of his innocence.*

"I am powerless to resist your armed force Captain Ketch, but you act without my permission and against my will."

"So be it", replied Ketch.

"You will remain here in this study until we have finished. I can post a man outside the door if necessary." Giles scowled but nodded his assent.

Ketch left the study but paused to listen at the front door where Stephen was addressing a small crowd.

"These are army matters, go home. You do not need to become involved, just get on with your business."

With Stephen there, Ketch was satisfied they would not be interrupted in their search. He turned to begin his task. He first found Holditch.

"I want you to commence the search upstairs. Take your time and be thorough. We have only this opportunity. I doubt that we shall be able to search here again"

Ketch with Tull then went straight to the kitchen where Mathew and Maria sat at the Kitchen table looking bewildered. Mathew was a twenty-six-year-old man, well under six foot in height, who was slightly built with light brown hair and an attractive face. With deep brown eyes and a soft chin, he looked more like a poet than a manservant. He was dressed in a grey shirt that had once been white and black trousers with non-descript shoes. Over everything he wore a dark brown apron. Despite his physical slightness there was an energy about him and an initially unseen inner strength. Ketch ordered Tull to guard the door. He then began in a toneless formal voice

." My name is John Ketch, I am a Captain in the army and your master Giles Middleton is thought to be a royalist paymaster. It is your task to convince me that you know nothing of this. To begin with I do not want to hear a word from you. You will submit to a body search and then you will open every drawer, every cupboard and oven, every shelf and pantry, reciting first what is to be found in there."

119

The two servants looked at each other. Whilst Mathew sat quietly awaiting events, Maria was very different. She was restless on her chair at the table, with her arms constantly moving. Her lightly darkened skin and jet- black hair suggested a Mediterranean ancestry. Her figure was robust and she was clearly used to hard work and a tough life, as her hands looked particularly large and strong. Her age was difficult to determine, Ketch thought her in her mid-thirties. She was not cowed by the two men in front of her for she scowled defiantly at Ketch.

"No man is going to body search me".

In fact, Ketch sent Tull to get Anne and the two of them completed the body searches speedily with a minimum of complaint. Ketch then left Tull to keep an eye on Maria in the kitchen. Whilst, he returned Anne to stay with Elizabeth and then escorted Mathew to his bedroom.

Mathew sat on the bed as Ketch began to search the room. It was a spare room with a window that looked out on to the market square. As well as the bed there was a table and chair and a wash stand. There was no cupboard and no ornaments apart from a pair of candlesticks. It felt the room of a priest rather than a young man. However, under the bed there was a small chest and a long wooden box. Ketch opened the chest and began to examine the contents. Inside there were quills, a bottle of ink, spare candles and a small leather pouch containing a few silver and copper coins. There was also a thick bundle of hand bills and tracts all of a political nature. Ketch moved to the window to examine these in more detail. Everyone was a polemic against the monarchy and praising the actions of Parliament. The most extreme were calling for a republic with toleration for all religious practices except that of the Catholic faith.

"You have strong views Mathew, why then do you serve a royalist?"

Mathew looked sharply at Ketch, he was clearly frightened but his voice had conviction.

" He is not a royalist. He has been through all this before. I was not here then, but in the past, he has been accused of being a royalist by a Members of Parliament. He had him beaten up yet nothing was proven. Despite that he has loyally run an estate that sends a regular supply of funding to Parliament. There has never been any evidence and I have never seen any royalists in this house."

"How long have you lived here, asked Ketch.

" For three years," came the reply.

"My father died and his debts forced mother and I out of our house and workshop. My mother on her own had a lot of help and attention from Master Middleton. He gave me this position and has regularly helped mother with small gifts of money. He has even found her a trading stall in the market where she can earn a little money selling lace, handkerchiefs, needles, thread and buttons. I keep some of her stock here in this box under the bed".

Ketch pulled out the box and indeed it contained items such as those disclosed, together with skeins of wool and some rather thick bone knitting needles. Ketch sighed.

"I have to ask you one more question Mathew. Do you know anything about a hoard of golden coins?"

"No Sir!" was the reply.

Ketch looked about him. There was nothing here remotely connected to any gold and it seemed clear that Mathew was not going to divulge anything but praise for his master. Ketch ordered him to stay in his room. He moved to the kitchen to collect Maria

Her room was basically the same as Mathew's, with bare floorboards, a single bed, chair, table and washstand, but she had curtains at her window and a cupboard. There were, however, numerous wooden boxes strewn about the floor filled with clothes, books and a collection of ancient and broken cooking utensils. Ketch first examined the cupboard finding only female undergarments and nothing else of interest. He inspected the various boxes. The strange collection of kitchen utensils contained a variety of devices he had never seen, but there were also the usual sieves, carving knives and meat skewers. Throughout the search Maria had sat on the bed with a measure of contempt in her eyes. She now gave voice to her thoughts.

"Have you found any golden coins yet soldier"?

"No", replied Ketch sharply, "and you would do well to take this seriously. Whilst Giles Middleton is a man of significance in this town. You are not and Stephen Hedllow and I could have you in the town gaol in an instant and I doubt many would complain."

He looked down into her face. "And I mean this. Gaol is not a pretty place for a woman".

Maria shrugged, but it was clear that Ketch had made his point. He decided that more detailed questioning should take place with Maria. He quickly established that she had a Huguenot family background and not originally from Northampton, but had been brought up in Oxford where her father had been a college cook. He thought it worthwhile to quickly touch upon Oxford.

"You say you were at Oxford some until ten years ago. I know much earlier there was an unhappy college fire when town's people were killed and crushed. Were you or your family involved at all?"

Maria seemed uninterested in the question.

"There are always fires in Oxford, timber houses, students and drink. They are always happening."

For a moment she hesitated but decided to continue.

"I remember the one you mention. It was not where my father worked but, it did cause a lot of bad blood between working people and the students. There were a number of fights."

Ketch was happy to leave that topic and move on, she had shown little emotion on the matter. Maria had worked at Wilmington House for two years, her work being the basic tasks previously managed by Elizabeth. He asked the same questions he had put to Mathew concerning any knowledge of gold, but as he began to probe as to her thoughts and knowledge of Giles Middleton, he detected a tension entering her voice

"There has been some information received concerning his treatment of women", he said.

Her response to that was guarded but not immediately flattering for Giles. As Ketch persisted, she could not help but let her true concerns emerge.

"He is our master and pays good wages but he would be kind to me, as he says, if I let him. But with Rose I'm not sure she has a choice"

Maria's arms were wrapped around her chest and she was leaning forward on the bed becoming distressed. Ketch thought it wisest to end his questioning.

"Thank you, Maria, that will be all".

He was happy to leave Maria to compose herself but as he and Tull went in search of Holditch he had little doubt about the more unpleasant side of Giles Middleton.   He was not enjoying this search and only the importance of the work maintained his pursuit of information. He felt the need for his wife's support. At this point he met Holditch loitering in the corridor having finished his search upstairs.

"Nothing Captain I have been thorough. Most of the rooms upstairs are empty and those that are not have very little in them. Unless it's under the floorboards or in the walls and roof, there is no cache of gold coins to be found there".

Ketch knew that in these matters Holditch was reliable. There was no gold upstairs. He had, however, another task for Holditch.

"Holditch, I want you to go to the front and if matters are peaceful let Stephen know that he can go or stay whatever he thinks best. I want to go the Castle Ashby tomorrow morning, but I must first see the Mayor. Ask him to invite the Mayor to meet me tomorrow at home for breakfast and after that Stephen can join us so that we can search Castle Ashby together."

Holditch set off to his task and Ketch, told Tull to wait. On Hilditch's return from Stephen, he instructed them to maintain a strong presence along the corridor especially keeping an eye on the study. In return for his instructions he got a quizzical stare from Holditch and a disgruntled look from Tull.

"What is the matter with you two," he demanded.

"This is all a bit gentle Captain," Holditch replied.

"We do not seem to be making any progress," added Tull.

"Look you two, our position here is not so strong that you can go ripping up floor boards and breaking down walls. The war is over. The army cannot just do what it likes. We fought against tyranny and the citizens of this town were strong for Parliament. They will not accept being subject to any physical interrogation or punishment. We are dealing with an important citizen and his blind wife. Just control your desires to force out information and follow my orders. Precisely!"

It was not so much what he said, but the tone in Ketch's voice was one that both men recognised. It was sufficient for them both to know that he would be obeyed. In a slightly sulky fashion, they both took up a position in the corridor He entered the large front reception, come bedroom, in which Anne had been waiting patiently with Elizabeth. The room was large with high ceilings and large windows. It was well furnished with carpets and curtains together with a large double and a single bed. It had, however, the feel and smell of a room for an invalid. He ordered Rose to her room. Elizabeth was sitting at one end of a chaise longue with Ann at the other. Ketch picked up a chair and sat facing them.

Chapter Thirteen

Whilst Ketch had been questioning Mathew and Maria, Elizabeth had been sitting with Anne occasionally exchanging the smallest of small talk. In reality her mind was going over events of that afternoon, the visit to the cellar, and then now the arrival of Captain Ketch and his interrogators. This woman next to her was his wife. She had quite liked Anne, but she was not deceived by this friendship she was now her enemy. Elizabeth knew that she must say as little as possible. In no way must she give a hint or smile or start that could suggest she knew about gold. But Giles had lied to her. He and Edgar had said the gold was for the Compton family, for rebuilding the family estate that had served the Middletons so well over the years. But in reality, Giles had helped fund the invasion of England by Charles Stuart. She could not forget that men and woman had been killed as a result. That was hard to forgive. She also feared for her own position. If Giles was to be caught who would look after a blind- woman whose husband was a traitor? These were just some of the fearsome concerns that once more captured her mind. There was still the matter of this man Dundas, here in Northampton who knew Giles was guilty of these treacherous acts. Amongst this whirlwind of frightful thoughts, she came back to the man in front of her. This soldier named Ketch.

Ketch leaned towards Elizabeth. Despite her affliction she remained a very beautiful woman and to Ketch she seemed tense but in control.

"Tell me about yourself, Elizabeth, he said, and be careful what you say. There is every chance that your husband is to be exposed as a royalist sympathiser and paymaster. If so, few would believe that such matters are not known to his wife, even one that is blind. The charge is that he has in his possession a hoard of golden coins. What do you know of this?"

Ketch understood that Elizabeth would be uncomfortable with this questioning, but he had no time for gallantry.

"If you are his accomplice, I can do little to save you unless you tell me all that you know, now! "
Despite her fears Elizabeth was not to be bullied.

"I am a poor blind woman and I know nothing of a royalist paymaster or golden coins. I knew that many years ago before we were married that my husband had been the victim of gossip and lying accusations of just this nature. It was not true then and it is not true now!"

Ketch sat quietly Elizabeth was on the attack.

"He was beaten up by Varley Brent and the retainers of Zouch Tate. He nearly died and nobody said sorry. He was left just to get on with his life. If these are the same accusations brought back to life, it is a disgrace!"

Elizabeth had made her point but there was no relaxation in her body. She knew she had lied, and that now she must defend it as best she can. She was still determined to give nothing away, nor respond to anything they he may say to her. Ketch, himself, remained calm but he had to continue his questioning based on fear.

"Let me quite clear," he continued.

"Gold, that was once thought to have been hidden here in Northampton has once more been found specifically after the battle of Worcester. This property and your husband are the sole regarded source. If we find these coins in this house or somewhere to your husband's knowledge, you both face death for treason"

Elizabeth spoke in a strong voice.

"Is no one listening to me. There is no gold, there never has been. Search away Captain, search this house, search my person, bring out the gold and prove your accusation!"

Ketch could not but admire the strength shown by Elizabeth and unless actual gold was found, he knew he had nothing as a basis for a formal charge, nothing but speculation. He turned to Anne for help. Anne, with a gentler voice, and in quieter tones recast the central nature of the danger facing Elizabeth. She spoke of family disgrace, the horrors of imprisonment for women, at the very least a life of poverty and misery, but to no avail. After further questioning they both realised that Elizabeth was not going to change her story. They both rose to their feet. Ketch issued a final warning to Elizabeth of her danger and leaving Anne to remain with Elizabeth he went to question Rose the maid. As he moved on towards Rose's room, he heard banging on the front door. He turned to see Holditch and Stephen grappling with someone on the steps to Wilmington House. They saw off the intruder and he made a mental note to inquire later as to matter. He moved on to his next task. He grimaced, he had another woman to question, but at least it was a girl. He opened the door to Rose's room swiftly, hoping that a sudden entrance would give him an advantage and indeed at his entrance Rose leapt to her feet. Ketch introduced himself and explained the reason for her body search by his wife and the search of her room. Rose looked about sixteen years of age and was some five- foot tall, small of stature, wearing a rather grubby dress and mob cap. Her eyes were dull and there was a lack of energy about her. Her room was similar in size and contents to those of Mathew and Maria. It had bare floorboards, a single window, wash stand, chest of drawers and a cupboard. There were few personal trinkets but a copper bowl of flowers on a bedside table. There was no small chest or box under her bed but he did find in the chest of drawers an old leather bag. Inside there was a collection of tools, a small hammer, a number of awls and a pair of sharp pincers. Holding these, Ketch turned to Rose.

"Sit on the bed Rose" he ordered and he took a stance in the middle of the room.

"I know you only as Rose ", he said.

"What is your full name and when did you become a maid to your mistress?"

"Rose Streetly is my name Sir and I have been looking after my mistress since the beginning of April. I replaced an elderly sister of milady who died at that time"

"Where are you from?" Asked Ketch.

"I was born and brought up in Kettering. My father was a shoemaker, but both he and my mother died from the sweating sickness and I was left with only an ageing uncle. It was he that found me a position through Master Giles."

"What are these tools for Rose?

"Just keep sakes sir. My father treasured them they were the tools of his trade. They are the only ones I have left."

Ketch grunted and returned the tools to the draw.

"And you get on well with Master Giles?"

Rose was not prepared for this question. She lowered her eyes and for a moment she seemed to draw into herself.

"I love my mistress Sir! But Master Giles can be sometime hard with me because I am foolish.

"Does he beat you?" demanded Ketch"

"No Sir He does not beat me.

Ketch was not happy with this, but he had to concentrate on his central task, the matter of the gold coins.

"What are your duties?" he asked.

"Anything milady needs, she replied.

"I help to bathe her, I fetch and carry things for her. I help her to dress and undress. I help her around the house Of course we do not go upstairs. For the rest, she is very independent in her movements. She can usually find her way about the house and even in the market. I am just there to protect her and to tell her to whom she is talking."

Rose fell silent for a moment and then thought of something else to say. "I have no skill for mending clothes but often Mathew will repair her clothes. He has skill with a needle and cotton."

Ketch came to his central question.

"Do you know anything about a hoard of golden coin Rose, either here in the house or elsewhere?"

Rose looked bemused, but finally shook her head.

"No sir, I know nothing of such matters"

Ketch looked at Rose carefully. She was obedient and seemed to answer his questions truthfully and being in the household only since April, it was unlikely that she was involved in any of the matters he had to investigate. If she had indeed seen or heard nothing, it was time to move on.

"Thank you Rose, tell Mathew and Maria that they can take up their household duties, but let them know I still have your master to question".

Ketch checked that Anne was still with Elizabeth. They seemed to at last found some common ground that allowed a low level of conversation. He then entered the study.

Ketch had left Giles alone for some time and Giles had spent minutes rehearsing answers to any questions that may be put to him. He felt confident that he would not face any physical harm and with his saddlebag safely in the tunnels, he felt he had little to fear. He had leaned back in his chair ready for the interrogation when a spasm of fear ran through him. Elizabeth had brought one gold coin back from the tunnels. He had forgotten all about it. If just one coin was found he would be lost. Exposure, arrest and possible death suddenly faced him. He bent his mind feverishly to what had happened to it. It took a long moment but with a gasp of relief he remembered. In his mind's eye he saw Elizabeth putting it into the left-hand side drawer of his desk. He immediately found it and took it out of the drawer. He thought desperately what was he to do with it. His study had yet to be searched He knew he had little time. He looked about him. On his desk was a large silver holder for his letter writing. It had two cut glass inkwells set in the silver with places for quills, sand, seals and wax. Raising one of the inkwells careful to avoid any spillage, he placed the coin into the resulting recess and then replaced the inkwell. It was the best he could do. Now he had to pray that it was sufficient. He knew his confrontation was coming he had to hold his nerve.

Ketch found Giles sitting at his desk apparently calm and controlled but he could see that this was a man whose body was rigid with concentration.

"There will be a reckoning for all this Captain Ketch!" the words were spat out in anger.

Ketch paid no attention to the outburst. He first examined closely the room. He paid particular attention to the two large cupboards in which were stored Giles's personal papers and the key documents of his business. He found the stock of cash but there were clearly no ancient gold coins. The drawers of the desk also revealed nothing.

"Show me the cellar!" demanded Ketch.
Giles rose slowly from his chair and led the way to the top of the cellar steps. Ketch noticed the ritual of running the hands through the pots of herbs. He guessed that the cellar was a very unpleasant place. Once down in the cellar Giles lit a candle and Ketch took to examining the bits of old furniture and other rubbish found there. He then looked at the metal door that led to the tunnels.

"Open it!" he said.

Giles took the key from its hook, and pulled wide the door. A draft of cold, damp air flowed into the cellar. It had its own unpleasant taste on the mouth and a musty smell of decay.

"You can go in if you like," taunted Giles.

"That will not be necessary," replied ketch. He was by now quite sick of this interview and having serious doubts about the success of his search and Giles's obvious growing confidence was a special irritant.

"Let us return upstairs. There is still more to do"

The two men returned to their original situations and Ketch once more began questioning Giles. He found himself endlessly repeating questions he had asked of the servants and getting the same replies. After half an hour, he decided that there was no purpose served by continuing.

"That is enough Middleton. We will now have the body search. You are the last, the rest of your household has complied and if you show any resistance, I shall call my two men here, to hold you down. Your choice!"

Giles gave Ketch a hard, black stare, there was a savage look on his face. Ketch was methodical examining everything. Eventually he stepped back. There was nothing.

"That will be all sir. My party are now leaving but it may be necessary to question you again."

Ketch felt pretty uncomfortable. He had done his job to no avail. He had to leave quickly with all the dignity he could muster. Giles laughed in his face.

"Just go soldier and do not come back again. Lord Wilmington will hear of your insolence and the damage you have done to my management of Parliament's estate.

Ketch gathered together Ann, Holditch and Tull and left Wilmington House in discomfort.

132

"Let us get home quickly", he said

"What a waste of time."

His companions kept silent as they made their way back to what was now called Derngate House. Ketch himself broke the silence.

"Tomorrow morning, I shall breakfast the Mayor and then we shall search Castle Ashby. I have little hope of finding anything there and then we shall end this exercise. I shall report to Thurloe that I have failed and that we wish to get on with other things. At best, if I get the chance, I shall continue to keep a watch on Wilmington House and Giles Middleton."

Back in Wilmington House Giles gloried in his success. He had seen off the army, he had confounded his enemies. He had been too clever for all of them. He burst out of his study into the corridor.

"Mathew, Maria bring wine and food, my wife and I will celebrate our victory!"

He danced into his bedroom, rushed across the room and picked up his wife and half tossed her into the air,

"Well done Elizabeth! Well done everybody. They will not come again"

He lowered his voice.

We are safe Elizabeth, between us we have removed that shadow. We are now publicly innocent. Sit I have ordered food and drink. We shall celebrate together!"

Elizabeth smiled back at him but she knew in her heart they were not free. That hidden gold will always be a source of danger.

Giles looked expansively around the room and smiled. He strode next door and faced Rose, who sat on her bed in turn smiling at the household happiness.

"I shall want to see you later Rose in my study. You can add to my happiness"

He turned and left. Rose fell full length on to her bed and bit her hand to stop crying.

Chapter Fourteen

The next morning news arrived that Charles Stuart was alive and in France. It had caused great concern in Whitehall and Westminster, but in Northampton for all but a few, it was noted discussed and then put to one side for life's more immediate problems.

For Ketch it meant that if there was gold to be found. His task had a new urgency and failure would become more serious. For Edgar Middleton it meant that he had to see his brother, who he knew was under clear instructions from the Earl that no gold must go to Charles Stuart.   It only added to the anxiety and indecision of Giles Middleton. He knew he could expect a visit from his brother, that Captain Ketch was bound to become troublesome again and he would have to deal with Dundas Stannard.

Dundas Stannard knew for certain that Giles Middleton had the gold. He had now to decide as to the likely course of action to be taken by Giles. Would he be the faithful King's servant and deliver the golden coins to the royalist cause, or will he seek to take the hoard for himself?

One man had little interest and paid no attention to the politics of England. Conrad Tauber sat in a window seat in his room overlooking the market square. In his hand he held the note from Giles Middleton denying that the estate of the Earl of Northampton had any responsibility for the poverty and wretched life of his betrothed. Clearly as things stood at the moment, she and her mother would receive no compensation of any kind. Controlling his anger, he decided he would not be treated this way and fobbed off with a piece of paper. He had travelled too far for the sake of justice and the rights of his future wife. He resolved that he would see Middleton again but, on this occasion, he would be prepared to use violence. Conrad Tauber was a deeply religious man and for him Giles Middleton's defiance was an afront to Christ himself. His community at home was made up of god-fearing men and women who closely followed the words of the bible. He like some of the other elders had visions when God spoke to him, and his visions told him, that Angelica's pain and suffering must be wiped clean before she could become his wife. He rose from his chair and from his saddlebag lying on his bed, he drew out a thin stiletto. If it was necessary and there was no atonement, there would be retribution. He may be a man of God but he was no weakling.

Varley Brent was full of rage. His anger was so intense that he was red in the face and shaking. He had just been told that the army were in Wilmington House undertaking a search. No one was going in or out and Stephen Hedlow had been stationed outside to ensure that they were not interrupted. Varley was sitting alone in the Laurel Bush, a tavern in then Northampton's main thoroughfare and the public room was abuzz with the news. A few brave souls cast a quick look to see how Varley would re-act and an unknown voice at the back of the room dared call out,

"Is someone's looking for your gold Varley?

There was a muted laughter in response. Varley looked around the room and with a snarl he rose to his feet, looking for the source of the jibe. The room went silent, it was best not to push Varley too far. His reputation was as an ill-tempered bully who approached his enemies from the back and preferably down a dark alley. There was no honour or mercy in him. He adjusted in his belt the cudgel he always carried, looked menacingly about him and left the tavern. He started walking down the highway making for the market square and Wilmington House. As he walked, his mind began to clear and his anger was brought under control. He started to think of what was the best thing to do. Although rough and violent, he was normally a man of caution and cunning and this had served him well in the past. He felt vindicated about his previous beating of Giles Middleton, but nevertheless he believed he had been made to look a fool. Now was a time for revenge. To the world he had been outwitted and deceived. His bottled-up hate for Giles Middleton burnt twice as strong within him. His rage was such that his normal caution was forgotten. It fired a deep determination to destroy Giles Middleton. Crossing the market square, he made for the constable.

The crowd that had pestered Stephen in the early morning, had reduced to an occasional enquiry. The constable was alone standing at the foot of the steps and thinking that he could now stand down and deliver Ketch's message to the Mayor, when Varley Brent approached him. He could see trouble coming.

"Now Varley! Do not get involved," he said, and made to hold Varley back. But full of righteous rage, Varley pushed Stephen aside and mounted the steps to Wilmington House's front door. He seized the large central boss, and began pounding on the door. Stephen followed him up the steps and grasped him around the shoulders. Varley turned and pushed Stephen down the steps. At that moment the door opened and Holditch stepped out and seeing Stephen on the floor pitched into Varley himself, giving him two hefty blows to the head. Stephen back on his feet, grasped Varley more firmly but he was again shaken off. However, Varley saw that there were now two men in the fight, and one of them was in uniform. He stood still, in defiant challenge, his breath coming in heavy gasps.

"Calm down Varley", shouted Stephen. "This is not for you! The army are in charge here. I will put you in a common cell if I have to."

"I was right!" Varley shouted back. "I was always right. He's been a stinking royalist all along and there is gold somewhere. Zouche knew him for what he was, he should hang."
 Having had the last word Varley stumbled off towards the market square.

Stephen turned to Holditch," Thank you, that was well timed. I don't think he will be back. He will drink now, but we may have trouble later."

After his morning the Constable was feeling tired.

"I cannot stay here all day. I will see the Mayor for Ketch and then return home. "

He waved to Holditch. "I shall see you all tomorrow in the morning."   Holditch smiled and waved him on his way.

Dundas Stannard had taken an upstairs front room in a popular local tavern called the Rood in the Wall. Its position at the top of Bridge street on the road to London afforded an excellent view of All Saints Church and the front door of Wilmington House. After breakfast in the main room he had retired to take up a vigil of Wilmington House whilst he thought over what he was going to do about Giles Middleton. He immediately noticed a small group of people talking and questioning someone, who appeared to be the town constable. There was much waving of hands and pointing of fingers. Dundas decided that this required him to keep a very careful eye on these events and eventually he witnessed the struggle between the constable and a rough working man. He thought to himself, who *is this with such an interest in*

Wilmington House? It must surely be related to what I think is in the possession of Giles Middleton.

He rose from his chair and hurried from the tavern in pursuit of Varley Brent. He was not too clear in his own mind what he hoped to gain, but at least this man may have useful information, perhaps he was a local ally he could use. He followed the rough looking man into the town centre.

Varley Brent was set on getting a drink, he decided that he would not go back to the Laurel Bush. They were an unpleasant and miserable lot, neither would he try the Peacock inn for in that place there were too many of those who thought of themselves as the quality. No! He would go to the Bull, just off the market square by the Northern Gate.

Dundas Stannard was a solid built, dangerous, looking man, and when he sat down at the table occupied by Varley Brent Brent sat back in alarm.

"Can I fill your tankard for you friend?" asked Dundas.

Varley looked at him with suspicion.

"No nastiness," added Dundas. "Just a nice friendly talk about gold" these last words were spoken very softly.

Varley stared at this stranger and then slowly nodded his head.

"I wouldn't mind a fresh drop of the best".

Dundas rose moved to the bar and collected drinks. He returned and once again sat opposite Varley.

"I saw you outside Wilmington House. You seem to want to get inside but the constable and a soldier from inside, prevented you,"

"And what's that to you?", retorted Varley.

Dundas thought he would take a chance. *He guessed that this man was called Varley Brent and was the man who Giles*

Middleton complained about to him and Skeffington, when they collected the gold shipment earlier in the year.

"I know for a fact that Giles Middleton guards a great treasure"

Varley sat very still for a moment. He framed a careful reply.

" Now Friend! what is your interest in this. Do you serve a gentleman who has recently been said to be in foreign parts, or have you a more personal interest?"

Dundas smiled. He had guessed correctly. He felt sure this was Varley Brent.

"Oh! my interest is very personal", he replied." I have a desire to spend my last few years in a warm and sunny climate." He paused, "I think you are Varley Brent and have a long-standing interest in what it is that Giles Middleton is hiding."

Varley was caught off guard by the stranger's knowledge of his name. He was interested in this man, very interested. but he needed to know a lot more about him.

""Who are you?" he demanded. "I need to know more about you."

Dundas chuckled. "My name is Dundas Stannard and earlier this year I collected a quantity of gold from Giles Middleton and took it to Charles Stuart"

"So!" interrupted Varley, you are a damned royalist and villain. We don't like such people in this town"

"Yes, once, but now we all live in peace and harmony and old enemies can now happily work together for their mutual benefit. I think we have a mutual interest in taking what is in Wilmington House for ourselves."

Dundas knew that this was the point in their conversation when Varley could stand up and denounce him or decide to join him in a joint endeavour. He hoped that greed would secure cooperation. He reached into his pocket, and brought out a clenched fist that held something within it. He quietly placed that same hand flat on the table and covered it with the other. He smiled and opened up his cupped hands. Nestling in them was a large gold coin. He spoke in a whisper.

"They are not all as large as this but there are many of all sizes, in the possession of Giles Middleton. I am sure that some could be yours."

Varley Brent's eyes opened wide and a large smile covered his face.

"I think we can do business," he said.

Chapter Fifteen

The Mayor of Northampton, Councilman Lugg, arrived early for breakfast with the news of Charles Stuart. The smell of frying bread, eggs and meat, convinced him that his journey had been worthwhile. He had known Ketch and Anne for some years and was one of those who fully understood how important Ketch's activities had been for the good of the town. Also, it was his office that had held all the legal documents relevant to Ketch's inheritance. He was a friend that they respected and wanted to keep.

Both Ketch and Anne ate with him in their dining room and when they had all finished and were drinking some warm cyder, they brought the Mayor up to date as to their activities at Wilmington House.

"I am sure you will receive complaints," said Anne.

"Giles Middleton was very upset and will want some sort of compensation"

"He is an important man in this town," stated the Mayor.

"He will not be easy to satisfy."

Ketch moved uncomfortably in his chair.

"The trouble is we found nothing and only caused upset,"

"Frankly Mr Mayor, with no evidence I shall have to apologise to him"

"Probably best," replied Councilman Lugg. "He is is important but not well loved. I think an apology will be sufficient".

Ketch was relieved. He now felt certain that the Mayor would deal with this problem in the appropriate matter. Having settled his main concern, the three of them fell into discussing old times and indeed the recent news of Charles Stuart. After half an hour there was a knock on the front door. It was Stephen. The Mayor was waved off and Ketch Stephen and Holditch prepared to ride out to Castle Ashby. Ketch was determined to stay no more than a morning searching the abandoned property. His hopes of finding anything significant was low, but it was the least that Thurloe would expect. They took the road to Bedford and after a few miles they turned into the village and avoiding the parkland rode up to the great house. In a desultory way they searched the bare and pillaged rooms. They found nothing and after three hours they re-joined their horses. They paused to admire the worded stone balustrade and then rode home. Ketch could see that both Tull and Holditch were not pleased at such a wasted effort.

"We had to do it, he exclaimed. "It would look strange back in London if we had not made the effort. Especially if we find nothing elsewhere"

Giles Middleton had taken breakfast in his dining room with Elizabeth. It was not a particularly happy event. Elizabeth had clearly been dwelling on the events of yesterday and she let Giles know that his confession of helping to fund the war aims of Charles Stuart upset her considerably. She kept mumbling about straining the loyalty of a good wife. The servants were just as unpleasant. Mathew was distant and constantly staring at him with open hostility. Giles was sure he had come to some unpleasant conclusion about the return he, Giles, demanded for helping his mother. Maria mentioned in a louder than necessary voice that Rose was unable to assist Elizabeth and had taken to her bed and she did not know why. Between eating his bread and meat he was also conscious that Dundas Stannard and Conrad Tauber were here in Northampton, determined to raise their pressing and unwanted business with him.

With a gesture of impatience, he rose to his feet and hurried to his study. When sitting at his desk, he in part recovered some good humour and he once more savoured his victory of yesterday over his enemies. These thoughts were soon clouded, however, by his immediate concerns on the two men, who would certainly call sometime today, Stannard and Tauber.

He resolved to prepare to meet them. He moved to one of the two large cupboards in his room and took out a wrapped cloth bundle and unrolling it on the top of his desk, he took up a long-barrelled flintlock pistol. The wrapped cloth also contained shot, a small packet of gunpowder, oil, new flints and a small ramrod. He prepared his pistol and placed it in the top right-hand drawer of his desk. He was pleased. He could defend himself.

Back from Castle Ashby, Ketch determined to gain a better understanding of his new inheritance. He was determined to involve Anne firmly into the details of their new- found wealth and its management. At the very least, they would require help in running their new home. James Hedlow had required a manservant and a housekeeper to deal with his domestic arrangements and they would need more than that, especially if they had long term plans to expand their family. They both sat at their new large dining table and began to review deeds and bonds and the cash that was in the box that Tull had collected from the Mayor's office. They worked long into the afternoon until it was time for candles.

Giles Middleton had spent his morning in a similar activity, although his was of a wider commercial nature. He had rents and loans to consider and correspondence with merchants and suppliers to the sequestered estate. He had taken his noon-time meal alone and the house had remained silent with a brooding and unhappy atmosphere. He had consoled himself with a bottle of claret and a little brandy. He was not surprised on returning to his study that he felt a desire to take a short sleep.

He was awoken by a heavy knocking on the front door and a raised voice demanding to see him. He was annoyed when Mathew showed his visitor straight in to his study and left immediately with an unpleasant look of satisfaction on his face. It was Conrad Tauber and he was clearly in a rage. He was wearing a large, dark cloak and he wrapped it around him before sitting in a chair opposite Giles. Tauber could see that Giles was slightly befuddled with sleep and decided to take advantage of the situation. From within his cloak he produced the reply Giles had sent him on recompense to his betrothed Angelica. He threw the letter at Giles and launched his words with venom.

"This is quite unsatisfactory! You are a no English gentleman! You are a disgrace to your country and to God. I will not accept it. Your Earl has ravaged a young girl and left her and her child destitute. All this has been explained to you and you have ignored it!"

Giles raised up his hands to stem the flow of words but Trauber was not to be halted.

"I have not travelled hundreds of leagues to be ignored. We will settle this matter now. I am quite certain that you have monies here in this room, and I will take what is owed to me"

Tauber was trembling with anger. He pulled from his cloak his stiletto and rose to get around the desk to take hold of Giles. Tauber's words had frightened Giles into full consciousness. He was in mortal danger. This foreigner was a mad man full of violent, religious piety. Giles was not without courage. He pulled from his desk the pistol he had primed earlier and pointed it at Tauber.

"Hold Sir! Or I will shoot you dead!"

Tauber had not actually meant to strike Giles rather to show him the stiletto up close. The sudden appearance of a pistol in his face pulled him up short. He froze and Giles with his pistol waved him back to his chair.

"Put your knife away Sir! I could shoot you where you sit. No magistrate or jury would find me guilty of a crime when firing at a man waving a knife and threatening me in my own home".

The two men stared at each other both with passion in their eyes.

"Pass me your knife Sir, or I will surely shoot you", continued Giles. He was gaining confidence. He would now tell Tauber some unpleasant truths, embellished with a few lies that would teach him to attack his betters. He would enjoy seeing him off in that way. Tauber knew he was at a serious disadvantage but he still had spirit. He scowled and murmured at his opponent. Reluctantly he tossed the stiletto on to the desk. Giles picked it up and with contempt threw into the drawer.

"Now Herr Tauber, let me tell you the full story of what happened in Italy and the girl called Silvrina, mother of your Angelica." He made himself more comfortable in his chair. He would enjoy himself.

"At that time in Italy, Silvrina was a young girl of some twenty years dark and strikingly handsome. She was the girl of the village. Young men flocked to her and she welcomed them all. Her favours were sometimes given freely but she always enjoyed presents. She loved parties and would drink and dance and disappear with the young man of the evening. When she found herself in the presence of rich foreign diplomats away from home and ready for entertaining, she favoured us all with great enthusiasm."

Giles was in full flow and Tauber's face went red with rage and then slowly turned grey with distress. He was not totally sure that Giles was lying.

"Of course, the Earl became her favourite. When he was not engaged in talks, she was always with him but she still had time for me and others of our party. My own time with her was short, as it was for so many others."

For some time, Giles regaled Tauber with details of the life led by his betrothed's mother. Pleased with himself Giles eventually called a halt to his tales and ordered Tauber out of his chair and waved him to the door.

"If you doubt me, question your betrothed more carefully or make a visit to the Valtellina. Ask the older men about Silvrina."

All the fight had left Conrad Tauber. He staggered to the front door and turned to Giles.

"You are an oaf and a swine! I do not believe you."

It was harsh but had little conviction. Giles was confident he would not return. For a moment he stopped and quickly returned to his study and collected the Stiletto and followed Tauber out of the house.

146

"Take your little knife and leave Northampton you foolish old man".

He laughed as he returned to his study. He needed a drink to celebrate another success.

"Mathew," he called.   "Bring me brandy"

There were those in the house who had heard much of what had passed between the two men and although he was the head of the household, they were beginning to see him as not the man he portrayed but as someone very unpleasant. For the rest of the day Giles continued to think on his problems not doing any sensible work but steadily drinking.   He found himself asleep in his chair when Mathew knocked on his door and announced that a gentleman called Stannard wished to see him.

"Ask him to wait in the dining room, replied Giles."

He felt stiff and old. He vigorously rubbed the hair on the side of his head and then the large, bald patch at the top. His mouth was dry and unpleasant. He moved to the Kitchen drank copiously water from a jug, and then ordered Mathew to show the visitor into his study where he would await him. Mathew felt bold enough to leave the study door slightly ajar as he saw Stannard into the study. He wanted to know more about this man he had once admired. A man whose treatment of women raised many questions.

Giles and Dudley Stannard faced each other suspiciously'

"Well Stannard what do you want?" These words were not said kindly.

"That is a harsh voice with which to greet an old comrade", replied Stannard. "You were pleased enough to see myself and Thomas Skeffington not so very long ago. No need to pretend with me. I know you for the royalist paymaster that you are and I know you still have gold hidden close bye. You have played the game of deceit beautifully, Giles, but now is the time to move on."

Giles was impatient that Stannard had thrown in his face the life of lies he had followed. He found Stannard's face with his dropped lip and smallpox scars both unpleasant and irritating. He wanted to be rid of him.

He repeated, "what do you want?"

Stannard leant forward across the desk with a leering confidentiality that Giles now found repulsive. It implied a relationship that he detested.

"The game is up for us Giles. Charles Stuart had his chance and he failed. I know he has turned up in France but he has nothing, no support. There will be no more military adventures no matter how much gold you have hidden away. Are you really going to give it up for a cause that is lost? With your gold Charles Stuart will be more comfortable but that is all. It could on the other hand comfort you and me in a new life."

Giles stared hard at Stannard and placed a re-assuring hand close to the draw with his pistol.

"That gold now belongs to James Compton and although he cannot claim it. I suppose it must be held for him."

Stannard laughed, "You are a fool Giles. He won't thank you for it. It may be years, anyway, before he can live openly here in Northampton. All that time you are at risk. The secret you carry could come out at the very moment that you feel safe and secure in your hidden life."

Stannard leant back in his chair to see how his words were affecting Giles. He noticed that Giles was thinking hard. It was time to really frighten him.

"Now take me in my position. I am a poor man a known royalist with no prospects in England, rather at risk of unpleasant punishment. I have to prepare for a new life abroad and my friend Giles has a large quantity of gold to hand. I know he commits treason and has done so for many years. I could finance my future with a trip to the magistrates and play the informer. I think I would be well received and almost certainly well rewarded".

Giles could feel the passion in Stannard's eyes. He saw him reach into his pocket and place on the table with great deliberation three gold coins.

"And I have proof," he chuckled. "Proof that respectable citizen Giles Middleton is and always has been a royalist spy and paymaster. Indeed, my few conversations in this town leads me to believe that there are those who would not be unhappy to hear such words "

This was Giles's worst nightmare. The moment he had faced Stannard in the market square this thought had been in his head. He had tried to banish it from his mind but now it was fully laid out before him. He knew Stannard was right. Informers were rewarded and forgiven. He was in mortal danger. He had the gold safely hidden, but Elizabeth alone knew how to get it. He hoped she retained her confidence in him he had to ask himself...

"If questioned could she remain silent could she face hardship or torture? In his heart he knew the answer was no! The truth was stark, he was in Stannard's power.

He spoke very slowly. "I repeat once again Stannard what do you want?"

Stannard smiled to himself. He thought this was going well.

"Well Giles we come to the very heart of the matter. I had thought a timely gift from you of say five hundred gold pieces and I would take my travels and leave you alone. But then another thought came to me that you in turn, having handed over gold could rush off to the Magistrate with some tale, perhaps my seeking to trade coins for silver and denounce me. I could be taken along with the gold."
He paused for breath and then continued but with amusement in his voice.

"What I am coming to Giles is that you and me we must stick together. Our fate if that gold is to be of any use has made us partners. I cannot have my share without trusting you and you in turn must trust me. The reality is that you must leave Northampton with me and the gold. It means a new life in another country for both of us. You could try to bring your blind wife but I suggest she be left to fall back on her friends. It is unkind but necessary."

Giles was appalled.

Stannard was determined to bring home to Giles the sacrifices that were inevitable.

" You could bring her on later but I really see no alternative than a speedy leaving by the both of us"

As he spoke. Stannard began to pick back up his gold coins, they had made his point.

"off course you may be thinking that you could quietly make me disappear violently, but I assure you, as an old man you would find that difficult."

Giles flushed. He really hated this man but then he laughed. Here he had an advantage.

"I must tell you that any violence towards me would be equally pointless. I do not know where the gold is hidden!"

A look of surprise and then fury crossed Stannard's face.

"What's this trickery? he demanded.

"Someone else who I trust, alone can produce this gold. There is no point in killing me".

Stannard continued with his black looks.

"Can you produce the gold or not."

He rose from his chair

"Are you with me or not. Do you swear that we will leave Northampton with the gold as partners?"

Giles knew that this was the moment of decision. He had no intention of going with Stannard he did not trust him. He saw him as a mercenary, greedy thug. But he had to satisfy him. There was only one answer he could give. It would give him time to find the real answer to his problem. How to get rid of Dundas Stannard. He must find some way to kill him.

"I am not happy Stannard but I agree. My life here has become dangerous. I had a visit yesterday from the army about this very matter of royalist gold. I must go away."

This news came as a shock to Stannard. If the army was about, he had better not linger.

"Alright Giles, this must all happen quickly. What arrangements do you suggest?"

Giles suddenly rose from his chair and motioned Stannard to be quiet. He had noticed that the door to the study was ajar. He moved to the door and quickly opened it. There was no one in the corridor. He turned to Stannard.

"I am just going to check the whereabouts of the servants." He moved cautiously towards the back of the house. Whilst Giles was out of the room Stannard stood up stretched his arms and wandered to the second of the large sash windows that lit the study. He unlocked the window not with any particular purpose but in his world little actions like that often-created opportunities that could bring great rewards.   Giles returned, the servants were where they were supposed to be. The two men began to discuss the details of their escape. Giles would recover the gold and Stannard would arrange horses and provisions. They agreed that Giles would make no farewells but slip out and leave with Stannard in two days' time. As they discussed the nature of their leaving Giles was in turmoil. *He had agreed to leave. He thought he could remove Stannard, but could he? Was he inevitably going to be drawn into this madness? If his courage failed him, he would surely have to leave with Stannard.*

For his part Stannard had little faith in Giles and thought that he might seek to betray or even remove him. But, he knew Giles was weak and he did not know of Varley Brent. He and Brent would be too much for Giles. He slowly returned the gold coins to his pocket.

"I shall come again tomorrow," he said, "to see how matters progress.

Chapter Sixteen

There were those in the house who had heard all that had passed between Giles and his visitor. Mathew, Rose and Maria sat in the kitchen whispering their concerns to each other. They were being abandoned, thrown out on to the street. Giles had been an unpleasant master but they knew that they enjoyed privileged and secure positions. If Giles disappeared would he be replaced? Would such a person continue to employ them? They were forced to realise that the answer to these questions was probably "no!"

Of the three Rose cared the least, Giles had abused her and she hated him. In her heart she wished him dead and gone. Maria being without any family feared that she would be quickly on the streets of Northampton begging for a new position or just money to live. Mathew felt passionately betrayed by Giles. He felt a fool that he had been so easily deceived about Giles's true loyalties. Although deeply concerned about their fate, this commonality of their concerns gave them a certain comfort. Each received and gave sympathy in return. It helped a little.

Elizabeth, however, was alone and distraught. She had heard everything and a deep bitterness filled her heart. She had been a loyal wife and he had taken advantage of that in his new arrangements for hiding the gold. She had been used by a man who had no love, no loyalty not even any care for her. She was to be abandoned, thrown over left to her blindness. She heard the visitor leaving. Her husband would come to her now with more lies and deceit. A fierce revenge filled her heart. She would not be treated with such disdain. She was determined to make her husband suffer before he ran off.

Ketch and Anne had spent two hours considering the nature of their new wealth and the new life it would give them..They had no thoughts of gold or Giles Middleton or Secretary Thurloe. But now, as they put all documents and money away, they felt the need to refocus on such matters. Ketch decided he needed to consult with Tull and Holditch and strolled into his parlour. The two men in their civilian clothes sat by the fire, Tull reading a book and Holditch looking around searching for something to ease his boredom

"Ketch", demanded Holditch, "What are we doing now. I am happy for your new wealth but we have a task to complete. For good or ill, Secretary Thurloe wants information about the hoard of gold, if not the coins themselves"

Ketch sighed, Holditch was right. They must re-new their efforts, yesterday's failures had to be forgotten.

"Enjoy your rest gentlemen" he said "Today is drawing to a close but tomorrow we are going in search of Edgar, the brother of Giles Middleton. He may be the person we should question. He once served the Earls of Northampton. In fact, if not him, I am not sure where we should turn. We will ride out to Wilmington Hall track him down and put him to the test."

It was unfortunate that Ketch did not know that at that very moment Edgar Middleton was striding up the steps of Wilmington House and knocking on its front door. He had heard that Charles Stuart was alive in France. He was determined to speak with his brother before anything foolish had been done over the rights of James Compton to his father's gold. As he entered the house, Edgar allowed Mathew to take away his large cloak but he retained his staff. He was then shown in to Giles in his study unannounced and Mathew once again left the study door slightly ajar. However, with some irritation Giles rose from his chair and pushed it shut. He turned to Edgar as he resumed his seat.

"Well brother how can I help you?

Whilst Giles had retained some affection for his brother, he was conscious that Edgar was his intellectual equal but vastly superior in strength and physique. He found it intimidating.

Sitting opposite Giles, Edgar could not but be surprised, at how tired and strained was his brother. He looked as if he had had no sleep whilst also showing obvious signs of having drunk too much.

"It is about the gold Giles, the gold that belongs to James Compton. I have seen him, he has spoken to me and his very words were.....
'The Stuarts have had enough. What is left must be kept safe for the future estate."

Giles was unhappy and confused, his brother was just another source of pressure upon him. Moreover, there was such a firm conviction in his brother's voice that he was clearly ready for an argument. Giles anxious to postpone conflict suggested that Elizabeth should be involved as they both had something to tell him. Edgar reluctantly gave his consent but clearly disliked the change of subject. Elizabeth was escorted in by Rose and some time was taken getting her settled comfortably in another chair.

"Yes! Yes! Rose!", muttered Giles. "Your mistress is comfortable you can leave us."

Giles turned to Elizabeth.

"Edgar is here about the gold. I think we should tell him about its new location"

Edgar threw an asking look at Giles. But Giles was unperturbed, he was pleased to be in charge of at least this part of the conversation. He covered in some detail how he and Elizabeth had found a new safe place, deep in the tunnels under Northampton and that only Elizabeth could retrieve it. He dwelt long on Elizabeth's unique ability and bravery hoping to regain some of his lost affection.

"And you are confident of finding it again Elizabeth," demanded Edgar. He liked his sister in law, and had a high opinion of her but she had to be absolutely dependable in this matter.

Elizabeth gave a short, cold reply in the affirmative.

Giles threw her an unhappy glance but took up the conversation. "When we have concluded business, I shall ask Elizabeth to show us how we can be sure of her recovering the gold"

"Well, let us deal with equally important matters first", demanded Edgar.

In his heart Giles hoped that talking with Edgar would help him to decide what he should do. Should he take on Dundas Stannard or continue to defy the army and its captain or hold the gold for the Earl? He could, 0f course, send it to Charles Stuart or just abandon everything and seek a completely new life elsewhere.

While the two men began the initial part of their discussion Elizabeth sat and fumed with rage in her chair. *"A further step in your get away plans Giles. You want the gold closer to hand", she vowed that she would not let that happen.*

Giles had moved on to asking Edgar's thoughts on what should be done now that Charles Stuart was in France and had he had any change of heart. Edgar was passionate in his reply.

"As I have just told you, I have seen and spoken to the Earl. He risked his life arranging for a meeting and his words still ring in my ears. The Stuarts have had enough from the Comptons...... and he is right Giles, successive Earls have given everything. The Italian gold is all that is left. If the estate is ever to be rebuilt, it must remain here in Northampton".

He turned to look at Elizabeth.

"Wherever you and Elizabeth have hidden it."

Giles was annoyed that the Earl had spoken with Edgar. It had only strengthened Edgar's opposition to what Giles had once intended. But now, as far as Edgar was concerned Giles would stand by his original arguments.

"Look Edgar, the actual estate is fine. It is largely in my care and managed as one and it can be made ready for the return of the Comptons. For that to happen you need a Stuart King and he is penniless in France. Everything still depends on the King returning to his own."

As the two men repeated their arguments, their voices rose with a growing passion. Elizabeth sat listening intently and as the minutes passed, she could detect a growing of disinterest in how Giles responded to the demands of his brother. She detected that he was coming to a decision to take neither of the courses under discussion. He was going to do something else.

Elizabeth had successfully understood the change in Giles's mood. He was sick of this debate, he was sick of the pressure, sick of this house and sick of this life. He had made up his mind.

Words slowly formed in Elizabeth's head. She rose to her feet.

"He is lying to you Edgar. He has no intention of holding the remaining gold for the Earl, or sending it to the King. He intends to flee, to abandon me and take up with an accomplice. They leave with the gold for France or Italy in two days' time. He had a visitor this afternoon and they planned their escape together!"

She fell back into her chair.

"Let him explain that to his brother. I hope Edgar beats him to the ground"

Edgar rose to his feet and glowered down at Giles.

"Is this true brother!" he cried, "you would betray us all! Your words are lies! You would discard your wife, your brother and your King. You are but thieving vermin. and not fit to live."

Giles rose to confront him, he well knew his brother's temper in such matters. But in a fury of passion, Edgar grasped his great staff and struck Giles a cruel blow on the head that sent him falling to the floor. As he fell, he received a further heavy blow to the head from the very edge of his desk. The antler tips at the top of the staff dug deep into the bald skin of Giles's head, blood flowed from where three tines had gone deep. It began to mingle with further blood from his head wound.

Edgar froze at the sight of his brother's collapse. Mortified he called for help and took a fevered glance at his brother.

"I have not killed him. It was but a glancing blow "

These words were cried out more in hope than real substance. Giles lay on the floor, he moaned. He was not dead but the few words he mumbled made little sense. Mathew the manservant had responded quickly to the noise. He rushed to the study and bent his ear low to hear the words of his master. Strange sounds continued to come from Giles.

"He has lost his senses. Help me raise him to the couch," cried Matthew.

The room became full of people as both Maria and Rose hurried into the room. For a moment they both stood still looking down at Giles body prone on the floor. After a moment's hesitation they helped Mathew place him onto the coach. Rose turned towards her mistress, who when the blow was struck and Giles had fallen to the ground, had shrunk into her chair with her arms over her head

" Your husband has been hurt ma'am by his brother! Come away with me."

Rose managed to manhandle Elizabeth out of the chair and guide her across the corridor to her own room. With soft words, Rose calmed her, insisting that she should have no fear of anything.

Leaning heavily on his staff, Edgar stood stunned at what he had done.

Mathew spoke sharply to him. "Edgar go find the doctor, your brother is not dead but your blow and his fall have rendered him senseless. You must hurry!"

Wide eyed Edgar took one quick look at his brother and immediately left the room to search for the doctor.

Fortunately,Edgar had met the doctor in the market square and they swiftly moved on to the doctor's house for his instruments and salves. They then hurried to Wilmington House. On arrival Doctor Benton ordered the room to be cleared apart from Elizabeth and Rose. He confirmed that Giles was neither dead nor dying but he was grievously hurt. He administered to Giles for a few minutes and then instructed Elizabeth and Rose in the basic care required.

"He must have complete quiet and rest. I have smoothed a salve to the blow from the study. The top of his head I have cleaned, but the blood will continue to ooze and then form scabs. What he needs now is sleep"

Dr Benton was a small slightly built man with a surprising lack of presence. He was, however, a long- time inhabitant of Northampton and generally well regarded. Importantly he was known to be discreet.

After a few more instructions to Rose, he decided not to become involved in a family dispute and he whispered his fee to Elizabeth and left. There was a short argument between Edgar and Elizabeth. He was determined to stay the night and oversee his brother's recovery. Elizabeth insisted that an overnight stay was inappropriate he should leave and come back in the morning. With some reluctance Edgar left informing them that he would take a room at the Peacock and return early tomorrow.

After he had gone, Elizabeth told Rose to take some rest in her own room. Once Rose had left, she found her way to the study and carefully felt all around the room, identifying the place of the desk, chairs and the couch. She found the sleeping Giles, and softly ran her hands over his head and body. When satisfied that all was clear to her, she left to rest in her room. Maria was in the doorway.

"Are you alright madam?" she inquired.
"Yes, Maria I needed to see for myself the full nature of his hurt."

Dundas Stannard had taken the first- floor front bedroom in the Rood in the Wall. He had positioned a small table and two chairs so that he and Varley Brent could observe the front of Wilmington house whilst they reviewed their next move. Stannard gave Brent the details of his conversation with Giles Middleton and Varley had his questions.

"Do you believe him Stannard?" "Do you really think he will give up everything to come away with us?"

Stannard smiled.

"Firstly, he does not yet know you are involved. That may be useful and secondly, he has no choice. He knows I will inform on him, and expose his treason. I showed him the gold coins that can prove it and send him to the gallows."

Varley was not entirely convinced but decided to go along with Stannard's judgement.

"It will be your task Varley to have horses and provisions for the three of us to leave Northampton early the day after tomorrow. I shall provide the necessary monies"

Varley agreed that this could be done. But Stannard had decided that some further action might bring their reward earlier.

"I unlocked one of the windows in Middleton's study. It might be worth a visit tonight. Just a little look around to see. We may find something, we may not. We may be found there. We may not. It does not matter it will remind him that we are close bye and he is ours"

Chapter Seventeen

There had been a stilted discussion in Wilmington House about what night time supervision should be made for Giles. Elizabeth had to leave matters to the household servants. At this difficult time, Rose felt that she should be with her mistress. Neither Mathew nor Maria had any great interest in caring for their employer. Thus, it was decided that as doctor Benton had required rest for his patient and as Giles was sleeping the best arrangement was for him to be left alone. A new candle was set on the ledge with the herbs, so that if he did awake, he would not be afraid. It was an unhappy household that finally determined that the day had ended. Rose and Elizabeth took to their beds in the front reception room. Mathew and Maria went to their separate rooms to sleep.

The October night grew cold and all was quiet in Wilmington House, when a pattern of footsteps was heard and a thunderous crash shattered the silence. It came from the study and members of the household, in a frightened state congregated outside the study door. Taking their courage, Mathew and Maria entered the pitch-black study and by their candles found Giles Middleton once more on the floor. His body seemed in slow convulsions as his arms twisted and his body quivered. His desk had been pushed aside and its silver ink stand had fallen to the floor. A pool of ink was settling onto the floor boards. In the semi-darkness it found the bare feet and shoes of everyone, including Elizabeth and Rose who had followed behind to find what had happened. Each of the servants held their candles high, the better to see the cramped and tortured body that had begun to slowly become calm.

"I think he must have had a seizure," suggested Maria.

Both Rose and Mathew nodded in agreement. Maria cast a look at Mathew. I think you must go for doctor Benton again."

"Should we move him," inquired Rose in a voice with little enthusiasm for the task. I do not think he should be left on the floor." Nevertheless, she unwound herself from Elizabeth and the three servants managed to avoid suffering any further ink and got Giles back on to the couch.

"I'll go for the doctor," volunteered Mathew. He went quickly to his room, collected a coat lit a lantern and marched up the corridor to the front door. As he left, he called back to those in the study.

This front door is open".

The three women stood still unable to tear their eyes away from the still and crumpled body on the couch. It was Maria who broke their reverie.

"This room is a terrible mess, wait here Rose with the mistress, I shall bring soap and water. We can then at least clean our feet and madam's shoes."

Marie, still clutching her candle, followed the trail of black footprints left by Mathew and after a few minutes, having cleaned her own feet as best she could, returned with a bowl of water and soap for Elizabeth and Rose. Having cleaned her shoes Elizabeth felt that she should make an effort to take charge.

"Let us leave everything in the study as it is for doctor Benton, and retire to my room. Perhaps Maria you will find us some food and warm drinks, warm brandy if you can find it. I fear we have a long night ahead."

It was some time before Mathew and doctor Benton arrived. The two men were pleased to get out of the cold and finding the women in Elizabeth's reception room, accepted a glass of brandy. When they had finished, she waved the Doctor towards the study.

"Be careful Doctor, the room is a mess especially the floor. There is a pool of ink to be avoided. We have all got ink on our shoes and feet. Be careful that you avoid it. We have left three candles in the room."

"What has happened", demanded Benton.

"Mathew says he has had a seizure!"

Elizabeth nodded her agreement.

"We heard a great crash and found Giles on the floor. His arms and legs were twitching. It was horrible to see. He became calm but looked more dead than alive."

Doctor Benton entered the study with Maria following. Rose and Mathew hovered at the doorway.

"We put him back on the couch, Doctor" offered Mathew"

Dr Benton gave a non-committal grunt and bent down to look carefully at Giles. The light, even with the three candles was not good. After a few moments, the Doctor straightened up.

"Yes! I think you are right. A nasty business, indeed a seizure! You cannot be too sure why or when such things happen. Of course, he is dead. It will have to be reported. I'm afraid Edgar is in a lot of trouble."

He turned to take his leave, but something caught his attention. He took up a candle from Maria and looked quizzically once more at the bald top of Giles's head. He made a sound of concern.

"This is not good. Everyone must go back into your mistress's room. The study door must be locked and I must have the key."

The doctor not only locked the study door, but chose to lock the entire household in Elizabeth's room. He shouted through the door.

"I must get the constable!"

The four occupants of the room were bewildered. The Doctor had acted with such speed and determination, that there had been no time or appetite for opposition. Now they sat around the room in silence, not at all sure at what had happened.

"Why are we here?" wailed Maria.

"What has upset the doctor, he seemed so nice"

"I do not know" replied Elizabeth

Rose together with Maria sat on her bed, while Elizabeth and Mathew occupied a sofa set by the door. Rose spoke in a voice strangled with fear.

"The doctor was angry because the master had been struck down by his brother and as a result had a seizure. He was not happy seeing him lying on the floor in his own study. "

"He thinks we are involved", said Maria.

"It is Edgar who is to blame, said Elizabeth He struck my husband"

Saying those words, brought back to Elizabeth that scene with Edgar in the study. She had betrayed her husband and that had led to the blow She suddenly realised her own guilt.

"All we have to do is wait, "advised Mathew.

"The doctor will fetch the constable. He already knew about Edgar, perhaps we are all to be witnesses. That is all. They will want details about how Edgar struck down the master."

No one was fully convinced by Mathew's words. It was plain that something else had pushed the doctor to his strange behaviour.

Sitting there, locked up in her own room, Elizabeth slowly came to terms with her situation. She could not think on her future, but she could consider more calmly, about Giles lying on the study floor with the household looking down on him.

"Had one of them hated him enough to want to kill him," she thought.

There was no doubt that Giles was dead and that could be the only explanation of the doctor's strange behaviour. She began slowly to consider her servants one by one. Rose, her maid she needed, she had made her life bearable. She knew Elizabeth intimately, better than anyone else. She not only cared for the physical needs of her mistress, but her close companionship had become a close friendship. She could not conceive of life without her. She was quiet, uncomplaining, her conversation was limited but she was loyal to her mistress. Reflecting on this, Elizabeth felt a surge of guilt.

"Had she been loyal to Rose?"

In the last few days she had sensed that Giles had taken advantage of Rose. Both Mathew and Maria had hinted as such, but she had shied away from raising the subject with Giles. But now as she placed it at the front of her mind, she had to face that some of the nervousness, she had sensed in Rose, may have come from the physical demands of Giles.

"If so, would a wounded Giles be seen as an opportunity for revenge."

To think that, of the woman sitting opposite to her was making her feel sick and unhappy. She desperately tried to remember when Giles and Rose had been alone together and then Rose's resulting behaviour. It added to her misery that she thought she could detect a pattern.

By his voice, Elizabeth could hear Mathew talking to Maria by the door. As far as she knew he had been a reliable and helpful manservant. Her husband had been demanding, but had rarely complained of Mathew and in matters of honesty Giles would soon have detected any misdeeds. As far as Mathew was concerned, at times it seemed to Elizabeth, that he practically boasted about his position in serving such a master. That, she had not understood and it was strange that Giles had been so supportive of Mathew's widowed mother.

Of Maria she had no complaints. The food she cooked and served was good, all shopping and washing was done well and as far as her blindness allowed, she felt she lived in a house that was clean. Maria was the one member of the household who was frequently out in the town shopping and running errands. She had enjoyed a number of male companions, but apart from this there was nothing different about her place in the household compared to anyone else. She had no reason to think badly of Maria. Elizabeth felt a reassuring smile from Rose. She sighed. They would all have to wait.

Doctor Benton's heavy knock on his front door had pulled Stephen from his bed. He was used to a night time summons, even if he disliked them. He carefully opened the door to his impatient visitor.

"Come in doctor, what requires you to see me now?"

The doctor pushed his way passed the front door. He was breathing heavily, and at first his words were unclear. Stephen placed his hands on the doctor's shoulders.

"Take your time doctor. Tell me slowly."

"I think Giles Middleton has been murdered."

Despite Stephens advice the words came tumbling out.

"And I think the household is involved."

The doctor proceeded to give Stephen the details of his examination of Giles and what he knew about the fight with Edgar. How he had left Giles sleeping, only to be called back to Wilmington house because of an apparent seizure. By now he had recovered his composure and his words were calm and measured. He spoke of his real concerns, the earlier puncture wounds from Edgar's staff and that on his second visit there were fresh wounds of such a nature that he had locked in the household and come straight to Stephen. The new wounds had been deadly.

"I have locked them all in one room Stephen, I think it is murder. Come quick, I will show you the wounds and then it is for you to decide"

Stephen dressed quickly and followed the doctor to Wilmington House. On entering the corridor, the doctor drew Stephen into the study. There was Giles's body laying heavily on the couch. To reach it they had to edge past the silver ink stand, that had fallen to the floor and a large pool of ink that spread from the desk almost to the threshold of the room. The ink had begun to soak into the floor boards but they were both careful where they placed their feet. The two men crouched before the body. There was but one candle in the room, the doctor took it and raised it to cast its light onto Giles's head.

"When I first examined him, I had three candles and yet I nearly missed the cause of his death. With just this one, it is difficult to see but look here at the bare skin of his baldness. It has three puncture marks. They came from the blow of Edgar's staff. The two brothers had an argument, late this afternoon."

Stephen leaned forward. When shown, they were very clear. One still oozed a trickle of blood, but the other two had begun to scab over.

"That is how I first found him and, in that state, we laid him on the couch", continued the doctor.

"Tonight, I was called back on the grounds that he had a seizure so violent that he fell from the couch and caused the upset we see about us"

He paused for a moment to both get his breath and prepare his words.

"The puncture wounds from the antlers on Edgar's staff were painful and damaging, but they have not cracked the skull. There was blood but no brain matter."

He pointed to the bruise on the forehead.

"On that occasion he was seen to hit his head falling to the floor. That, together with the blow from Edgar, would knock him unconscious, give him great pain and a very nasty headache that would last days. I do not, however, think that these injuries killed him."

The doctor carefully moved the light of the candle to the hair line. With his hand he gently disturbed the hairs, and revealed two further puncture marks. These looked very different.

"These are larger and much deeper than the others. The skull has been penetrated and there is brain matter in the blood. It is an unhappy thing to say Stephen but to me it looks as if his assailant hoped that they would not be noticed or thought to have come from Edgar's staff."

The two men stood back. In a low voice the doctor made his final point.

166

"This is an evil and cunning blow Stephen and I think it must have come from the household. That is why I have locked them away."

Stephen stood silent, deep in thought. This was a terrible murder, but the victim was central to the investigation into royalist gold by Ketch and his men from London. He saw difficulties ahead. He turned to the doctor.

Doctor Benton, thank you for your swift action. This is a very important matter and there is more in this than I can tell you, but your actions have been of great significance."

He gently ushered the doctor to the door.

"I know it is late and you will want to get back to your bed, but may I ask one more service from you. It is important that a Captain Ketch also knows about this. He lives in the house of my late uncle, in fact we are his joint heirs. It would help enormously if he is immediately involved. Please knock on his door and tell him what has happened and that he should come at once. Leave the details to me but let him know that Giles Middleton has been murdered."

The doctor sighed. He had hoped to get home.

"Alright Stephen, at once. Will you need me in the morning?"

"No!" Replied Stephen. "But a report will be needed. We are without a coroner, as no one has yet replaced my uncle. I think you must formally report this to the Mayor as our Justice of the Peace"

It was not long before Stephen heard the clattering of boots on the front steps. Ketch had brought Tull and Holditch. Stephen asked them to man the corridor whilst he explained matters to Ketch in the study.

"Beware of the ink Ketch! It still covers much of the floor, and is to be found up and down the corridor."

Having given his warning, he directed Ketch to the corpse. Ketch had brought a lantern and under its light Stephen recounted all he had been told by the doctor, the fight between Giles and Edgar, the antler blow and its puncture wounds and those that were the real cause of death.

"This does not favour the household," murmured Ketch

"There has been a deliberate attempt to deceive with knowledge know only to them"

He paused.

"But, of course Stephen, Edgar also knew of this. Where is he?

Stephen thought for a moment.

"After striking Giles, he seems to have gone to the Peacock inn for the night, intending to return tomorrow morning. The household are locked together in the front room"

Stephen mumbled his reply, for his attention had been drawn to something about the ink. He had seen a black disc shape amongst the small pools. He bent down, prodded and then picked it up. Underneath was a flash of gold.

"A gold coin!" he exclaimed, "John, look at this"

Ketch took out a handkerchief and held it out to Stephen. The coin was dropped into the cloth and after a quick wipe, Ketch held up a clean gold coin.

"Very ancient", he cried.   "Here we have a coin from the hoard totally denied by Giles. It seems he has had access to it. This is proof that he was a royalist paymaster. One, no one suspected but Zouche Tate and Varley Brent."

His face was a broad smile.

"At last some certainty Stephen. I was doubting the existence of this, but now there is purpose in my mission. Murder is a terrible crime, but there has been murder and treason in this house. We must separate the household. "

Ketch had a sudden moment of reflection. He turned to Stephen.

"There are some important matters of authority in this. The murder, for it surely is murder, is a civic matter and you must manage any investigation. But the army has an interest in this and there are matters of treason to be considered"

Ketch moved to make certain the door was closed.

"I think the Mayor will be happy if we conduct a joint operation but under your full control.

Stephen nodded his acceptance. "Much the best approach"

Ketch had more to say. "I suggest early on we stress the treason issue, I think the members of this household need to grasp the full measure of their situation"

Seeing Stephen's agreement, Ketch moved out into the corridor. Asking Stephen to unlock the door to the front reception room and flanked by Tull and Holditch, he entered to face the suspects. Uncertainty and fear had produced a room that was hot and full of body sweat. Half lying on the floor Maria was wiping traces of ink from her feet, and she and Rose gave off kitchen smells especially onion. Mathew was dabbing a handkerchief at a small graze on his wrist and a strong smell of rosemary came from both him and Elizabeth, as they sat together on the couch. Ketch felt a spasm of sympathy for them all. Three, possibly all four were innocent of any involvement in the death of Giles but he had to be thorough in the treatment of them all.

Chapter Eighteen

 Dundas Stannard Lay on his bed in the Rood in the Wall fully clothed. By the light of his solitary candle any observer could have seen the strained and worried look upon his face. He had abandoned any thought of sleep. His mind was full of his meeting with Giles. He kept reminding himself that Giles had agreed to leave with him for France the day after tomorrow. He had agreed that there could be no turning back, no other course of action. Wife, friends, position all were to be given up. He went over this again and again. But a nagging voice reminded him that this agreement had only been arrived at only after much argument and persuasion. Giles had not welcomed what was inevitable. Stannard could easily picture Giles going over in his mind the arguments and thinking that in some miraculous way he could overcome all the dangers of discovery and arrest. In such a way he could change his mind and not only tell all, but also expose Stannard to the authorities.

 He rose from his bed to look out of the window. He expected to see nothing but darkness, but to his surprise he could see lights in Wilmington House. This caused him some concern. There was no reason why there should be household activity at such a late hour. There were shadows moving in that house. He resolved to find out what was happening. He quickly left his room and holding high his candle, crept down the stairs to the large public room. He passed through the lobby to the front door. With some difficulty he released the chains and bolts to the front door and he left the tavern waking no one. He had snuffed his candle before leaving and in the darkness was forced to move slowly with outstretched arms towards the lights of

Wilmington house. As his eyes grew familiar with the darkness, he was able to make his way to the portico of All Saints church. From this vantage point he could easily observe any late visitors and any other of the towns people with such late- night purposes. Within a few minutes he could hear voices, it was if the whole household was awake. Unfortunately, he could not hear enough to understand why they were up so late. After some twenty minutes a dark figure emerged and by the light of his lantern he saw briefly, a man not at all known to him. He considered the value of pursuit, but held on waiting for further insights into events inside the house. That judgement was rewarded when three men of military bearing knocked heavily on the door and were given immediate entry. It was clear to Stannard that events of some purpose were taking place. Although he could see he was still unable to hear anything. He was tempted to risk the window to the study that he had unlocked earlier, but regarded it as too dangerous. He was certain of one thing he would call on Wilmington house at first light. As he made his way back to the tavern his mind continued to think on Giles Middleton. *Should I consider more carefully my demand for five hundred gold pieces. I had rejected it as a serious possibility, fearful of being denounced by Giles. But would Giles really take the risk of everyone examining everything about hidden gold and Northampton. Perhaps this is the best option for all*. He was as uncertain as his victim. He returned to his room restless.

Dundas Stannard was not the only one unable to sleep that night. In the Peacock inn Edgar Middleton sat on his bed with his head in his hands. Whilst Dundas Stannard fretted about the future, Edgar was trying to come to terms with the past.

Remorse at having struck down his brother lay heavily upon him. At the moment, he felt sure that, no one outside the household, knew of his fight with Giles, but at first light he had to present himself to the constable and explain his offence. This was not going to be easy. Everyone in Northampton knew that the brothers were on good terms. He could not give the real reason for striking Edgar. He needed a plausible option. It was not immediately obvious to him. He realised that was a minor problem for by lashing out in his rage, he had lost the opportunity to determine Giles's real intentions.

"Was he going to leave Northampton and Elizabeth?

"Steal the money of the family he had served for thirty years?

"Was his destination France and Charles Stuart, or Germany and a life elsewhere?

In truth Edgar could not understand what was happening. The central core of his life was falling apart. He exhausted his mental energy constantly thinking of these things. Edgar resolved to concentrate on the fact, that at the moment Giles was in Northampton. He was grievously hurt, but at least this gave Edgar time to pin him down on the present location of the gold. If he could prise this out of his brother, then he could meet the requirements of James Compton whatever happened.

After some hours sleep, he decided that he needed food and made his way down to the public room to secure his breakfast. Whilst sitting and eating, he was pointed out to a well- dressed man who was clearly from foreign parts. He had reluctantly accepted the stranger's drink, but had been required to listen to a most unpleasant tale. The man was undoubtedly a strong Evangelical Christian and spoke of his demand for compensation for the hurts done to his fiancé's mother by Spencer Compton, nearly thirty years ago. It seemed his brother Giles had sent him away with nothing and having identified Edgar, the stranger had turned to him for support and recompense. He was indignant almost threatening, paying little heed to Edgar's size. After a difficult conversation in which Edgar gave him no satisfaction, his final words were...

"Your brother will pay one way or the other!"

Before Edgar could take the matter further, he had risen from his chair and left the room. He could see that this was a further intrusion into his brother's life at a time he was beset with difficulties. For a brief moment, he could not help but give a fraternal smile at the current state of his brother's life I had to date been one of regular peace and progress, when the rest of the country had been at war.

Back in Wilmington House, Ketch determined that immediate action was required and that if future questioning was to secure the truth of the night's events, then the household must be separated. He looked to Stephen for a nod of approval to continue. With a slight nod in return from Stephen permission was given.

"Listen everyone! It is still dark and you have had a terrible night. Murder has been done. You will all be questioned separately. Go to your rooms and stay there until you are called to account for yourself. But for the moment rest and if possible, sleep. The constable and I will want to see you in the morning. We will be patrolling the corridor. He turned to Tull and Holditch.

"Escort them to their rooms and then we will give thought to our arrangements".

When all was done as Ketch required and Tull and Holditch had taken up their positions in the corridor, he and Stephen moved into the dining room. They sat at the table. It was a quiet moment between them. They looked at each other and smiled. "Our lives seemed locked together Stephen. Your uncle's will and now this murder and my hunt for gold, they all conspire to make us a partnership."

"For myself," said Stephen. "It is a most happy chance. These are weighty matters John, and in the past, we have worked well together. I would not wish it any other way."

For a moment they sat in companiable silence. Then of one mind they took up the matters before them.

"It is late Stephen, I suggest you get some rest. I and my men will hold down things here and, in the morning, I think you must first tell the Mayor all that has happened and possibly get a note to Lord Wilmington. We must see Edgar Middleton in the morning, in fact it is probably best if you question him first".

Stephen pondered for a moment.

"Agreed, we must follow the formalities. We must be within the law. With my uncle's death we have no replacement coroner, so it is important that our investigation has the approval and support of our two Justices of the Peace".

He stood up and stretched his arms.

"I am for home and my bed, I shall be back at first light and tomorrow, together we can take these matters forward. Is there anything else?"

" Unfortunately, yes!" replied Ketch.

"It would be a great help if early tomorrow you inform my wife as to what is happening and arrange for her to come here with as much food as she can carry. We will be here for a few days and we must be fed. Also, given that we have three females to question, to have a woman involved will be a great advantage"

Stephen laughed. "You sound quite distressed John. I am sure that Ann will arrive as substantial support on all fronts".

Ketch was not yet finished. "Further more Stephen, we must do something about the body. I think the Justices will want it placed somewhere safe.

Stephen interrupted him.

"The cellars of the Council House are used as a mortuary. Tomorrow early, I shall bring some men and we shall take it out of the back door and around by the market square to the Council House. It will all be done quietly and swiftly. That will relieve those who live here and meet normal procedure."

Ketch nodded.   "Our joint efforts are working".

The following morning, Ketch could see that he had no choice but to allow the normal life of the household to proceed. Food had to be prepared and fires brought back to life, Rose had to attend to Elizabeth. It was strange, however, that all these activities were taking place in complete silence. No one had any desire to talk, or call more attention to themselves. It was with some relief, that ketch went to open the back door in response to Stephen's knock. He watched Stephen with two helpers wrap the body in blankets and carry it away. He followed them to the back door and was gratified to see that there were only a few stalls and not many customers about that early. The less attention to their activities the better. He was relocking the back door when there were insistent blows on the front door. It was Tull who stepped forward, and opened to the visitor. He was confronted by a large man in a full length, black, cloak. Before Tull could say a word, the newcomer had thrust his head in Tull's face.

"Who are you he demanded? Where is the doctor? Where is the constable?"

For a moment Tull was overwhelmed by the size, energy and passion of the man in front of him. Ketch came forward to Tull's aid.

"My name is Captain Ketch, together with my men I am investigating Giles Middleton on a matter of treasonable holdings of royalist gold, I assume you are Edgar Middleton here to explain to the constable your ferocious attack on your brother yesterday afternoon"

Before Edgar could reply Ketch continued. "I am very sorry to have to tell you that your brother is dead. The doctor has stated not from your blows. But his death again is of great interest to me. You are in serious trouble Edgar Middleton. I am dealing with treason. The constable is now in the Council House and he will question you there. I also will want to question you later today. Do not leave town."

The rapid flow of words from Ketch, and their serious tone, had by the time they were finished, quite rebuffed the initial aggressive intent of Edgar. His reply was a stuttering of panicked responses.

"My brother is dead? I did not kill him? I do not understand. Where is he? Where is Elizabeth?

It was Rose who came to Edgar's assistance. She cast a quick look at Ketch, who with a nod gave his assent.

"Come with me master Edgar, Miss Elizabeth is in her room. She will tell you all that has happened here. I suggest that you then have another word with Captain Ketch.

Ketch was determined that no un monitored conversations were to take place.

"Tull go with them, be helpful but stay in the room.

The conversation between Edgar and Elizabeth was in fact quite short. The news that Giles was dead had hit Edgar hard. He was in a dazed state. To comfort him Elizabeth rose from her couch and held out her arms to him and he stepped into them to receive consolation. They stood silently hugging each other for some time. It was with a tightening hold on Elizabeth's arm and the whispered word "Careful" that Edgar conveyed the need for them both to be extremely cautious in what they said about the death of his brother. It must not lead them to forget that they were both conspirators in the matter of the gold. Elizabeth's reply of a similar tightening of hand on arm conveyed that she understood him. Thus, their conversation was a controlled exchange of sympathy and Edgar soon turned away and Tull escorted him back to Ketch. He was given instructions to report to Stephen in the Council House for questioning and that there, he would find the body of his brother. As Edgar stepped out of Wilmington house, he passed on the steps, Dundas Stannard on his way to talk to Giles Middleton. Stannard was shocked to see military men in the corridor. He stopped abruptly, his mind in a whirl.

"Something has gone wrong! Why are they here?

He tried to hide his discomfort and forced himself to keep climbing the steps and face Ketch. However, his recovery of manner had not deceived Ketch.

"And who are you? He demanded.

"Aaah" spluttered Stannard. "I have just realised that I am in the wrong place. I had thought to meet Lord Wilmington here in his house, but I recognise neither you or the young man who has just passed me. Is Wilmington here or at the Hall.?" Stannard recognised the thinness of his tale but it had been the best he could come up with in the circumstances. The tale did not deceive Ketch but he had no grounds for any action against a possible innocent party and he had quite enough problems without getting involved in something else.

"What is your name", demanded Ketch who was becoming irritated by the delay in his questioning of the household, the arrival of Edgar and now this person was a hinderance.

"Martin Shoesmith", replied Stannard now in full control of himself. "I am so sorry to have disturbed you. I shall take my leave"

Ketch allowed him to walk away. He had a suspicion that he had been given a false name, but he had got a good look at the intruder and would remember him.

When a good distance away, Stannard sighed with relief, He had no idea what was happening in Wilmington House. Various possibilities flowed through his mind.

"Has Giles been arrested? Has the gold been found? Is the name Stannard involved? Is it time to leave Northampton?"

He decided to search for Varley Brent. It was not yet time to give up on his hopes.

Chapter Nineteen

Ketch had decided to make the study his place for thinking and discussing matters with Holditch and Tull. The questioning of the household he would undertake in the dining room. He called his two friends into the study.

"Before I forget Tull, you got a good look at our recent visitor. Remember his face, I have no idea what he wanted but I feel certain he was intent on mischief."

Tull grunted in reply. He had made himself comfortable on the couch and appeared unaffected by the fate of its last occupant. Holditch had taken to leaning against the wall by the large cupboards. In between looking at his feet he looked out of the far window.

"This is what we are going to do for the rest of the day," explained Ketch.   "In part this murder of Giles Middleton is a blow to my investigation into the whereabouts of the gold. Our main source in finding it has gone. But we now have proof that he had in his possession a coin such as we seek. The murder gives us a solid case for remaining here and posing questions about anything to anyone. It is also a strong possibility that the gold is in some way a motive for murder."

His two colleagues gave each other a look which said, *"We already knew this."*

Ketch came to the nub of his instructions and turned to Tull

"I am going to commandeer the dining room for the questioning of the household so I want you to remain with Rose and Elizabeth in their bedroom. They are not to leave it"

Tull raised his hand. He had a point to make, but Ketch waved it away and carried on.

"Holditch! Mathew and Maria are also to be confined to their rooms with the same conditions and that will be your job. When I am ready, I will call our suspects one by one for interrogation into the dining room."

Both Tull and Holditch indicated a wish to speak, again they were waved silent.

"Hopefully in a few minutes Anne will arrive. She will take over the household duties, namely feeding us and if necessary, escorting those women not being interviewed, to the privy."

Tull nodded that his question had been answered.

"One more thing" said Ketch.

"I want you to search again the room of whoever Is answering my questions. Giles Middleton was killed with something of the order of a hard, metal spike. I am not sure exactly what so use your brains."

Now Ketch waited and his final words were delivered in a tone that was easily understood.

"Any questions?"

They both understood that none were required and set to their tasks. Ketch had nothing to do but await the arrival of his wife and clarify in his own mind how he would deal with the four main suspects. After a few minutes he could maintain his patience no longer and he collected Maria from her room and began to question her in the dining room.

The dining room in Wilmington House had always been well used, both in the days of Lord Wilmington and Giles Middleton. As a result, there were fine curtains at the windows and a large Turkish carpet of intricate design. The table itself, was made of best walnut and had been well cared for. There were also two large sideboards, with heavy sets of silver dishes, canteens of cutlery, and condiments. There were a number of candlesticks set about the room and sconces on the walls. Ketch placed himself one side of the table and motioned Maria to a chair on the side opposite to him. He was going to take his time.

He began by setting out why she was being questioned and the treasonable activity of Giles Middleton. He emphasised that the nature and timing of Giles's murder placed her as one of the prime suspects. He explained that it was her duty to make it plain to him that she was not involved in treason or murder. Initially Maria had shown the same truculence of her previous interview, but as Ketch outlined the facts of the matter the anger in her face was replaced with fear. He first asked her thoughts on Giles Middleton.

"What was your opinion of Giles Middleton?" Maria looked very uncomfortable and became a little hunched into herself. In her own mind she finely balanced the truth with the consequences of its telling, but she soon brought herself to an answer.

"He was a rich man, but I never saw any large quantities of gold or any gold for that matter. I was grateful for my position here. It meant regular employment and regular money. He never beat any of us, but I was told he was a hard man in business. I do not think he was a good man. "He!" At this point she stopped, uncertain as to where her words were leading her. After a short pause she decided to carry on,

"It seemed to me that his feelings for his wife became less constant after her accident. One moment he was adoring and the next, not rude, but distant. What was horrible was his behaviour with Rose. She became terrified of him, so much so, that she dare not tell the Mistress. She had to bear his foul actions and participate in actions that made her sick. She always looked strained and unhappy." Having delivered her indictment of her Master, she gave a great sigh, breathed heavily and looked at Ketch expectantly.

"All right Maria, that was brave. But the man is now dead. In this matter we can leave judgement to God."
Ketch turned towards other matters.

"What visitors had there been recently? Any new or unusual visitors at strange times?

Maria had expected to be questioned on this and she had thought through her answers.

"Yes, we have had new visitors. First there was a foreign gentleman, perhaps aged fifty who came to see the Master. Then two days after, confronted all of us in a very angry way, when we were shopping in the market place. He kept taking hold of the Master's arm, such as in the end he was pushed away and we made an escape through our back door."

Maria was pleased that she was getting her story in the right order. "He came again yesterday morning and there was a heated argument with the Master in the study. We all could hear it. When the foreigner pulled a knife, the Master took out his pistol, made him give up the knife and chased him out of the house. He even threw his knife back after him".

This was important news to Ketch.

"Did you hear a name? What sort of knife was it?

Maria said that unfortunately she knew no more.

"Any other visitors?", prompted ketch.

Again, Maria gave an affirmative response and enthusiastically explained the visit of Dundas Stannard. It had been longer than that of the foreigner and the visitor had left in a happy mood although the Master was thoughtful rather than pleased. When pressed on the substance of the meetings, Maria spoke about the nasty and unhappy words between Giles and the foreigner. Of the meeting with the English gentleman, she had heard nothing, but Mathew said he had heard parts of it but had not shared it with her.

"And then, "she said. "Mr Edgar came and quarrelled with the Master, I do not know what it was about, but I heard the blow and the crash to the ground. The whole household came out and we helped him to the couch and left him to rest".

Ketch was pleased with the progress he had made. But he could see that Maria was becoming tired and was starting to falter.

"I know about the blow from Edgar, but tell me about later in the evening when the household had retired for the night."

Maria was indeed very tired, but she thought to herself.

"This man must understand what a shock all this has been for all of us," but she nevertheless gathered herself to make a final effort. "After the doctor had left on his first visit, he had given us strict instructions that the Master needed rest and quiet. We had left him in the study on his couch. We placed a large candlestick on the ledge, by the pots of herbs, just to give him some comfort and light.

"What happened then?"

"It was hard to sleep with all that had happened that day staying in your head. But I was sleeping in bits when I did hear some light footsteps in the corridor. I thought it was Rose or the Mistress going to the privy, and thought no more about it"

"Yes, go on "said Ketch.

"Later, there was a terrible crash. It sounded all around the house. I got up, but my candle, my night light, had gone out. It took me a moment to light it from the fire in the kitchen. Then straight away, in my night shift and bare feet and carrying my candle, I slowly went into the corridor. There up ahead of me, dressed the same, except he had the sense to wear shoes and carry a bigger candle was Mathew. He was just outside the study door. I crept up behind him and then Rose with her candle came out of the Mistress's bedroom. We all three waited as we were fearful what to do. Then, the mistress came up behind Rose and when Rose told her we were all there. She told us to go in together."

Ketch could not forbear to ask his question.

"What did you see."

"Mathew led the way in. It was pitch dark in the study but three candles provided a good light. The Master was on the floor twitching. When we moved towards him, Rose and me felt we had wet feet., Parts of the floor, near the door were covered in black ink. Mathew and the Mistress both had shoes, but they still got ink on them. The house was to be covered with ink marks eventually. The Master had knocked the silver ink stand to the floor. The mistress told me to fetch water and clean what I could. I took a candle, collected a cloth and a basin of water and I removed the worst from my and Rose's feet. But Mathews shoes were totally covered, thankfully the Mistresses were not very bad."

"I know about the ink stand, "said Ketch. But, did you see any footprints to the front door before you went into the study?"

"I'm not certain. I do not think so. There were to be ink stains everywhere".

"How long was Giles twitching?"

"He soon stopped, he looked horrible lying on the floor.

We restored the ink pots to the table and tried to make him comfortable. Rose went to get another candle and again, we placed a lit candle on the ledge by the pots of herbs, shut the door and left him to rest "

"Did anyone enter the study after that?"

"No".

The certainty of that answer was important to Ketch He continued with his questioning.

"Were the front and backdoors locked?"

"Mathew always locks up when the Master is away. Last evening, I saw him lock the back door. I do not remember the front."

"You all looked at Giles on the floor and then you placed him back on the couch and Mathew went to get the doctor."

"Yes," replied Maria.

Ketch could see that Maria was visibly wilting and no longer thinking carefully about her answers. He decided to end the interview.

"Thank you, Maria. That was very helpful. I suggest you take up your normal duties, I do not think I will have to see you again. In fact, my wife will be here soon and you may help her as you can."

Gratefully Maria returned to her bedroom and threw herself onto her bed. There she found the half- eaten onion of the night before. She took it up gratefully.

Ketch poked his head out of the dining room door.

"Well! He cried, "What have we found, anything? "

Holditch, in the corridor, held up a pair of steel meat skewers.

"These may be of interest"

Chapter Twenty

Ketch carefully examined the meat skewers found in Maria's bedroom. They certainly looked vicious weapons, but when he tried a stabbing motion with them his hand slipped along the steel. It was hard to get a purchase on them and difficult to see them puncturing a head. Frankly, Ketch could not imagine them being used by Maria, or anyone else in the household, to murder Giles. He was discussing this with Holditch when Anne emerged from the Wilmington House kitchen.

"I am sure you all could manage something to eat. I suggest we eat together in the dining room and leave the household to its own affairs".

This suggestion received unanimous assent. Anne went and informed Mathew and Maria that they could get on with the household lunch. She then went to the kitchen and carried two large wicker baskets into the dining room.

As they were arranging themselves around the dining room table, there was a heavy knock on the front door. It was Stephen and of course they invited him in to share their meal. He gladly accepted and took up a place. The first full mouthfuls, were eaten in silence, with little conversation other than appreciation expressed for the food and drink. As their hunger diminished, ketch considered it a good time to have a review of their investigations. He began with his latest interview.

"The Maria woman was very helpful and gave a clear account of the events last night as she found them, but knew nothing about gold or treachery and I am inclined to believe her."

He went on to give details as to how she had heard early footsteps in the corridor during the night, the loud crash and meeting Rose and Mathew outside the study door. He repeated in some detail what Rose said they found inside and how they were locked up by the doctor. She had been unable to state whether or not the front door had been locked. The information was listened to carefully and when he had finished, Tull leapt in with an early question.

"What do you make of these footsteps?"

Ketch knew his answer would be unsatisfactory.

"Honestly I do not Know. It is likely to be nothing more than a visit to the privy. I hope it is not more sinister than that, but I shall remember to find if anyone owns up to being in the corridor at that time."

Tull grunted he most certainly thought it was worth following up.

"And the skewers?" interrupted Anne.

"They are dangerous things to be found in a kitchen"

Ketch explained the problem of a lack of purchase, if they were to be used as a weapon and the company agreed with his judgement on this.

"She was not very helpful on the front door," chipped in Holditch. "If that door was open other persons than the household could be involved, the brother Edgar, the foreign gentleman and the man at the door who you think gave a false name."

Ketch turned to Stephen.

"Can you help us with any of these visitors?"

Stephen sat thinking for a moment. "The body of Giles Middleton lies in a temporary mortuary in the Council House. Virtually next door I have Edgar locked away. This morning I questioned Edgar. He does not deny that he struck his brother a blow that could have been mortal. However, I have had another conversation with Doctor Benton and he believes that the blow, although savage, is not what killed Giles. Edgar was also clearly seen, straight after that, going directly to the Peacock inn."

Ketch, Tull and Holditch all smiled in remembrance of the Inn, having been billeted there some years ago. It was where Ketch had been made Corporal and where the struggle with the Witch-Finder General had taken place. Stephen continued with his news. "Edgar says he was there all night and denies any night assault on his brother, and I am inclined to believe him., Most of us who know the landlord, Porteus Botterill, know him as not the most likeable of men. But he locks up the Peacock Inn like a prison every night. Nobody goes in or out without Botterill knowing. He says Edgar was there all night."

"The man named Conrad Tauber has disappeared. He was last seen in the Peacock Inn talking to Edgar Middleton and Edgar has confirmed this. He has not paid his bill, but his room still contains his additional clothing, washing material, and his horse is still in the stables. I do not think he has run off but he still cannot be found. I have asked some people to keep an eye out for him. If I have any news, I will tell you at once."

Stephen looked at each person around the table. They were his friends. He had known them for some years, he knew they were as individuals intelligent, witty with formidable minds. He felt it a real challenge to keep up with them, and devoutly hoped that he would not let them down.

"Any questions," he inquired

Ketch looked to see if Stephen had anything else to say. As he kept silent, Ketch took up the matter of the unknown caller.

"I have no idea who he was, and I rather wish I had bothered more to question him when the opportunity was there. Tull! You caught a glimpse of him. When we are next out and about make a special effort to look out for him."

It was Anne who took up the conversation.

We seem to have eliminated Maria and Edgar from the murder. John has still to question the rest of the household and we have to find Conrad Tauber."

There were nods of agreement around the table.

"In terms of finding the gold coins, we know that Giles was involved although we only have one coin. For myself, I cannot see Giles trusting or involving his servants in something that was so secret and as treason, so dangerous to himself. I think Stephen would agree that Giles was a very private man. In such a matter as this he would have very few friends, very few other people he dare bring into his plot. In the matter of the gold, I think we should concentrate on his wife Elizabeth and his brother Edgar."

At this point Ketch decided to lay out a plan of action.

"Following the wise words from Anne, I intend to complete the interviews with Rose and Mathew. I will concentrate on resolving what we can, as to the responsibility of the household for the murder. Elizabeth I shall question about both the murder and the gold. May I suggest that Stephen, with Holditch and Tull seek out Conrad Tauber and also try to find out more concerning the unknown caller. If you have time Stephen, you may try an interview with Edgar about his brother's treason."

He looked up expectantly. They all clearly agreed.

"Shall we begin?"

Their meeting broke up as they went their separate ways.

Dundas Stannard was struggling to control his rage. He had just received news that Giles Middleton had been killed, probably murdered. His expectations of an exit from Northampton with a saddlebag of gold and two companions, had just disappeared in smoke. He was sitting in the window seat of his upstairs bedroom in the "Rood in the Wall." Opposite him, lounging on the bed was Varley Brent. He was the cause of Stannard's emotional upset.

"When did this happen, Varley!?"

"Late last night. It was all over the market this morning. There are army folk from London and they are questioning the household. Stephen the constable has taken Giles's body and locked it away in the cellar of the Council House."

These words came out in short bursts as Varley sought to placate the angry Stannard with information. It was enough for Stannard to ponder carefully these details.

"I was there early this morning he admitted. It is good that I gave a false name. No surprise then that they looked at me with suspicion."

"Are we finished," asked Varley? No hope of getting our hands on those lovely gold coins."

It took a few moments for Stannard to reply. He didn't answer the question. He rather voiced the thoughts of his mind.

"It must be that that either, they have the gold and are now trying to find the person who has killed Giles, or they have the murderer but not the gold."

"No! No! cried Stannard to himself, they may have not found the gold or caught the murderer. I think we still have a chance of success in finding the gold."

He looked directly into Varley Brent's face.

"When I spoke with Giles Middleton yesterday morning, very reluctantly, he agreed to join us in leaving for France, taking the gold with us. I could see in his eyes that he desperately wanted some other choice, but…." Stannard chuckled.

"He understood that I had him in my power, and I could expose him for what he is."

"As I have always said," interrupted Varley. "I have always said this, Zouche Tate always agreed with me, but they simply would not listen. Giles Middleton was a fraud, a liar, and a Royalist paymaster."

Stannard was cross at the interruption, but carried on.

"He wanted time to wriggle like a fish, to find some other way. His excuse for waiting a few days was that he did not know exactly where the gold was to be found, that knowledge was with a trusted friend."

Varley Brent looked astonished.

"He doesn't know where it is!! This is hopeless. We may as well give this up. You have been no use to me Stannard, you had better get to France."

Dundas Stannard looked very hard at Varley Brent, who in the face of such a frightening look of anger, shrank back on the bed.

"We are not done for yet. Think! A trusted friend. How many friends does Giles Middleton have?"

Varley Brent began to understand the point of Stannard's question.

"I do not think he had any friends. He kept himself to himself. He was a hard man of business, many acquaintances but no friends. He was not liked."

"Exactly! Exclaimed Stannard

"Now! of the people he did know, which of them would he trust.

Varley Brent went straight to it.

His brother or his wife. The wife is blind, it must be the brother."

"I think not", said Stannard.

"You tell me the brother is in the cells because he broke Giles's head with his staff. There doesn't seem to be much friendship or trust there. Giles could never have entrusted such a secret to him. On the other hand, who better to entrust with your greatest secret than your blind wife. There may be ties of love, but there are certainly ties of dependence. No! Varley. It is the wife"

Varley Brent, with a smile, acknowledged he was convinced by the argument.

Dundas Stannard rose from his seat, walked around the bedroom, returned to the window and stood looking up the road to Wilmington House.

"At the moment, there are soldiers and probably the constable in Wilmington House, but when they have gone, there will only be a few servants between us and Elizabeth Middleton. It will be easy to take her. We will then find somewhere quiet and ask her to help us"

He smiled.

"Well Varley we have things to plan, some details to arrange.

Chapter Twenty-one

Ketch was growing weary of his questioning, but he knew of no other way of seeking out the murderer or the hiding place of the gold. However, he still sat at the desk in the study trying to find the energy for the final interviews. He was pleased when Anne walked in to join him. She bent and kissed him on the cheek and then sat on the couch. The various stains on the floor and couch had dried. She felt no ghost of Giles Middleton on her shoulder. The husband and wife looked at each other.

"You still have much to do" said Anne, as both a question and a statement. Ketch grimaced in reply.

"Yes, whether they add anything to what we know already is uncertain. I am gathering a conclusion about the murder but have made little progress on the gold."

"You have searched this room and the cellar? It's just a thought, you haven't mentioned it," queried Anne.

"You're right!" exclaimed ketch.

"I made a cursory look on the first day, but it was with Giles watching me at every turn. Let us do this, we may find something and at least it delays for a moment these interviews."

They both rose to their feet.

"I shall go down to the cellar," decided ketch

"I shall start on the room", replied Anne.

Ketch moved to the stairs, descended to the wooden door.

He pulled up short. The October afternoon light would be of little use. He would need a candle. He was about to re-trace his steps when Anne called out.

"John! Come and look at this, I have found a pistol."
His wife was holding up in triumph the pistol she had found in the desk. She waved it at Ketch.

"Well done Anne! That is a fine pistol, but please point it at the floor. It is probably loaded. The best of our cavalry regiments had two of those dog- bolt pistols for each man. Very effective but it is only one shot."

He quickly crossed the room to her, unloaded it and gently replaced it in the open draw.

"It is useful to know it is there, but let us get on with our search."

Lighting a candle, he moved on down to the cellar. He was rather disappointed at its failure to produce anything of interest. There was an old wine rack, an empty chest and a musty damp smell. He took some time examining the metal door. He unhooked the key and opened the door. A fetid smell of decay swept over him, choking but at times strangely sweet. He felt the darkness facing him was intimidating and he remembered the warnings of Lord Wilmington. He was happy to return to the room above. As he approached the top of the stairs, he took more time to examine the pots of herbs. There aroma was a pleasant change from what was below. Ketch had a background in herbs. In the years he was in Europe, he had for a while worked for a Dutch purveyor of herbs and spices. He especially liked Rosemary. He ran his fingers through the prickly foliage. He stopped! His hand picked out of the earth a wooden handle which revealed the spike of a shoemaker's awl.

"Anne", he called out.
"Come and look at this."

They both tried the awl in their hand. It was a perfect weapon for punching holes.

"It has purchase. I could swing this with sufficient force to puncture a head," declared Anne.

Ketch held it tight.

"We have found the murder weapon and unfortunately I recognise it. It was amongst a collection of tools found in Rose's room. She said they belonged to her father."

"There is also a little blood here "said Anne, and with her fingers of both hands, she parted some fronds to reveal a short, stubby, hard piece of branch about an inch long projecting up from the soil. A smear of blood was on the jagged wood.

"Whoever has tried to hide this has damaged his or her hand," she said.

"Whether or not it belonged to Rose, whosoever plunged this into Giles Middleton's head, had little time to dispose of it. It was the nearest and most convenient place."

Ketch felt it was time for him to share some thinking on the murder.

"I have thoughts on the culprit. Overall, my evidence is weak, unlikely to convince magistrate or jury but, still I think I am correct, the questioning of Rose will add important confirmations. Bring her to the dining room"

Anne collected Rose, brought her into the dining room, and gently settled her into the chair so that she was facing Ketch across the table. They both could immediately see that Rose's hands although worn and blemished had no sign of a wound. They smiled at each other, that was good news. Anne left and Ketch began to present the background to his questioning.

"There are some things that you should know Rose. Matters have moved on since our last interview. We have found gold in Giles Middleton's study and this is fresh evidence of treason., and..."

Here he paused,

"I must put this as carefully as I can."

"The weapon that murdered your master was an awl. I think it one of your father's shoe making tools, kept in your room. Before this interview I have been to your room and seen that the one in your room is now missing. Can you help me with this?"

Ketch's worst fears were realised. Rose burst into tears. Her hands covered her face and her whole body shook. Between sobs and breathlessness, she spluttered out groups of words.

"This is unfair! I know nothing I did nothing! Someone, help me!" Her crying and wailing slowly got louder and she was clearly becoming hysterical. Ketch rose to his feet, trying to calm her down.

"Rose! Rose! No one is saying that you are guilty of anything. I just need you to answer some questions."

The dining room door flew open and Anne came into the room. She threw a look of impatience at her husband and went immediately to put her arms around Rose. With gentle words and huggings, Rose's cries of distress slowly subsided. Anne turned with a cross face to her husband.

"John Ketch I sometimes think that you know nothing of women. Rose here is barely seventeen, she is no murderer and you know it. Give me some time with her."

Ketch knew it was time to withdraw. He left the dining room and returned to the study. Here he slumped into a chair and to calm himself began examining the pistol left in the drawer. After ten minutes Anne joined him.

"She is better now. You really frightened her with your talk of treason and the murder weapon, but if you let me stay in the room, she has promised to answer your questions"

Ketch grimaced, it would have to do. Husband and wife returned to the dining room, where a red-eyed Rose was still snivelling but in control of herself. Ketch tried again.

"Now Rose! Mrs ketch is going to stay in the room, and from the beginning I want you to understand that no one is making any accusations against you. I just need some answers to my questions."

Deep inside he was holding himself in check. He knew half a dozen men who would push him aside and simply use hard violence to get their answers. He knew that was not his nature, not in this case. Rose looked at Ketch and gave him a weak, encouraging smile. Ketch tried his questions.

"Have you noticed anyone in your room, anyone at all?

Have you noticed any of the household behaving in an unusual way? Any other unusual strangers?

To all these, Rose shook her head. Ketch had now reached a point at which Rose had to speak.

"Just tell me what you know about master Edgar striking his brother."

He waited and in a low voice Rose spoke.

"I didn't see anything, but we all heard the noise and we saw the master on the floor groaning with blood on his head. Mathew went for Doctor Benton. He looked at the Master and said he was hurt but not dead and he should rest."

"And you all helped him onto the study couch," interjected Ketch.

"Yes, and as it was beginning to get dark, we left him a candle for comfort and light and closed the door."

Ketch felt matters were improving.

"Excellent Rose. That was fine. Now I want you, with as much detail as you can, tell me about what happened to master Giles later that night and especially the state of the room."

Rose paused for a moment. Telling her story was much easier than facing talk of treason and murder.

"Well there was a very large crash from the study. It was very late at night and everything was dark and a bit frightening. The mistress and I were sleeping in the front reception room and we did not know what to do."

"But you did go to investigate2, added Ketch encouragingly"

"Yes," replied Rose.

"The mistress got from her bed and said we should find out what had happened. So, I lit a candle and with mistress holding my shoulder I led the way out of the room"

"And what exactly did you see? Demanded Ketch

"There was Mathew and Maria outside the study door. They looked too frightened to go in".

"Was Mathew in front?"

"Yes, Maria was crowding behind him"

"And then?"

"Mistress said we should all go in together. So, Mathew pushes the door and we go in with our candles but it was so dark that no one saw the spilt ink and it was all over our feet. Mathew and the Mistress had shoes on, but me and Maria were in bare feet It was nasty and ink was everywhere. Mathew as first, was especially bad, he even had ink on his night shirt. The master was making a horrible noise and shaking on the floor, and then went quite quiet"

"That is fine Rose, tell me about the doctor."

Rose took a series of deep breathes, she was beginning to falter, but a word of support from Anne gave her the courage to continue.

"Mathew went and brought Doctor Benton again. The doctor took a good look at the master and was about to go, when he asked for all three candles to be held up close to the Master's head. Then very slowly he looked at us and pushed us into the mistress's room, demanded the key and locked us in."

"You are sure there were only three candles Rose?"

"Oh yes," she replied, "only three."

Ketch looked at Anne.

"Thankyou Rose, you have been most helpful."

Anne took charge of Rose, and suggested that she went to her room and rested, but Rose stated that she was better now and would go and sit with her mistress.

Anne accompanied Rose to the front reception room and left her to talk with Elizabeth, she then went to look for her husband and found ketch coming out of the kitchen.

"Husband I was just making sure that everyone is still here, both Mathew and Maria are in the kitchen, they are there preparing a meal, so all is in order."

"I have some bread and cheese which we can enjoy with a small flask of wine," stated Anne.

"Shall we eat in the study"

Ketch and Anne made themselves comfortable in the study and whilst eating, once again began a review of the investigations. Ketch felt it was time to reveal what he knew and to get Anne's reaction.

"In terms of the death of Giles Middleton, unless we can find any intruder is involved, the culprit must be amongst the household. Mathew is the obvious suspect. This murder has an evil aspect about it. Not only is it a horrible way to die but there is also a low cunning attempt to shift the blame onto Edgar, hoping the puncture marks would be taken as coming from the antlers."

"That was foxed by the skill of Doctor Benton," noted Anne.

Ketch continued.

"Mathew looks a nice enough young man, he even has a sort of sensitivity about him, but I must admit I cannot really see the ladies in this household acting in such a swift and deadly manner. There is also the motive of his heavy astonishment and feeling of betrayal, at the discovery that Giles was a secret royalist of importance. It is true, however, as the chief suspect we only have the flimsiest of evidence against him. It is the obvious innocence of the others that we rely upon."

"What is the evidence that you have?" exclaimed Anne.

Ketch collected his thoughts.

"Firstly, there is the matter of the candles. If you remember, after the attack by Edgar, Giles was left on the couch in the study, with a candle for light and comfort. Both Maria and Rose stated that the room was dark when they entered. What happened to that candle? Both Maria and Rose had candles, so did Mathew. Thus, there should have been four of them in the study, but there was only three. I believe Mathew crept up the corridor in the dark entered the study, killed Giles with the awl, quickly placed that in the pot of herbs, swiftly picked up the lighted candle and took up his position outside in the corridor. It thus appeared he was the first to arrive at the study door in the same manner as Rose and Maria. There is no other explanation".

Anne pursed here lips.

"You are sure that the original candle in the room did not just go out," she suggested.

"I think not," replied Ketch.

"I did, at the time look for the candle."

"Well carry on<" suggested Anne.

"What else?"

Ketch drew a deep breath.

"Then there is the issue of the ink. Maria and Rose only suffered ink to the soles of their feet, as did Elizabeth to her shoes, but Mathew had it all over his shoes and on his night shirt. I believe that he was in the room striking Giles when the ink stand fell to the floor."

He sat back looking for comment from Anne.

"Yes, that is more substantial. Anything else"

"Surprisingly yes," replied Ketch.

"Our recent discovery of the awl is possibly linked to Mathew through the particular aroma of rosemary. The awl is undoubtedly the murder weapon. It was hastily placed amongst the rosemary by our murderer as he races to take up position outside the study. As such he may have a hint of rosemary about him, along with a damaged hand."

"Does any of this fit with Mathew" asked Anne.

"Well, we have yet to actually look at his hands for damage but on the night of Giles's death, when I entered the room, holding the four members of the household, locked up by the doctor. I noticed amongst the smells of discomfort, those of sweat and onions also a faint aroma of rosemary. This came from those sitting on the sofa. It was Mathew and Elizabeth."

Ketch suddenly smiled. "And now I think on that moment, I believe I remember Mathew nursing his wrist."
He shrugged his shoulders.
"Another weak link, but they do add up."

"I think we must examine his hand now, "suggested Anne.

"You must do that next and confront him with all this evidence."
The study door was suddenly opened and Tull and Holditch stepped into the room.

"We have found Conrad Tauber," cried Tull.

"Actually, I found him, "continued Holditch.

"Stephen told us to search the market square, and then take our separate ways, to more easily cover the town."

Tull interrupted.

"Now you have to understand that not one of us had actually seen this man, but Stephen took us to see the landlord of the Peacock Inn, who gave us a general description, which initially was of little help."

Holditch stepped in again.

"He did much better on Tauber's clothes. He was seen to be wearing a black cloth cap with ear flaps, and his black coat had very wide sleeves, and you do not see that clothing in Northampton."

"There was nothing in the market," said Tull.

"But", Holditch started walking up Abington street and was about to turn back when."

"I saw him, "claimed Holditch.

He was with three other men who were dressed as strict puritans. They were deep in conversation and strolled into what looked like a meeting house."

Ketch held up his hands. He was impatient to confront Mathew, but it was important that the place of Conrad Tauber in the crime was cleared away so he allowed the tale to be told. He hoped this was not going to be a long and detailed account.

"Just give me the outcome," he demanded.

At that moment Stephen stepped through the door and joined the conversation. In a firm voice he gave the heart of their findings.

"Tauber had met three men from Lancashire. They had been brought to a new life by a preacher called Fox. He had formed a new sect and they call themselves "Tremblers" or "Quakers". They fear God but believe in peace and universal brotherhood. They shake when the talk about him. Tauber has completely taken up with them. They confirm that he has been in their company for two days, ever since he left the Peacock. He has become one of them and has spent that time talking and losing his anger. He was with them sharing their vigil when Giles was murdered. He embraced us all and put himself at our disposal. I told him I did not think he would be needed".

"Well done Stephen," said Ketch

"It would seem that we have no need of Conrad Tauber."

He rose to his feet.

"I can tell you all that Anne and I have reviewed what little evidence we have on the murder, and it is strengthened by the elimination of Conrad Tauber, I am convinced that Mathew is responsible for the death of Giles Middleton and I am going to confront him now!"

He turned to his army colleagues.

"Go and get Mathew and bring him to the dining room, Stephen and I will confront him together."

He turned to Stephen.

"You will get a chance to review what evidence we have"

Stephen smiled. It was a relief to have some answers.

The two men moved to the dining room where they sat side by side waiting for Tull and Holditch to bring Mathew.

The door burst open. It was Tull.

"He's gone! We can't find him anywhere! I think he has made a run for it.!

Chapter Twenty-two

Ketch was annoyed he had been too lax in his supervision of the household. Having identified Mathew, he had been too anxious to get on with his other task, the search for the royalist gold.

"We must find him quickly. This death of a royalist traitor in our midst is important. It cannot end like this Stephen. He must not escape. This is your town, I feel you must manage the search."

"Of course," replied Stephen.

"I shall start at once. He cannot have gone far. Northampton is not such a large town, nevertheless a full search will require extra men. Let us go to the market square. I shall enrol deputy constables and together we can scour the town for him."

" What if he makes for the fields and forests, cried Tull.

Stephen was confident in his reply.

"He has no food, no transport, on the roads we would soon find him. The forests and fields are more difficult, but he is a town boy, it is October. He will find it unpleasant, he will take risks for food and shelter. He will be eventually found by farmer or woodsman."

These words of certainty gave them all a confidence that the fugitive would soon be secured. Stephen led them all to the back door of Wilmington house and out into the market square. Before leaving Ketch had a word with Anne.

"I want you to stay here, the three women will feel some fear and concern at Mathew's guilt, but also some relief that they are no longer under suspicion. It may well be best if you remain and be reassuring. In such an atmosphere there may be some words relevant to our main purpose."

Anne smiled at her husband.

"I understand your need in this, but hurry the faster you leave the greater your chance of finding him."

In the market square, Stephen together with Ketch, Tull and Holditch, went to secure the men they would need for the search.

In their watch on Wilmington House, Dundas Stannard and Varley Brent had originally taken turn and turnabout, in watching from the window and loitering around watching the front door. However, the planned abduction of Elizabeth, involved equipment and that involved Varley moving about the town. Fortunately, their requirements were minimal, a large hand cart, an old blanket or carpet, some cloth and strong cord would be sufficient. The plan was that to avoid suspicion, Varley together with the cart and its contents would settle in the market square, hidden amongst the daily activity of a market. Stannard would be stationed at the front of the house. Any exit from the house would thus be covered. Finally, Dundas had decided that there was no time for a secure property that could be obtained for the planned interrogation. Rather they would have to find a place in the fields or woods, which would be private enough for the task in hand.

"I can find what is needed," enthused Varley."

Dundas grunted.

"Good, now where would we take her?"

Varley had to give this some thought, and for a few moments his mind could be seen searching and discarding options. Finally, he made his choice.

"Down by the river, there are plenty woods towards what is known as Cow Meadow. There, no one would interfere."

Varley did not take long to acquire all that was required. They decided that when there were no men in the house, they would move the cart to the front, then both enter by the back door, take Elizabeth wrap her up and then bundle her out of the front door, into the handcart. With their preparations complete, the two men had a drink together in the public room of the Rood in the Wall. In a quiet corner where the could not be overheard, they discussed their plans to become rich. Each, felt it necessary to be reassured by the other that they were determined to play their part. They were a pair of tough, hard-bitten and ruthless men. In a strange way these similarities had built a bond between them. They hardly knew each other and they well realised that the other could not be trusted, but a common desire for gold kept them together. They had each weighed the risks and accepted them to the same degree and they enjoyed their common villainy.

They had decided that they would take up their vigil for two days. If the soldiers were still there after that time, they would temporally abandon their kidnap and try again a few days later.

However, Mathew's flight from the house provided them with an immediate opportunity. It was as he occupied the steps to the central market fountain, drinking a cup of water, that Varley saw the four men leave by the back door of Wilmington House. He watched Stephen trying to gather his posse and the problems he was having. He purposely kept his head down, although no one would have been surprised at Varley Brent failing to volunteer. Slowly rising from his place, he began pushing the handcart out of the market and around to the front of Wilmington House. When it was in position, they hurried around and entered the back door. Their plan required them to move through the house quickly, find Elizabeth, and proceed to the front door. Finally, Elizabeth gagged, was to be placed in the cart and they would make their escape.

For privacy Anne had guided Elizabeth into the study. Maria and Rose, she left scrubbing the corridor to remove the last of the ink stains. Elizabeth sat hugging herself and gently rocking backwards and forwards in her chair. Anne saw how, even in the midst of her upset and misery, she looked beautiful. Her wayward blonde curls fell out of her lace cap and framed a beautiful face. For the first time Anne noticed how her clothes complemented her beauty in an understated way. She wore a simple light blue shift, with a belt of dark blue, fastened with a simple silver buckle. Short sleeves revealed well formed, and blemish free arms. But, beyond the beauty, in her own mind Anne saw the difficult life facing Elizabeth.

"She is now a young widow but with Giles gone. What is she to do? Where is she to go?

She reached out and touched Elizabet's arm and the rocking stopped. Now they were comfortably seated, Anne took up the conversation.

"Elizabeth you must be totally shocked and bewildered by what has happened these last few days, Edgar's behaviour, the accusations against Giles of treason and his murder by Mathew."

Elizabeth began to speak.

"I don't know what I am to do Anne. I have no money. I am blind, I am the widow of a royalist traitor. My servant murdered my husband. What will happen to me?

Anne felt it was an appropriate time, when conversation may not only benefit Elizabeth, but also help Ketch, her husband. She had not discussed it with him, but it was her belief that if anyone knew anything about the gold under Giles's stewardship, it would be Elizabeth. What she had to say may unlock this.

"I sympathise, Elizabeth, your situation does look bleak, but I would like to put to you an idea that might go some way to helping you."

She paused. She knew that in this she had to be very delicate.

"John and I have just inherited a fortune with a new house. Our former property in the market square, is now empty at the moment. When you leave Wilmington House and I think you know in your own mind that this will be soon, John and I would be happy for you to use it. It would solve your immediate problem of somewhere to live."

Elizabeth raised her head, she smiled. Anne knew she had made a good decision. Elizabeth looked alive and hopeful.

"You are a saint Anne. I have thought of little else. I know I should grieve more for Giles, but in truth, I have been sick with worry about where I would live. I was not certain that my father would take me back."

Anne was delighted at Elizabeth's pleasure and she determined to take matters a little further.

"Now I am sure that Maria and Rose would go with you, but with your sight the presence of a male protector would be very desirable."

Elizabeth sat up straight in her chair, uncertain as to what was coming. Anne continued with carefully chosen words.

"We both know of a person near bye who has also recently acquired a fortune and would most willingly throw the warmth of his protection about you."

Anne was delighted to see Elizabeth blush.

"Anne you are shameful, I am just made a widow, my husband is not yet in his grave, and you are matchmaking"

For Elizabeth this happy bit of realism was the most enjoyable conversation she had for weeks. For a few moments more the two women, disgracefully early, gave their opinions on the suitability of the newly wealthy constable as a future husband. Anne felt that the good nature of this conversation could be guided to benefit Elizabeth in an equally important matter.

"I do not know how much money you have to hand Elizabeth"

Elizabeth replied quickly.

"I can pay rent Anne. I am not yet totally destitute."

Anne held up her hand.

"No! Elizabeth, never mind that. Whether or not our plans for Stephen take place, you have a need for money. Servants must be paid and the daily round of life is not cheap. There is also the matter of Giles's treason and the gold coins he is reputed to possess."

Again, Elizabeth made to say something, but Anne ignored her.

"It would be very helpful if the beautiful blind wife of the royalist traitor was to provide a clue, that would lead to the recovery of the gold. A grateful town and indeed the army, would see such a person, as both a victim and a heroine, undoubtedly one deserving some monetary reward for her efforts. Any idea that she herself was a royalist traitor, or even helped a royalist traitor would be obvious nonsense."

Anne held her breath as she finished and there was a long silence in the room. Then Elizabeth spoke.

"You are a clever and persuasive woman Anne, and you give me good advice. You cannot know how much I have longed to have rid of a terrible burden."

Anne continued, desperate to help Elizabeth to help herself.

"I can see a future for you Elizabeth where you do not have to carry the crimes of your husband as your own.

At that moment Anne heard a crash and loud shouting in the corridor.

Dundas Stannard and Varley Brent had entered Wilmington House in a great rush. As a result, they collided with Maria and Rose kneeling on the corridor floor with their buckets, water, and brushes. Varley fell over Rose and Dundas kicked over a bucket. They were not amused, rather they were cold with anger. They lashed out at the two women and drew blood on each of them. No one came to interfere, so they took their time, dragging their victims into the kitchen, where they cruelly bound and gagged them. They returned to the corridor still in an angry mood. They saw Anne by the study door looking at them.

"That's not her hissed Varley. There must be two women."

As they quickly moved to take Anne, she retreated into the study, and swiftly turned the key in the lock.

"Elizabeth, there are two men in the corridor, they mean to harm us."
A series of heavy blows fell upon the study door. A loud cracking sound, showed its weakness.

"Quick Elizabeth help me push this desk against the door, it will give us a little time. I'll keep it jammed up against the door, while you call for help out of the window."

This resistance to their plans infuriated the two men. That two women were obstructing them, gave added impetus to their blows on the door. Elizabeth together with Anne, managed with great physical effort to slide the desk up against the door. For a moment they held each other in fear as the banging continued, and the door gave evidence of breaking up. Freeing herself from

Elizabeth, Anne moved to get the pistol that she remembered was in the desk drawer, but she was held back by Elizabeth.

"No time for that Anne," she cried.

"Guide me to the top of the cellar stairs, take me down to the cellar. Hurry trust me."

Anne could see only temporary relief in the plan, but no real solution. There they would be trapped, but she did as Elizabeth ordered. Elizabeth's words came tumbling out.

"Now, take me down through the wooden door into the cellar! With it open, there is just enough light for you! In the cellar there is a metal door! The key is on a hook beside it!"

Having gained the cellar Elizabeth's voice became calmer.

"Open the door."

As Anne followed the instructions, they heard the study door break open and the sound of running feet.

"Take my hand Anne, instructed Elizabeth. They will not follow us into the tunnels"

Anne could not believe it. All her time in Northampton, she had been told how dangerous they were, how terror from their darkness had caused injury and death.

"Do not linger Anne, they are coming"

As their two assailants rumbled down the stairs the two women disappeared into the darkness.

Chapter Twenty-three

When Ketch called Maria into the dining room, for questioning on the death of Giles Middleton, Mathew took the decision to leave Northampton immediately. He knew he had been stupid, he hated violence, he never got enraged, but this time he had committed a horrible crime, in a most deceitful way. He had become deeply ashamed at his own behaviour, but Giles Middleton had behaved so badly that for the first time in his life, he, Mathew, had lost control of himself. Giles had made a fool of his mother, he was plotting to abandon his blind wife, he had been a deceitful royalist, one who had provided money for the recent Scottish invasion. Men had died because of this. But, above all he had deceived Mathew himself, he had only pretended to embrace the cause of Parliament, and that he could not forgive. But from recent events, Mathew soon realised, that the crime would be laid at the feet of someone in the household and that he was the obvious suspect. He had tried to divert suspicion elsewhere to Edgar, to Rose, to an outsider, but he had no evidence that this had worked. If he stayed, he would most certainly hang.

Sitting on his bed he managed his thoughts to leave.

"Now is the time to go, the two soldiers will not be a problem. Under the cover of my normal servant duties, I shall make my way to the kitchen, the store rooms, the privy, and the privy- gate, into the side alley."

He determined to see his mother. He felt sure that in time, she would forgive him, especially as he was determined. she should know everything. Giles had for years been a secret royalist, holding gold for their cause, and that he intended to flee to France with Dundas Stannard and the gold, and thus abandoning his blind wife. She would find it hard to accept that he was the cause of the death of her lover, but later he would contact her again after his treachery is well known, then she would forgive him. He had also given practical thought to his future. He had few friends in Northampton, none who would give refuge to a murderer. He had to make for London and he had to take the risk of the South Gate. Once successfully beyond the town, he felt he could avoid pursuit, in the hustle and bustle of a major highway. He could not face the countryside, always cold, damp and bare in winter. He stood up, he collected what money he had. In the kitchen, he filched some food and made his way out of the house.

Stephen stood amazed. Mathew was wrong. He had friends in Northampton, whereas, Giles Middleton, the royalist paymaster, had none. There were no keen volunteers to track Mathew down. Mathew's mother was a trader on the market, and whilst many a wife frowned at her relationship with Giles Middleton, most husbands thought that "*a poor widow must live*". Both sides of the debate, however, had sympathy for Mathew. Ketch was becoming anxious and he could see that Tull and Holditch were becoming bored. Tull turned to Ketch

"Captain this is all very important for catching Mathew, but we do not know Northampton, and there are other things that we could be doing"

Ketch made no immediate response, but Tull was absolutely right. *He should be questioning Elizabeth, they were wasting time.*

"Stephen, we are of no use to you here. We will get back to Wilmington House"

Stephen looked unhappy at this, but grasped the reality of the situation.

"If you must John, fine, I will carry on here".

Ketch, Tull and Holditch crossed the market square and went straight into Wilmington House. It was strangely quiet, but seeing part of a splintered study door at the end of the corridor, he thought it best to hold still for a moment. It was Holditch, who had taken a glance into the kitchen, who exclaimed.

"Captain look at this!"

"Good god! Free those women" demanded Ketch.

"Tell me quickly! What had happened?"

Tull and Holditch removed the gags and the bindings from Rose and Maria. They were both extremely upset. and for a few moments could do nothing but draw breath and groan. Trying to curb his impatience Ketch spoke softly.

"Maria, Rose, what has happened. Are there intruders in the house?"

Maria only could reply.

"Two men, one was Varley Brent, I do not know the other. They have gone looking for my mistress and your wife."

Ketch turned to his two men.

"follow me!

They moved silently to the study door and listened. At first, they could hear nothing but then there were voices coming from the cellar. Two men were arguing.

"I tell you Stannard I am not going in there. People get lost and it's dangerous. If you fall or cut yourself you will get sores that turn bad and you can die. No! Let's get out of here."

A second voice spoke more loudly and with greater authority.

"They are tunnels, yes they are dark and dangerous, but we can easily find lanterns, and with light, find these women. This is our best chance Varley. If you want gold, then this is the only way, and we must hurry"

Ketch remembered the pistol in the desk draw He collected it and he knew it was unloaded loaded. He tried it as a club in the palm of his hand. *"This will do"*

He turned to Tull and Holditch.

"Have you weapons?"

Tull, always carried a knife, He showed it to Ketch, he was ready. Holditch, also had a knife, but he left it in its sheath. Of the three he was the most used to brawling. His right hand grasped a collection of coins in his pocket, a blow from this would be very heavy indeed.

With his two men behind him, Ketch approached the top of the cellar steps.

"You! down in the cellar come up and explain yourselves."

A quiet, descended on those in the cellar as the talking stopped. Strained ears in the study could hear whispering, but not what was said.

"It's those soldiers," hissed Varley Brent.

"These tunnels seem our best choice," re-joined Dundas Stannard.

"No! I have told you no! Better to take on what's upstairs."

"They may be armed"

"They may not. I have faced pistols and swords before".

"You are a brave man Varley Brent. Alright, let us see what awaits us."

Dundas and Varley Brent, carefully made their way up the steps to the study. Ketch, holding the pistol in front of him, together with his two comrades stepped back into the middle of the study, ready to confront the two men, as they emerged. Ketch recognised Dundas as the unknown man at the door, but did not know his name. Holditch saw him immediately as Dundas Stannard, from the description he had been given in Chester. Both groups of men eyed each other, their minds spinning as they estimated their chances.

"I do not think that pistol is loaded" whispered Stannard.

Varley Brent thought that the three soldiers did not look at all frightening.

" *They may look lean and fit but the taller one looks too old to be of much use in* a struggle."

They both carried a similar thought.

"*We can take these men.*"

They looked at each other, then Stannard picked up a pot of herbs from the ledge, and threw it at Ketch. He followed this with a head down charge. Varley Brent prepared to spring forward as the momentum from Stannard, drove Ketch straight through the splintered door of the study, and into the corridor. Here they both crashed to the floor kicking and punching. Varley Brent although big, had not the physique of Stannard. Where Stannard was hard muscle and bone, Brent was slack fat. Nevertheless, he strode forward, confident that he could master the two men in front of him. However, Tull, the tall, old one, gave him a hard, sharp kick in the knee, that caused him to stumble. At this, Holditch took the opportunity to land a heavy blow to the throat. Varley Brent ended up on the floor gasping and choking. Holditch and Tull exchanged looks.

"I can manage, help Ketch!" said Tull, and promptly sat on Brent, pinning the coughing man to the floor.

Assured that Tull was in control of his opponent, Holditch moved out into the corridor. Stannard was on top of Ketch, the pistol was on the floor. but Stannard had blood in his hair. Nevertheless, he was bearing down on Ketch with both hands reaching for ketch's throat. Ketch's own hands were clamped tight around Stannard's wrists. A trial of strength was taking place. It looked stalemate. Holditch bent down beside Stannard and spoke in an inquiring tone.

"Dundas Stannard."

Stannard could not forebear from turning in response to his name. At that moment Holditch gave him an all mighty punch with his hand holding the coins. Muscle and metal knocked Stannard senseless and he rolled over onto the floor.

"That is one you owe me Captain," Holditch said with satisfaction.

The next few minutes were taken with securing Stannard and Brent. They were dragged to the kitchen, tied to chairs and Maria and Rose recovered some spirit by inserting the prisoners' gags. There was also some strong language from both women, which described with some colour their views of them. While this was taking place, ketch was acutely conscious that neither Anne nor Elizabeth were present.

"Stannard where are the women?"

Rose eased the gag from Stannard's mouth, and to everyone's surprise, but satisfaction, gave him a stinging slap across the face.

"Where is my mistress? What have you done with her?"

Initially taken aback by the sharp blow from Rosa. Stannard shook his head and snarled a reply.

"We have nothing, we never even saw them. They both disappeared into the tunnels. We left them there and as Brent here would not go in, we came up."

With that he gathered in his mouth to spit at Rose, but too quick for him she grabbed his nose squeezed and slipped the gag back.

Varley Brent was making noises in his gag, trying to give his version of events. He was ignored, Stannard had given them the information they required.

Ketch moved quickly to the study followed by Maria.

"Be careful sir, do not go into the tunnels straight away. They are very dangerous, they swallow people up, First take some time to light a lantern, then from the cellar, call out to them and keep the light shining into the entrance."

Ketch was grateful that Maria had foreseen what was necessary. As they prepared the lantern, he thought more of her and her future.

"You are a wise woman Maria, but with Giles Middleton dead, Lord Wilmington will want a new agent in Wilmington House".

Maria took the comment kindly, she had considered how recent events would affect her.

"Yes sir, but unless it is a person with their own servants, there is always room for someone like me. I hope to stay on in Wilmington House, I feel certain that Rose will go with Miss Elizabeth.

The return of Elizabeth and Anne was soon achieved. They were very careful to make certain that it was Ketch who was calling for them and when they emerged, they were dusty and although triumphant, beginning to realise how close they had been to real harm. Anne was tired but unhurt. Elizabeth had sustained a blow to the head and needed to be helped upstairs. Between them the two women carried a heavy saddlebag which was allowed to fall to the floor. Ketch retrieved the saddlebag and carefully saw them through the damaged study door where they were joyfully welcomed by everyone. They were made to sit in the front reception room and glasses of brandy were put into their hands. Neither Rose or Maria accepted brandy but the three soldiers felt that they too deserved it.

As they sat around re-telling their stories there was a knock on the door and Stephen entered the room.

"What a wonderful smell of brandy, ketch. Are we celebrating? I hope so for my own day has not gone well."

His eye then fell upon Elizabeth, sitting on the couch with a bandaged head, bravely holding her brandy but looking very tired. He fairly leapt across the room to kneel at her feet.

"My God Elizabeth! Has someone hit you? Ketch what has happened here. I put high value on this lady. She is not strong enough to suffer blows to the head".

The constable's normal, open and pleasant face was drawn with concern. He held both of Elizabeth's hands in his own. He rose to his feet, as if ready to give battle on her behalf. Ketch also rose to his feet to calm him.

"Steady yourself Stephen. No one has touched her."

Ketch turned to the assembled company.

"Perhaps we can take a moment to tell Stephen what has happened here."

There were sympathetic murmurs so Ketch continued.

"On return from you in the market place we found that Maria and Rose had been tied up in the kitchen by two intruders. We quickly found them, and there was a tussle, and my two soldiers got the measure of them. Elizabeth and Anne had been forced to enter the tunnels to escape them. Maria and I took a lantern down to the cellar and guided them to safety. They are both well now, but Elizabeth struck her head whilst navigating them to safety. The wound has been cleaned."

Stephen looked a lot happier, and ready to speak, but Ketch hurried on with his tale.

"They have not only saved themselves but, done wonderfully well. They are both heroines. There on the floor you see, a very heavy saddlebag stuffed with gold coins. This, they brought out with them. I think we will discuss that later."

Stephen made to question these words, but Ketch forestalled him.

"We have the intruders locked up and If you have any room in the Council House, I suggest they be transferred there. But first you may wish to hear, what I think has been happening in Wilmington House, that has led to the death of Giles Middleton"

Stephen stood still for a moment, and then took a chair and placed it next to where Elizabeth and Anne were sitting on the couch, facing Ketch. Maria and Holditch were sitting on the floor, just below the window that looked out to the front. Rose and Tull had chairs side by side on Ketch's left. They all looked weary, but he had their attention. Ketch stood in the middle of the room.

"I will be brief, but it is just as well that you all know everything for a day may come when we will all have to account for the death of Lord Wilmington's factor or agent."

Chapter Twenty-four

Ketch took a long moment to make sure that he had the full story clearly in his mind. He received an encouraging smile from Anne and began.

"By his flight from Wilmington House, Mathew has confirmed my thoughts as to his guilt for the murder of Giles Middleton. In my mind's eye, I see the events that led up to the actual murder of the victim. Mathew sits in his room, unable to sleep, and endlessly examining the reasons, for his terrible anger towards Giles. He curses the deceit that Giles has played upon the town. He was a royalist paymaster, not the servant of Parliament. He had made foul use of Rose and his own mother. He finally resolves to kill him."

At this point Rose shifted uncomfortably in her seat. She did not enjoy her shame being brought to the attention of others. Tull leaned across and whispered some comforting words, which brought a weak smile to her face.

"In anticipation of such a deed, he had already stolen the murder weapon, the shoe maker's awl, from Rose's room and once Elizabeth had returned from the privy, he moved in the darkness to the study. Here by the light of the one candle left, he struck the two blows that killed Giles Middleton and as he hoped, would point the finger of guilt to either Edgar or Rose."

Rose's face darkened against her betrayal by someone she thought a friend and ketch paused for a moment before taking up the threads of his argument.

"What Mathew did not consider was that such blows would cause Giles to rise up in a great spasm and strike the desk, causing the ink stand to fall, and throw ink all over the floor. His shoes and nightshirt were badly marked. Nevertheless, his mind moved quickly. At this point he was at grave risk of being discovered. He gets rid of the murder weapon by hiding it in the Rosemary plant, where he suffers a small cut to the wrist He then picks up the lone candlestick and hurries into the corridor, closes the study door and turns around just in time to be thought arriving, along with Maria and Rose, in response to the noise, Maria and Rose both line up behind him, each with their candle and all three appear to be standing, reluctant to enter the study".

Maria whilst listening to ketch had also been receiving whispers from Holditch, but at this point she spoke up.

"He was very clever, he was there waiting for us with his candle at the study door. He really looked worried and unsure of what to do."

"I think he was worried replied Ketch he was making up his story on the spot."

Ketch continued

"Elizabeth now comes and suggests that they all go into the study together. All agree it is in total darkness and they all get their feet covered in ink. It is this first information that gives us doubts about Mathew. Then everyone also agrees that the doctor examined Giles by the light from three candles, but of course there should have been four, the one originally left burning and the three brought by Mathew, Rose and Maria. The only explanation is that Mathew did not bring a candle, he used the one in the study."

Ketch looked carefully at his audience. He willed them to see the importance of his explanation. His listeners sensed that he needed their understanding to continue and they nodded their heads, with varying degrees of enthusiasm. Ketch accepted this as a sign to continue.

"The issue of the ink was more straightforward. Mathew's covering of ink was more substantial than that of the others. Their feet had stepped into pools of ink. Mathew's feet were covered and his nightshirt was splattered because he was in the room when the inkstand tipped over."

Elizabeth released her arm from Stephen's grip and raised it to make a point.

"He also tried to deceive us by saying that the front door had been left open when he went to get the doctor".

Ketch nodded encouragement to Elizabeth and Stephen once again secured her arm.

"These were our initial thoughts and they were supplemented by later discoveries. When I first arrived after being summoned, I entered this very room and you were all here. I straightaway detected a trace of Rosemary coming from the couch where Mathew and Elizabeth were sitting. He was also nursing a slight graze to his wrist. When Anne and I later discovered the murder weapon, the awl. It was in the pot of Rosemary and together we noticed a smear of blood, on a small, pointed stump of the bush."

Anne nodded in agreement, but she looked at Ketch and directed his gaze to Elizabeth who was clearly nodding with fatigue. Ketch was nearly finished and he hurried on.

"These are the things that pointed me towards Mathew, they are I admit small matters, not likely to be enough for a jury or magistrates. I am not fully clear in understanding all Mathew's angry motives or why indeed he had bolted, but his flight does seem to confirm our suspicions."

Stephen with obvious reluctance released Elizabeth's arm and rose to his feet.

"I think you all agree, that this feels like the truth of the matter, but we must now speak with Stannard and Brent. I am sure they have important things to say. But everyone looks tired and need rest. I suggest you and I Ketch, take the prisoners to the Council House and allow everyone else to rest this afternoon. Ketch agreed and the men, taking the saddlebag with them, assembled in the corridor, leaving the women to their own devices. Ketch spoke quietly to Holditch.

"News of what we have here will eventually become common knowledge and there will be many who will consider they have claims on this gold. I want you to return to Derngate

house, with Tull and Anne, collect your horse and ride to the garrison at Bedford, find the most senior officer you can."
He paused.

"You still have your letter of authority from Cromwell?"
Holditch nodded,

"Good! Tell him you need ten troopers. If necessary, you can settle for six. But you must have them here as early as you can tomorrow, remember not infantry, troopers! You will not make Bedford before dark, but get well past Lavenham. "

Holditch was well pleased. He had not enjoyed the sedentary life, trapped indoors." "At once Ketch"

Ketch called Anne into the corridor, informed her what was required and then turned to Tull.

"I want you to go with them and stay with Anne overnight. I am sure the nature of events will soon be known in the town, and that may make some think, that Derngate House may be worth rifling. It will need protection, more than that produced by a stable boy.".

Tull took the instruction in his usual unruffled fashion and he began to gather a few things together from the kitchen. Ketch then hurried them out of the door. Anne was not pleased that she was being taken away from the centre of matters. However, she understood that Derngate House should not be left unguarded and Holditch had to be sent off quickly.
Stephen was waiting for Ketch in the kitchen, looking at Brent and Stannard sitting tied to chairs, with their gags in their mouths. He removed the gags, they were after all to be questioned. The two prisoners took the opportunity to complain loudly about their treatment. Stephen waived it all aside.

"Captain Ketch and I have a lot of questions for you attackers of women. You are both in trouble. Usually those involved in treason go to London, to the tower for special questioning and punishment."

Dundas Stannard just swore a foul oath, but Varley Brent's face turned pale.

"Treason! He cried.

"I have been crying treason for the last seven years and no one has listened. I knew about Giles Middleton from the beginning"

"Shut your mouth," cried Stannard.

"Just keep quiet."

Ketch entered the kitchen.

"You need to help yourself Varley Brent," suggested Ketch.

"That man will lead you to the gallows. Stephen, let us re-gag master Stannard and untie the legs of prisoner Brent. We can question him in the more comfortable dining room."

They hustled Brent into the dining room, placed him in a chair and each pulled up one for themselves close in front of him. He looked at them both wildly.

"Constable, you know I am not one for treason. I have a hard life, here in Northampton. Now and then you have had to speak to me about some of the problems I get into, but you know I could never get involved in treason. Haven't I always been one for Parliament?"

Stephen's reply was unforgiving.

"Problems! You are a petty villain Brent, always in trouble., Thievery, intimidation, is what you do, but you have cooked your goose this time."

Ketch intervened.

"The Constable is right Brent. You have been seriously led astray, your only hope is to tell us all you know about Stannard, and what he intended to do."

Brent looked from one man to the other.

"You will speak for me. Remind people that I was with Zouche all those years ago trying to get Middleton to confess."

Ketch was getting impatient.

"Yes! Yes! But start talking, not about then, about now!"

Brent visibly relaxed. It was possible to see the flow of cunning returning,

Stephen tapped him on the knee.

"Remember, I know you Brent. I shall know when you are lying."

The prisoner took a deep breath, once more surveyed his captors, and began to talk.

"Stannard came to me, he somehow knew my dislike of Giles Middleton. He said he had proof that Middleton was a royalist traitor who kept a cache of gold, some of which Stannard, himself, had taken to Scotland to Charles Stuart. He showed me three golden coins and it proved beyond all doubt that I had been right about Giles Middleton all the time."

He looked almost beseechingly at Stephen.

"You see constable. I was right!"

"What were you asked to do," demanded Ketch.

Varley Brent swallowed hard, Stephen could tell that he was marshalling the very best arguments for saving his own skin.

"First he was very happy with blackmailing Middleton. He wanted five hundred of those gold coins, but we talked it over and realised that he could turn the tables on us, and inform the magistrates that we were the royalists. So, it was decided"…..

Here Brent paused. He needed to get his part in the plot explained to his best advantage.

"Carry on!" demanded Stephen.

"Don't stop!"

"Stannard decided he would see Middleton and suggest that it was best all round, if all three of us were to take the gold and get away to France. Stannard thought I was going with them, but I was getting ready to turn them in."

Ketch and Stephen looked at each other, Ketch spoke ignoring the obvious lie.

"Did Stannard actually put that to Middleton?"

"Yes, he did and Middleton agreed to join us and that is what we planned. We were to go tomorrow."

Stephen turned to Ketch.

"If that conversation was overheard, or made known to Mathew in some other way, I can the better understand, why he would want to kill him. This is quite enough without the other concerns for his mother and fellow servants."

Ketch could not but agree.

"You can understand why few people liked Middleton."

Stephen motioned ketch to the side of the room and in a lowered voice explained a special concern.

"It is clear that Stannard is a much more important captive than we first thought. I feel we must keep him well away from Varley Brent, definitely separate cells."

Ketch noticed Stephen was looking uncomfortable.

"Unfortunately, Ketch we only have two cells in the Council House, and with the body of Giles Middleton in the cellar, the other cell is occupied by Edgar."

Ketch recognised the problem.

"I think we can let Edgar out; the doctor was quite positive that he did not murder Giles. I do not think he will follow Mathew's example. It will also be good for Varley Brent, to be next to a Dundas Stannard, who will soon be very angry with him. Being threatened by Stannard will keep him honest."

Stephen spoke to Varley.

"Listen carefully Brent, you are certainly going to be punished for what took place at Wilmington House, punishment for anything else will depend on how the magistrates view your part in the plot. You, are going to occupy a cell for a while and I suggest you make every effort to behave. I am going to untie you now and you will walk alongside us as we take the other villain to his cell in the Council House.

"Ketch let us two take a firm grip on Stannard."

The party left Wilmington House by the front door and made their way to the Council House. Ketch was unhappy leaving the saddlebag in the company of the three women, but he had no choice.

They had expected to see a quiet and darkening Council House as it was now evening, but instead inside, it enjoyed not only a strong candlelight, but also a loud buzz of conversation. Pushing open the great doors to the large entrance area, they saw the Mayor, Council man Lugg. He was together with a few of his colleagues, standing around the wooden table, where much of civic business was discharged. On this occasion, however, it was laden with platters of food of every description, meat, cheese, bread, fruit and cakes. Each man there was drinking beer from pewter mug or wine from a glass. There were also a number of guests unknown to Ketch.

"Well what have we here?", exclaimed the Mayor.

"Civic and army authority with prisoners?"

He caught sight of Varley Brent.

"And, Varley Brent is going quietly to the cells. My! My!"

"We are setting Edgar Middleton free, Mr Mayor, and finding a cell each for these characters."

"Well hurry up I have lots to tell you," enthused the Mayor.

Stephen and Ketch took their time ensuring that Edgar was happy with his new status and ready to return in the morning and that Stannard and Brent were securely imprisoned. They then returned to the Mayor.

"Constable Stephen Hedlow and Captain John Ketch, I would like you to meet our newly appointed Clerk to Northampton Council. Mr Nicholas Baker who comes to us from City of London Corporation and is an Inner Temple lawyer." Introductions done Ketch and Stephen had a careful look at the man replacing their friend and Uncle. The new Clerk was dressed in lawyer black, about forty years of age, of medium height. His hair was plentiful and deep, shiny black. He had an open clear face which was welcoming in repose. He looked the part of a civic lawyer. The Mayor led off the conversation.

"The Council has been extremely busy Stephen. We have not only appointed our new clerk, but we have, subject to your final approval, appointed two deputy constables. With your new inheritance I fear you will not be with us for very long."

Stephen laughed. "Wisely done Mr Mayor you have read my mind. I do intend to resign; my dear departed Uncle has left me new responsibilities."

Stephen turned away from the Mayor and whispered to Ketch.

"I know you will fret about what is left pretty well unguarded in Wilmington House. I suggest you get away now. I will explain matters to the Mayor and our new Clerk"

Ketch made his goodbyes. As he made for the door, he heard the Mayor telling Stephen that the new Clerk was dealing with the body of Giles Middleton and had recommended the re-opening of the old jail. He soon returned to Wilmington House where Maria, Rose and Elizabeth were enjoying a meal in the kitchen. Ketch joined them and for a while they all were in animated conversation about their recent experiences. Even Elizabeth was moving her head about and smiling. After a while, however, the strains of the day began to tell and a common consent arose that it was time to sleep and to rest. The three women agreed to sleep in the front room. Ketch decided to sleep on the kitchen floor, with the saddlebag as his companion.

Chapter Twenty-five

Ketch awoke to the sound of a carriage wheel coming to a halt outside the front door. It was followed by a heavy knocking. Ketch had slept fully dressed, but in a few minutes he emerged fully clothed from the kitchen. He felt stiff, sleepy and uncomfortable in his clothes. He saw that the front door had been opened by Rose, but she was pushed aside by an angry Lord Wilmington who made straight for Ketch.

"Good God Ketch! What have you done? I have come back from North of the county to find my agent murdered and my outdoor steward in jail. I warned you to be careful, to avoid upset, to be discreet. Instead you have been a disaster. You had better explain yourself."

Ketch inwardly sighed. He had expected this response, in fact he had expected it sooner. But undoubtedly Lord Wilmington must have an explanation.

"My lord, let us go into the dining room and I will explain everything to you. You are right to be concerned."

Ketch ushered the furious lord into the dining room and sat him down at the table.

"Sit down my lord I have much to tell you."

Lord Wilmington did not like being told what to do, especially by an army Captain, who had totally disorganised his well-organised life. He was about to re-knew his abuse of Ketch when Ketch slapped three gold coins on to the table. He then looked hard at Wilmington.

"These my lord, are gold coins taken from a hoard, kept here in Wilmington house, by Giles Middleton, on behalf of Charles Stuart. They were found and taken from a messenger, currently held captive in the Council House. This messenger is named Dundas Stannard and he is accused of carrying a large quantity of these coins to Charles Stuart in Scotland before the recent invasion. There is also a large supply of these coins, present here and now, that I have taken into army custody."

These words left lord Wilmington stunned, not quite certain what he was being told. For a moment he was speechless, but a slow dawning of their meaning began to form in his brain. Given his advantage from this pause, Ketch continued with his explanation.

"What I am saying Lord Wilmington, is that for many years Giles Middleton has deceived you and the citizens of this town, as to his true loyalties. All the time as your agent, he was a royalist holding gold for Charles Stuart. The man we hold, the messenger, the go-between Stannard, had a local accomplice, who you undoubtedly know by the name of Varley Brent. He is quite clear that Stannard admitted to him, his role in everything. Stannard is a dangerous man and must be kept secure." Wilmington was determined to assert his presence with a question.

"Brent is a low-level ruffian, Ketch, can you believe his story?"

"My lord I think these gold coins are proof enough."

Lord Wilmington sat back in his chair. A worried frown seemed to become permanently lodged in his face. He was beginning to grasp some unpalatable facts.

"Giles a traitor! He looked sharply at Ketch.

"What about Edgar! Surely he is not a royalist?"

"Hard to say my lord. For a time, he was held in the Council House, not as a royalist but because of a terrible fight with his brother, in which he gave Giles such a blow with his staff, that it brought him near to death."

Deep concern was in Lord Wilmington's face.

"He killed his brother?"

"No! He severely hurt him, but Giles Middleton was murdered by someone else, who tried to incriminate Edgar."

"Who was that?" demanded Wilmington.

"The manservant Mathew who has now fled and as yet cannot be found.

Ketch thought it best to give Lord Wilmington time to digest the implications of this uncomfortable news. There was a tap on the door and Tull's head appeared.

"I am here with your wife Captain, would his lordship care for some refreshment?"

"Is it too early for a glass of brandy my lord?" inquired Ketch.

Lord Wilmington accepted the offer of brandy and expressed a desire to remain closeted with Ketch.

Ketch held a glass of water rather than brandy.

"I need a clear head whilst delivering unpleasant news to aristocrats. "

He renewed his conversation. "There is another difficult matter to draw to your attention my lord. This long-term deceit, and the sheer size and gravity of Giles's treason, providing gold to Charles Stuart, will impact on your own stewardship and honour. There will be wagging tongues unfavourable to your lordship."

It was clear that Lord Wilmington had already grasped this.

"Spit it out Ketch! I have enemies enough, who will charge me with knowledge of treason and even treason itself. I have been made to look a fool by Giles Middleton and he has paid his price in being murdered. No doubt I will be called upon to pay mine."

He took a large sip of brandy.

"I cannot believe that Edgar was involved to any degree in treason. His attack on Giles would indicate total opposition to his brother."

Ketch felt he had to make the situation clear.

"The point is my lord; did he know about the gold and fail to report it?"

"I hope we can free him from any charge of involvement," insisted the aristocrat.

Lord Wilmington. leaned forward in his chair, and rested his elbows on the table. He realised that, far from being someone to chastise, he now had need of this army Captain. It was important that Ketch was convinced of his own innocence and that of Edgar. Ketch took up the conversation.

"May I suggest my lord that we take breakfast together. As we are, I can answer your questions in detail. I think all interests are served by early action on this. Yourself and the Mayor are the town magistrates and you should deal quickly with Stannard, Varley Brent, the manservant Mathew and Edgar."

In a more determined tone, he re-stated.

"I shall maintain a hold on the gold."

With a steady look at Ketch, Lord Wilmington agreed to breakfast, but his mind was already moving on to his next course of action. *He must see Council man Lugg. He and the Mayor must manage events, they can no longer be left in the hands of this Captain, however well-intentioned he may be.*

Lord Wilmington left immediately breakfast was finished, and for the rest of the day Ketch was left to his own devices. A normality returned to the lives of those who had been most intimately involved in the murder of Giles Middleton. Maria, Rose and Elizabeth occupied the kitchen, cooking, cleaning and gossiping.

The release from the lordship of Giles Middleton had produced a lighter, happier atmosphere. Elizabeth in particular was heard to laugh and lead the talk.

Stephen met his new Deputy Constables, he agreed to their appointment and set one to take the road to Wellingborough in pursuit of Mathew, whilst the other was sent down the road to Bedford. They had clear instructions to ask questions at properties on the road, not to harass travellers. After a noon time meal, Stephen paid a visit to Wilmington House and spent a long time in close private conversation with Elizabeth. They both emerged after an hour from the front reception room, slightly blushing but continuing in their pleasure of each other's company. Rose in particular thought there was an unusual strong euphoria in their behaviour.

After passing the South Gate, Mathew had opted for the road to Towcester. He then had to spend a night in the hay loft of a farm just outside the town. He was inevitably to greet the day cold, stiff and hungry. He successfully risked begging a draught of cream from the early milking, which helped him on his way. Nevertheless, he began to realise that even on the road his flight to London would not be easy. Nevertheless, he was resolved to find a new life in London and one day invite his mother to join him.

Ketch and Anne returned with Tull to Derngate House. The two men washed whilst Anne produced a second breakfast. After which no one felt ready for the chores of the day. All three sat around in the parlour smoking their pipes, in defiance of King James, and talking over the last few days. In the afternoon, Ketch and Tull were sent into the garden, whilst Anne tested the suitability of three new servants. After an hour they were allowed to return to be informed that Judith was the new housemaid, Mrs Langley the new cook and William the new manservant. Thus, a new management structure for Derngate House was established. By the late afternoon Ketch and Anne were already enjoying the benefits of new servants. Together with Tull, they were back in the parlour, drinking ale and eating cakes, when the sound of horses' hooves were heard in the courtyard. Ketch immediately hurried outside. It was only one horse, he had this sudden concern that Holditch had failed? Fortunately, his concern was set aside as Holditch slowly eased himself to the ground, handed his reins to the stable boy and smiled.

"The Bedford commander was very helpful. Cromwell's authority and the name of Secretary Thurloe still carry weight with the army. I have ten troopers walking their horses down by Becket's well."

Ketch was relieved at the news from Holditch and invited him into the house.

"That is well done Holditch. I want you to take them to the field, I now own at the back of the garden. Tell them to make their camp there. They will be fed in an orderly fashion from the house. "

Anne came to join them to see exactly what was going on. Ketch quickly explained his need of the new arrivals.

"It will require a large effort from the kitchen to feed these men. I suggest that Holditch and William be sent to purchase all the stores required and Mrs Langley and Judith prepare the kitchen for the task ahead. I must leave you my dear to manage this. Hopefully for no more than a few days."

Anne laughed at his serious face.

"Of course, all will be done as you request. I am sure we will all enjoy the challenge. Mrs Langley and Judith, I have np doubt will manage soldiers very well. William seems a willing enough young man, and Holditch is always good company. You should have no concerns. We will manage."

Well satisfied Ketch went out through the garden to await the arrival of the small troop, and to brief them and Holditch as to the role they may have to perform.

Chapter Twenty-six

The following morning, Ketch received a note from Lord Wilmington, inviting him to a meeting of magistrates in the Council House at ten o clock. There was a definite formal feel to the invitation and Ketch decided that he and Tull would attend that meeting in full uniform, but without weapons. Before leaving he briefed Holditch to have the troop ready for instructions at any time. His mind then turned to the saddlebag of gold, he had kept upstairs in their bedroom. He had considered it the safest place and resolved to leave it there. But before leaving, he informed Anne, and requested that for the morning, all persons were to remain downstairs.

On arrival at the Council House, Ketch and Tull were directed by the new clerk into the Council Chamber. The chamber was a high ceiling room, about fifty-foot square and enjoyed plenty of light from three large windows, such that candle light was rarely needed during the day. The council membership was not over large and rather than benches, the councillors had sat in especially well constructed and ornate chairs, behind a series of oak tables. In meetings they were normally faced by the Mayor and the Clerk sitting side by side at their own table. However, for the purposes of this meeting, the two magistrates sat facing the audience, with the new clerk occupying a table of his own to their side. At right angles and against the wall, sat Stephen and his two constables and they had been joined by two of Lord Wilmington's retainers. Ketch and Tull were motioned to the tables facing the magistrates. Also present, behind Ketch were

Edgar Middleton and Varley Brent. Right at the back of the chamber were Elizabeth Middleton, Rose and Maria.

Taking their seats, Ketch and Tull extended smiles and greetings to those they thought deserved them. They received formal responses from the Mayor and Lord Wilmington, a subdued smile from Stephen and broad smiles and waves from Rose and Maria. Lord Wilmington opened the proceedings.

"Captain Ketch together with two of his men was sent by the army to Northampton. They were to investigate rumours of a cache of gold being kept for treasonous, royalist purposes, by my agent Giles Middleton. He was advised to focus in or around Wilmington House. In the course of his investigations, my agent Giles Middleton was murdered and an attack made by two ruffians on Wilmington House. Captain Ketch's investigation has indeed been successful and a cache of gold has been found and treasonous activity uncovered, He is to be congratulated on a job well done. These I believe are the facts of the matter."

Lord Wilmington paused and looked about him for any, who would challenge his version of recent events. Receiving none he continued.

"I must stress that this meeting is not a court of law, but a gathering of interested parties to determine what is to be done."

He turned to the Mayor for comment, but councilman Lugg just nodded in return. Ketch on the other hand had definitely something to say.

" My Lord, you are totally correct, in your summary of the facts. concerning the gold. However, I would like to stress that in the matter of the murder, the army presence has been in support of your own town constable, Stephen Hedlow, who took the lead on all matters to do with the murder"

. Stephen rose to his feet, to indicate his assent, and Lord Wilmington decided to move on.

"As to the murder, I understand the manservant Mathew was identified as the likely culprit and his guilt has been confirmed by his fleeing the town. What is happening with respect to his capture?

Stephen again rose to his feet.

"An attempt to raise an immediate "Hue and cry" was not successful, but the town has just appointed two deputy constables whose first task is to hunt him down."

Lord Wilmington looked at the two constables and grunted.

"The likelihood of success?

"Unclear my Lord. He has a day's start.

Both Lord Wilmington and the Mayor were clearly unimpressed.

Let us get on," suggested the Mayor. "We have the question of Edgar Middleton to resolve. In front of witnesses...."

At this point both Maria and Rose stood up, but were waved to sit down. The Mayor would not be interrupted

"At the moment we do not need to question them. In front of witnesses he struck his brother with his staff, punctured his head causing him to collapse, suffering major damage to his head."

Lord Wilmington intervened.

"This is a criminal act, however a blow from the victim's desk when he fell, did contribute to Giles's injuries, and Edgar by his actions did disable a dangerous traitor who was contemplating flight to France. In addition, the doctor was quite clear, the wounds from Edgar's blow did not actually kill his brother."

"Quite so." added the Mayor.

Ketch was convinced that he was watching a well- rehearsed set piece between the Lord and the Mayor.

"His lordship has strong feelings for Edgar. Some sort of pre-arrangement has been made."

The Mayor was speaking again.

My recommendation is that Edgar Middleton should be released and placed in charge of Lord Wilmington who will decide on his future."

"Lucky Edgar, thought Ketch.

"Are we all agreed," demanded the Mayor.

There was silence in the chamber'

"Note that was agreed mister Clerk."

The two magistrates went on to deal with Varley Brent and Dundas Stannard. Varley Brent was to have the choice between public chastisement, which was unspecified or six months incarceration in the jail, when re-opened. His early recognition of Giles Middleton as a traitor was noted.

"The local men of power have looked after their own. What on earth are they going to do with Stannard?"

These muses by Ketch were interrupted by the answer.

"Dundas Stannard at the moment remains in the cells. He is a hardened royalist. He will be placed in the custody of the army, for transportation to London and the questioning and punishment he will undoubtedly receive there,"

Ketch's cynicism reached new heights.

"Masterly, he is someone else's problem and we will leave it to the army."

The decision was noted by the clerk. The meeting was clearly coming to an end and Ketch whispered in Tull's ear and he quietly left on an errand for ketch. Lord Wilmington had a few final remarks to make.

"That finishes our main business, both the Mayor and I have actions to take. There are of course a number of other matters, to be decided on Wilmington house tenancy for example, but these can be covered informally. The Mayor has provided for us some victuals in the main entrance, and I hope all will join us." Everyone in the chamber followed Lord Wilmington and the Mayor to the entrance hall and the food and drink. Ketch noticed that Stephen and Elizabeth were in deep conversation. He felt they would not resent his intrusion.

"I am happy to confirm Elizabeth that both myself and Anne are agreed that you and Rose will move into our property on the market square. I have no doubt that Lord Wilmington will want a new agent as soon as possible."

Elizabeth smiled and held on to Stephen more tightly.

"That is very helpful news Ketch".

It was Lord Wilmington who spoke having overheard the remark.

"Yes! I will need to secure the house for my new agent and your generosity meets my main concern. I am also able to tell you that Maria has agreed to stay on in Wilmington House with the permanent position of Housekeeper, for whoever I appoint."

"Well these are all happy outcomes," declared Elizabeth and thank you Ketch for your kindness."

Ketch felt it was a delight to see the pretty girl so happy,

As time wore on, Tull re-joined the assembly and the Mayor made a fulsome but short speech. Ketch found himself taken aside by Lord Wilmington for some private conversation.

"Well that seems to have gone well Ketch, but there are still some other matters to bring to your attention. There is the issue of Edgar. I think it right that you should know my plans for him. I do not think that he can remain in Northamptonshire. His brother's treason will be soon so well- known and it will blight his life. He is no longer a young man, but he remains strong and he deserves a fresh start. I shall send him to the New World, to America."

Probably best my Lord," agreed Ketch.

"I have a family friend in the West of the county, called Lawrence Washington. Unfortunately, his affairs have gone badly and he is forced to sell up his estate, Sulgrave Manor. His son, John Washington, intends to work his passage to America as a seaman. I have written to Lawrence, offering to pay for John's passage, if he will act as companion and give support to Edgar on the crossing. I am sad to see Edgar go and he will be missed by many people."

Lord Wilmington looked quite morose for a moment, but he visibly gathered himself and adopted a more serious manner. Ketch found himself surrounded by an unhappy looking Stephen, his two constables and Lord Wilmington's retainers. Lord Wilmington looked grave.

"You have done well Ketch in recovering the saddlebag of gold and exposing Giles Middleton, but we must resolve the issue of the ownership of the gold. I must insist, that plainly it is part of the Northampton estate and must therefore be placed into my custody. In due time it will be sent on to the House of Commons. These gentlemen will accompany you to wherever it is located and you will hand it over to the Constable. I must add that the Mayor is in full agreement with this and if you do not comply you are to be detained."

Ketch looked at Council man Lugg who gave an unhappy nod of the head. Ketch looked about him searching for Tull and was dismayed that he could not find him. But Tull was already pushing open the great doors of the Council House and Holditch and ten troopers came filing into the entrance hall.

Lord Wilmington looked progressively stunned and then angry. He grimaced, looked about him, snorted and looked hard at Ketch.

"Well you are a man of action Captain Ketch and my little force is no match for yours. It looks as if your title to the gold is stronger than mine, Take the money to you Secretary Thurloe. I have no doubt your Cromwell will be well pleased. You have unmasked a traitor and provided your General with funds for which he is always needing. You may, however, in time have to face an unhappy House of Commons".

The aristocrat thought for a moment and seemed to measure Ketch as a man.

"I would take it kindly Ketch if you make it clear in London that my own honour in this matter is unblemished, that I had no knowledge or part in treason."
Ketch offered his hand his lordship.

"You have no fear on that score, I will be your man in London on this whole affair."

The aristocrat and the Captain shook hands and Ketch left with his troop and they made their way back to Derngate House. His men soon learnt why they had been used in this way and there were a few smiles and smirks that powerful people had been bested.

"Well done Captain," whispered sergeant Tull.

Husband and wife enjoyed a satisfying lunch in the parlour, throughout which Anne demanded the details and full story, as to what had happened that morning. Ketch had ensured pressing army matters were being fully attended. Holditch was managing the camp and Tull was in the kitchen with two men guarding the gold.   After a knock on the door, William, the manservant announced the arrival of Stephen and Elizabeth.

The two visitors entered, hand in hand and Anne guided them to seats in the parlour. She had an inkling as to what was to come.

"I am sorry about this morning", began Stephen. I was under some pressure from both the Lord and the Mayor."

Ketch waived his words aside.

"You were doing your duty Stephen, it generally must override friendship."

Stephen looked relieved.

"Thankyou Ketch, I am particularly pleased that I am forgiven, in that you and Anne have been so generous to Elizabeth in providing her with a temporary home."

He stopped for a moment and with a smile on his face continued.

"I say temporary as after a suitable period of mourning, Elizabeth and I intend to marry."

Ketch was surprised and delighted. Anne could not contain that she knew all along.

"There is something else," cried Elizabeth.

"But you must keep it to yourselves for a while. It is slow, but it is gradual that I am beginning to see again. The blow to the head that I received in the tunnels seems to have jolted my eyes back into working."

The delight of the party was total. Glasses and bottles were produced, gin and wine were consumed with enthusiasm, toasts were given and everyone wished everyone else happiness.

Eventually the party broke up. Elizabeth would go to her new house, where Rose was awaiting her. Stephen would now be a frequent visitor. Both Ketch and Anne saw their happy visitors to the door. As the evening drew in, candles were lit and their new servants kept them warm and comfortable. Sergeants Tull and Holditch were still about their duties and ketch and Anne knew that they also had to have an important conversation. It was Anne who started the discussion.

"Well husband, you leave for London in the next few days, what is our life to be? Is your home here with me, with your inheritance or in London, serving the republic and Secretary Thurloe. If necessary, I will move to London to be with you."

Ketch had thought long and hard on this matter and he had a reply ready for Anne.

"Peace is returning to England; the enemies of the Commonwealth are now overseas rather than at home. Thurloe has many agents who, better than me, can operate overseas. I like Northampton, I am a lucky man, I have a wife and an inheritance to manage. Both will be demanding and a joy. My place is here in Northampton with you."

"A long and lovely speech my love"

Anne' face was full of happiness.

"I shall be a good wife."

Husband and wife rose and held each other tight. Their married life was now much more of a partnership. Ketch took Anne's hand.

"Let us go into the garden, enjoy the last of the October sunlight and look about us at what we have to enjoy."

Author's note

On 3rd September 1658 Oliver Cromwell died.

On 25th May 1660 Charles Stuart reclaimed the Crown of England.

On 20th September 1675 the great fire of Northampton destroyed the town centre.

Printed in Great Britain
by Amazon